The

MAYFLY

Stories

Ben Rogers

www.readrogers.com

ISBN: 978-1-7343067-2-9 Paperback
ISBN: 978-1-7343067-4-3 Ebook
ISBN: 978-1-7343067-3-6 Paperback (Large Print)

"The Caretaker" was originally published as "Cutting Curtis" in *The Nevada Review.*
"Hillbilly" was originally published in *Prick of the Spindle.*
"Mayfly" was originally published in *Wags Revue.*
"On The Rejuvenating Effects of Arch Theft" was originally published in *PANK Magazine.*
"The Young Man and the Mountain" was originally published in *Arroyo Literary Review.*
"The Unbridled Underestimation of Racehorses" was originally published in *Dark Sky Magazine.*

TABLE OF CONTENTS

Here's to brothers, blood & otherwise.

ON THE REJUVENATING EFFECTS OF ARCH THEFT

ABSTRACT

The authors ditch a mechanical engineering conference to partake in tomfoolery. They have one hell of a time, inspiring them to sanction a new conference in order to partake again, on an annual basis. The authors get old. One of them gets pancreatic cancer. The remaining authors become once again inspired, this time to illegally remove a monument from its foundation and transport it across state lines for reasons that may or may not become clear to the reader. Initial data, albeit anecdotal, suggest tomfoolery cannot cure pancreatic cancer but can produce levels of joy unobtainable with more conventional treatments.

BACKGROUND

The first meeting of the American Society of Mechanical Engineers (ASME) convened in New York in 1880. Exactly one century later, in 1980, the ASME Conference on Education was held in San Francisco, CA. Among the professors in attendance were the authors of this study. These five gentlemen were already casually acquainted, having attended many such conferences together. Their camaraderie had increased as a function of time, owing at least in part to their mutual disdain for the ASME annual conference—a gathering characterized by the tameness of the attendees' neckties, the sameness of the conference rooms regardless of host city, and the sobriety of most everyone at the welcoming mixer.

During a mid-morning break on the second day of the 1980 conference, the authors stepped outside to commiserate in private (i.e. outside the auditory radius of fellow nerds). Ambient conditions were 63°F with 38% relative humidity and cloudy skies. The conversation included mockery of: (1) the sexual proclivities of a certain plenary lecturer, (2) the sordid past of the hotel bedding, (3) one another. The topic then shifted to the sanctioned evening activity—a bus trip to a newly built, state-of-the-art HVAC control center on the campus of Stanford University. Various alternatives to this tour were proposed and debated. Due consideration was given to the fact that the dinner at the campus dining commons would be complementary.

Diversions abound in San Francisco for the best minds of one's generation (Ginsberg, 1956), although the author of that study concludes such minds are often left "destroyed by madness, starving hysterical naked, dragging themselves through the negro streets at dawn, looking for an angry fix." It was an option.

The authors of *this* study (who shall be referred to here as Berkeley, Irvine, (San) Diego, Cambridge, and Eugene) were willing to consider other options, and soon made a fateful observation of an incontrovertible fact: the distance from San Francisco to Reno is 218 miles. Further, a rental car averaging 75 mph can cover this distance in under three hours. Prior studies of Reno focus on divorce (see, e.g., A. Miller, 1961) and cowboys (Ibid.). J. Cash (1956) conducted a well-known experiment there in which a man was shot merely so that his subsequent death could be observed. Of greater relevance in the present case is the city's proximity to the 1980 ASME Annual Conference; specifically, the following relationship:

Eq. (1) 218 miles > separation needed to ensure zero encounters with fellow ASME attendees

Also relevant in this case: Reno's deep-rooted association with the field of statistics.[1]

A Pontiac Grand Am was rented in San Francisco at 11 am on Friday, June 27, 1980, and returned at 3:30 pm the following day. Because Reno ≠ Las Vegas, The Code does not apply. What happens there is not required to stay there.

What happened in Reno: Diego received a lap dance from a homeless woman, for which he grossly over-tipped; Irvine snuck onto the Circus Circus trapeze between shows and described long arcs on a swing through the dark, high above the bustling midway—naked but for his black socks, and yet totally undetected; Eugene ingested and regurgitated an Awful Awful cheeseburger + accompanying basket of fries + 750 ml of Old Crow (earning him the nickname Old Crow), then ingested an unknown number of Mentos and Rolaids— also regurgitated; Berkeley forded the Truckee River while holding forth on the elegance of plate-fin heat exchangers; Cambridge met an off-shift cocktail waitress at the Club Cal Neva sports book, with whom he later co-investigated the suspension limits of a parked Subaru Justy.

In this initial assessment of the city, it was found that the equation balanced: Reno took the authors' money, but gave back 28.5 of the most liberating hours of their careers.

Our careers. We—the authors.

We were assistant professors in those days. We spent our days slogging through bureaucracy, writing 50-page proposals doomed to go unfunded, spoon-feeding thesis hints to grad students, lecturing to the stoned, and stepping gingerly among the political landmines of our respective mechanical engineering departments. We spent our evenings pulling weeds, unclogging pipes, wiping asses, and coaching sports we no longer got to play ourselves.

Of course, there were weekends. Spring and winter breaks, too. Often these were the times we locked ourselves in our labs to finally got some work done. We lived busy lives. Full lives. The stress led mostly to harmless, elastic deformation, which is to say, typically, we bent but did not break.

Some plastic deformation did occur. Our waistlines and brows warped inalterably from much sitting and furrowing. Diego got divorced, squared. Cambridge lost a lot of money in Atlantic City, a lot of times. Eugene's son got arrested (for possession of marijuana) (stolen marijuana) (marijuana stolen from his father).

So we were tested, yes. As are we all. But never were we strained to fracture. Never were our characters compromised. Our passion for work and life did not diminish. We—the authors—wish to state here our gratitude for this. To still be standing, like Roman arches, thanks to engineering and luck.

Later in our careers, curiosity turned to mastery, passion became profession. All five of us eventually obtained tenure. Two decades went by, somehow. Our attendance at ASME Conferences declined—the perfunctory parading out of research results no longer necessary for job security. We stayed in touch in small ways. We would host one another for invited lectures at our home campuses. We would forward hilarious, distasteful items from the internet. We would leave voice messages for one another, reading from whomever's paper had most recently been published, in a booming, self-aggrandizing voice, or at least a British accent.

Such things keep men in touch, yes. But that is not enough. Idiotic as we may have been during that fateful first trip to Reno, we'd had sense enough to realize even then that we needed an excuse to get together on an annual basis. Someone—most definitely Diego—proposed an alternative conference. Early on, while selecting the locale for this event, we determined the group's centroid. This was the point at which, if a huge and rigid map of the United States were built and each assistant professor were to stand at the location of his university, said map would balance on the head of a pin. Three of us taught in the University of California system; one taught in Oregon; one not only taught at MIT, but was quite overweight, which, he argued imparted extra eastward influence. The centroid was determined to be Enoch, Utah. Had it been, say, Las Vegas or even Denver, we might have trusted this calculation as fate. Of course, the Enoch centroid was quickly dismissed for what it was: mathematical masturbation. And every summer from 1986 to 2008 we returned to Reno.

A full report on the findings from these meetings has not been published, nor would such an account be germane here. Suffice it to say that Reno is our Mecca. Our annual pilgrimage has affected the scheduling of weddings, family vacations, birthday parties and two funerals.

The agenda each year is the empty set, denoted { } per convention, with one exception. The sole artifact of our seminal trip to Reno is a photograph, snapped as an afterthought on our way out of town. In it, we stand abreast across Virginia Street, underneath the Reno Arch, denoted here by $\prod$. Writ large across the arch is the city's famous (and unverifiable) claim to fame: "The Biggest Little City in the World." We look like death and, at the same time, 200% alive. In it, one can clearly see Berkeley's still-damp slacks clinging to his thighs, and a vomit stain on the lapel of Old Crow's sport coat. Eugene's eyes are closed and his head is tossed back for reasons never explained.

Months later, the film was developed by Diego's

girlfriend, who inquired as to how it ended up on her camera, and, more importantly, why she hadn't been told about a visit to Reno. Apparently, this solidified her already gelling concerns regarding capital-T Trust, and her relationship to Diego was soon nullified. The next year—and every year since—the only required activity at our meetings has been a re-enactment. The authors arrange themselves under the arch in the same positions. To hold with tradition we present a handful of casino chips to the passerby who snaps our photo. We then mail a print to the ex-girlfriend—a gesture she appreciates enough to have kept us informed of address changes over the years.

The rest of the conference schedule is improvised. Cards, golf, and *Romeo y Julieta* cigars are customary. Old Crow whiskey is strictly forbidden. Reno's contradictory claim has been adopted for our purposes; the gathering is "The Biggest Little Conference in the World."

$$Eq.\ (2) TBLCW = \{\ \prod\ \}$$

MOTIVATION

In January 2009, one of the authors (Old Crow) was diagnosed with pancreatic cancer. By February, the condition had been deemed inoperable. Symptoms included abdominal pain, appetite loss, odd-colored stools, tiredness, nausea, vomiting and weakness.[2] He was placed on bed rest in May. His wife took to caring for him at their home 15 miles east of Eugene, Oregon.

On the morning of June 26, 2009, $\{\ \prod\ \}$ convened under cloudy skies. By mid-afternoon, a thunderstorm had darkened downtown Reno. Rain buffeted our hotel windows. The decision to convene the conference at all had been made to honor our friend. Old Crow had insisted via email that { ∏ } not suffer just because he was suffering. We made unsuccessful attempts at (a) merriment, (b) debauchery, and (c) depravity. We eventually holed up at a bowling alley bar. We talked about our friend a little. We drank. By 4:30 p.m. we were at a hotel buffet. We ingested gummy slabs of prime rib. We constructed and then deconstructed gooey architectures from the nacho bar. We gaped into the caramelizing flames of bananas foster, sick to our stomachs with sadness.

The storm passed. We rode the elevator to the pool on the roof. Mothers were thumbing magazines, their children frolicking in the shallow end of the pool in the dim orange light. We found a table off in the corner and stunk it up with bitterness and cigar smoke.

The next morning we walked over to the arch, only to forgo our annual rite. To take the photo without the full complement of founding members was, in { ∏ }'s view, entirely fucked up.

One of the authors (Cambridge) completed his doctorate work at MIT. His thesis on finite element analysis is still widely cited, though perhaps less often than his contribution to MIT's storied hacker legacy. As is custom, he never took credit for his hacks; but when pressed, he has no alibi for Halloween night, 1966, when the campus' Great Dome was cleverly transformed into a jack-o-lantern wearing a mischievous grin. This stunt, coupled with the authors' ancillary interest in heists (see e.g., D. Ocean et al, 1960, 2001; T. Crown 1968, 1999), and monument magic (D. Copperfield, 1983) prompted a re-evaluation of our annual photograph, as well as ourselves. That is to say, we stood staring at our reflections in the gilded girders of the arch, facing new and alarming questions—questions that became the genesis of this study: What *real* good had been done over the course of our respective careers? Beyond incremental technological and philosophical advancements within our chosen niches, what had we to show for ourselves? Who had we truly helped? What had we contributed that wasn't out of professional obligation? To whom had we brought joy?

We came up empty set, { }.

And yet, we considered ourselves men of means. Sure, we lacked the bravado of youth. But we were salty. We knew things. We kept in decent shape. We played racquetball, ate salmon. We made enough money to buy new European cars every five years. We wore Mephistos. We gripped purse strings—but also an occasional wrench. There was leverage in us. Mechanical advantage. All we lacked: purpose. All we needed: someone who needed us.

Over decades of testing, the city of Reno had been proven to possess rejuvenating powers for the authors. The hypothesis tested here is that a surrogate for this holy land can be equally restorative. We posit that the Reno Arch is such a surrogate. Described herein is our attempt at stealing this hallowed structure and moving it. In this case, to our good buddy's place outside Eugene, Oregon.

MATERIALS & METHODS

There have been many Reno arches over the years, and we expect there will be more in the years to come. The arch in our first photograph was the fifth one. It spelled out 'R E N O' on four glowing plastic octagons and was topped off with a spiky star. The spiky star rotated. Its look complemented the "mod" signage by then no longer in vogue along Reno's main drag, Virginia Street, or any street for that matter. Our next photo, from 1986, featured the sixth and current arch, the design of which incorporates hints of its predecessors, including a spiky star. It is the biggest, gaudiest version yet, with more than 2,000 light bulbs. It, too, spans Virginia Street and is flanked by casinos that never close. On Christmas mornings, these casinos are open. On September 12, 2001, they were open. After thirty seconds of reconnaissance, we concluded that stealing this arch would require a Sikorsky heavy-lift helicopter, liberal volumes of smokescreen, an oxy-fuel cutting torch, and access to the city's electrical controls, among other unobtainables.

In contrast, we came to believe that the fourth Reno Arch —the one spanning Virginia Street from 1934 to 1963, but later erected as an historical landmark a few blocks away, on quiet Lake Street—was simply begging to be ripped off. Examine the thing. See its unadorned steel skeleton. Marvel at the rudimentary electrical housing at the base of its western tower. This arch makes a statement. The statement buzzes in all-caps neon: STEAL ME.

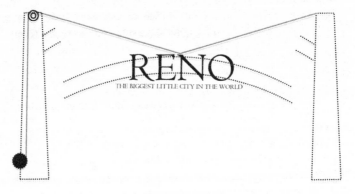

Figure 1.

The authors took a stroll down Lake Street on a Friday afternoon in June 2009 to case the old arch. Its supporting towers were framed out of slim steel bars, bolted together in a hollow arrangement that made the structure resemble a scale-model steel bridge. The towers were about three stories tall. The arch was attached midway up the towers, its apex slightly lower than the tower tops. Signs bearing the city's name and motto faced both directions of traffic. The joints at the base of each tower were welded. All remaining connections were made with standard nuts and bolts. We jaywalked from sidewalk to sidewalk, pacing off the span: 65 feet, approximately.

We returned Sunday night at 2:00 a.m. and parked down the street from the arch. We wore matching khakis, work boots, dark green polo shirts, hard hats and walkie-talkies on belt holsters. The street was nearly deserted. We were heavily caffeinated. At 2:17 am, a police cruiser trolled by. As soon as it was gone, three of us jumped out of a rented SUV and set to work.

A 9500-lb reversible wench was secured to the base of the east tower. The nimblest of the authors (Irvine) then scurried up the framework with the wire cable attached to his waist and spooling freely from the winch as he ascended. When Irvine was halfway up the tower, the cable snagged on a rivet, jolting him enough to sever two of the belt loops on his khakis. His hands started to shake. We told him to take a few deep breaths. He swore down at us. When he had collected himself, he descended to fix the snag, then started climbing again.

Once at the top, he strung the cable through a 9,000-lb pulley he fastened to the top of the tower, then crawled on hands and knees out to the middle of the arch, where he strung it through another pulley. We needed him to move quicker, but didn't dare say so. We did not want to distract or discourage him. We cringed as he scooted along, two stories above our heads. When a car came he would press his body to the girders and wait for it to pass underneath. Finally, he anchored the cable with a clevis hook to the top of the opposite tower.

The winch was powered up. The gears began to grind. Though we'd tested the winch beforehand, the ratcheting sound it made seemed especially conspicuous on such a quiet street. A dog down by the river started to bark. Another dog joined in. We looked around, waiting for something to happen. The cable tensed, forming an obtuse 'V' above the arch. The nimblest author at this point employed a power drill to remove 34 separate bolts, one by one. Within 20 minutes the arch had been separated from the supporting towers and was kept dangling in position between them by a wire. To the casual observer, however, the structure appeared intact.

We radioed Berkeley. He was idling two blocks away in 53-foot flatbed semi we'd rented the day before in Stockton, California.[3] He drove up to the arch from the south and, passing below it, slowed nearly to a stop just as a rowdy group of drinkers surprised us. We paused and smiled and did our best to look official. One of the drunks, an attractive young woman, asked what was up. We explained that the arch was being retrofitted to handle earthquakes. She nodded as if this was quite logical. She was unable to stand without assistance. Someone in her party joked that *she* could use some retrofitting. She nodded again, then retched in a planter. Another car went by. We waited.

When the street was again clear of cars and drunks, we radioed the truck. A minute later it was straddling the road's center line, the flatbed directly under the arch, perpendicular to it. We engaged the wench. The arch steadily descended, leaving the towers standing. See Figure 1. Two of the authors tugged on lines tied to the newly free ends of the arch in order to rotate the dangling portion by 90° and set it down lengthwise on the flatbed. Because we'd taken less than the full 65-foot span, the arch hung off the back of the trailer by only two feet. A taxi pulled up behind the trailer. The author standing closest held up his palm to the taxi driver, who rolled down his window. The author apologized for the inconvenience. The taxi driver saluted and lit a cigarette.

Minutes later we reconvened in an empty parking lot a

few blocks away and finished lashing down the arch. We piled cardboard boxes on it in a few places to mask the trademark curvature, then covered the whole thing in a giant canvas tarp.

Irvine let out a laugh. It was a tentative laugh, akin to a hissing release valve, and we realized just how nervous he'd been—how nervous we'd all been. What the hell were we doing in this parking lot in the middle of the night, risking jail time and our jobs for a prank, well-conceived/intentioned though it may have been? What were we trying to prove?

Well, for starters: our capability to create good in the world. But more than that: this was a game of chicken, where none of us wanted to be the one to back down, to call off the fun. Further, we had each accumulated, over decades of reasonable, respectable lives, a pot of social capital. And no point dying with Brownie points in the bank. And at this point, debate was moot. It was too late to re-hang the arch. We looked around at each other.

Irvine made an observation. He said it looked like we'd kidnapped a dinosaur.

RESULTS

We fled north by northwest to Eugene, Oregon. Two of us in the semi, two in the SUV. We drove through the night and could see little of the country we covered. The homely florescence of off-ramp gas stations tugged at our psyches—offering cups of coffee, slices of pie, urinals. We didn't so much as slow down.

Eugene and his wife had retired to a sizable homestead bordering the Willamette National Forest. Daylight found us on worn, two-lane highways that led through cool forests. Pink and yellow wildflowers speckled the ditches, the embankments. More than once, the semi's oversized side mirrors struck overhanging branches. An occasional gap in the trees provided a glimpse of mountains. Blankets of cirrocumulus muted the daylight. We yawned and felt fortunate.

The drive had passed uneventfully, though we'd clinched our teeth and anuses at every highway patrol cruiser, every dopplering siren. Was there an APB out for the Archasaurus?[4] Or perhaps city officials had been too embarrassed to act at first, waiting for business hours to make calls, assuming the best: something authorized but insufficiently documented was afoot. Retrofit rumors, et cetera.

Despite our somber destination, spirits were high. Within the warm cabins of our vehicles we shared stories about noteworthy vacations and exorbitant veterinarian bills, tricky desert golf courses, impending colonoscopies. We talked about Old Crow. A few times we mistakenly, innocently, referred to him in the past tense. We saw our own fates in him. He had been more alive than most anyone we'd known. Now, suddenly, he was less.

It had come to this surprisingly soon. We felt vulnerable, though this feeling went unvoiced. It made us feel better, though, to be affecting the situation. To be proactive. We were by this point like an engine driven by peer pressure, lubricated by testosterone. Though we hadn't known each other in high school, we postulate this is what it would have felt like.

None of us had been to the house before. In fact we passed his nondescript mailbox without realizing it until we passed a better-marked box down the road bearing the subsequent address. We weren't ready to go straight to his house, so we drove another half mile and pulled off the highway onto a gravel road that led uphill through the pines. A few miles in we came to an abandoned barn, behind which we parked the semi. It was 11:45 a.m. We got out to stretch and collect ourselves in the sunshine. Birds shrieked and whistled from the forest. Any other day, we might have been tempted to nap. We all piled into the SUV and drove back from whence we'd come. We visited various retailers in Eugene in search of a particular item and, having secured it, ate lunch twice, the first meal having failed to get us adequately stuffed, or buzzed.

Five hours later we were back at the barn. Afternoon shadows crept across the field. A pair of squirrels scurried out from under the big tarp as we pulled up. We sat on the tailgate and opened a bottle of Old Crow and passed it around, cursing cancer through gritted teeth and priming ourselves.

At 6:45 pm we headed to the homestead. We were clinically intoxicated. Pulling off the road onto the drive, we plunged through a thicket. Here we slowed to a halt amid sighing airbrakes. Crickets throbbed. A diffuse purple darkness hung in the trees.

We parked the semi in the weeds beside the drive and all loaded into the SUV. Driving on, we climbed a few switchbacks up and over a rise and emerged onto a plateau where a driveway circled an unmowed lawn in front of a house. The house was a nouveau, ranch-style place with red metal window frames, granite accents, and a wraparound paver porch. Flowers spilled from copper pots tethered to oversized wood beams. To the west there were a pair of outbuildings and a pond dotted with ducks.

A garage door yawned open. When it was midway up, a woman ducked under it and came out to stand in the gravel, arms crossed. She had a bandana tied about her neck and wore leather gloves. We had met our friend's wife years before and this looked much like her, except the hair was whiter, the body droopier. We waved and climbed out to greet her. She squinted at us, reaching into the pocket of her overalls for a pair of glasses. One of us said her name. She nodded, then asked what we were doing on her property. We started to explain. A 16-ounce bottle of Yoo-hoo containing

>15 ounces of urine tumbled from the SUV and cracked against the running board.

We were not invited inside the house. This was a wall of a woman. We'd come some 470 miles through three states, and our first substantial roadblock was five-foot, four-inches tall. She berated us. She expressed disgust with us. She pointed suggestively back to the road. We held up our palms. She shook her head. Her husband was extremely frail, she explained. He was in and out of consciousness.

We were skeptical. We'd seen his emails. He'd seemed okay in his emails. We told her as much.

She scoffed. She told us that he'd barely had the energy to hold his fork at dinner that evening. And that his wishes were simple—peace, dignity, *solitude*. She was damn well going to grant him these things. Visitors were strongly discouraged, particularly uninvited fugitives. She called our arrival an "ambush."

An accurate enough characterization, we agreed. But we knew: our motives were honorable. Unassailable. We were grown men, and we had come to help one of our own.

How? she asked. Well, we said, isn't this all pretty funny? Wouldn't it be a real kick in the prostate for our old pal?

You're drunk, she said. All four of you. She pulled a cell phone from the breast of her overalls and started to dial.

No, no, no! we said.

It went on like this. She stood with poise throughout the debate. A few times she held a handkerchief dramatically over her mouth and nose, perhaps to mask the smell of urine, or of us. Eventually, we detected some wear on her defenses. We were getting to her. Our operating assumption was that, deep down, she was a wild one. After all, she *had* married Old Crow, which at the very least implied a laissez-faire stance on marijuana and an appreciation for J. Garcia et al. But did she also love the second amendment, like our friend? Was she, as we spoke, slipping the safety off a pocketed 9mm?

One thing we knew for sure: she loved her husband. Probably more than we did. She wanted him happy. So did we. Therefore, by the transitive property:

Eq. (3) What The Wife Wanted = What The Authors Wanted

Still, it took considerable posturing and postulating to derive this equation. It was at least 35 minutes after our arrival before we were finally invited in. At which point we disclosed to her that, actually, we had a sizable gift we wished to fetch. Our unwillingness to further disclose the specifics of this gift led to ten additional minutes of haggling. Reluctantly, she consented to wheel Old Crow into the front room of the house, where he'd be afforded a view of the yard, while we retreated back down the drive in our SUV.

Back at the semi, we performed various, gratuitous, unfair impressions of The Wife. We stumbled around, urinating in the bushes like nervy dogs, then set to freeing Archasaurus.

Diego yanked the starter cord on a generator. Nothing. He yanked again, and again. Nothing, and nothing. We looked around at each other. It was suggested that the carburetor might be gummed up. Old spark plugs were also blamed. Meanwhile the one who'd rented the thing (Diego) kept furiously tugging. Using his legs and hips. With each try came a promising whir, then the sad little zip of the retracting cord. Eventually the question on all our minds was broached. Of course he took offense, but we insisted. He unscrewed the fuel cap. Bone dry.

Two gallons of diesel and two inspired yanks later, the generator coughed gray smoke and, after some fumbling with the choke, rumbled to a steady din. The forest flickered and then lit up, bathed in the brilliance of an electrified noble gas. Yellow and white neon penetrated deep into the trees. It was bright as day. Three of us climbed atop the flatbed and sat dangling our feet like kids on a hayride, while Berkeley jogged up to the cab. With a high-horsepower lurch, we were off.

We drove up to the yard, rounded the gravel turnaround and parked outside the picture window. Through the glass we could see Old Crow slumped in a wheelchair, The Wife standing beside him. Before she could take aim and shoot us, we hopped down and took up our customary positions under the fully lit arch, leaving an obvious vacancy where Old Crow was supposed to be. The whole side of the house was awash in light. Insects were already congregating above us. The generator hummed. The big letters of RENO reflected in the window. Through the reflection, Old Crow was smiling ever so slightly, his eyes bright with wonderment. His wife put her hand on his shoulder. His hand crept out from under a blanket and gripped hers. This moment is now referred to as The Biggest Little Moment.

We entered the house as heroes. Tea was served. We will not comment on our friend's condition except to say he was sicker than shit. We managed a short chat. He asked us questions about the arch. We recounted our adventure. He laughed and coughed, laughed and coughed. We didn't wish to overstay our welcome. The Wife was giving us the eye. We were grateful she had humored us. We shook his hand and looked him in the eye. He told us the cancer had stripped away all of the bullshit and exposed him for what he was, which was a weak old fool. It was only half true, but it made us sad to hear him say it. His hand felt cold when we shook it.

On our way out he said he wished to God he could go get arrested with us.

The primary question asked in this study was, can a stolen span of steel adorned with neon provide comfort to a man facing down death? Our answer: you bet. No further research is necessary. Note: the comfort is fleeting. But, then, so are arches. What's important is that men continue to find good reasons to build arches, to cherish them, and, when necessary, to steal them.

The authors wish here to cite the singular work of D.B. Cooper. In 1971, Cooper hijacked a commercial flight, collected $200,000 in ransom money, demanded a fuel stop at the Reno airport and then, once airborne again, strapped the money to his chest and leapt from the 727's rear stairway hatch somewhere over the Pacific Northwest, never to be seen or heard from again. The authors can't help but admire Cooper's panache, and further attest to the innumerable hiding places provided by the lush woods of the Pacific Northwest. Places where a dinosaur might be released back into the wild. For aspiring archeologists to discover and enjoy.

Further research is encouraged.

---

1. The authors here disclose a more-than-casual interest in blackjack.
2. Coincidentally, this is a subset of the symptoms commonly reported by TBLCW attendees.
3. Berkeley's sister owned a winery in Sonoma. Since college, he had helped haul cases of cabernet to customers up and down the state during a few weekends each year. His Class A license was valid.
4. That's what we'd taken to calling her.

THE YOUNG MAN AND THE MOUNTAIN

HIS FIRST ATTEMPT IS IN EARLY SPRING, snow still on the summit. Not to threaten the record. Just to confront it. After the ride Aaron hangs his bike in the garage and with a marker he writes the difference between his time and his hero's on the unfinished sheetrock. The snow thaws and recedes, leaving patches on the north faces. The patches vanish. Weeds sprout through cracks in the road. The summer sun rises behind the mountain a little earlier each day but until it rises high enough the mountain casts a shadow over everything.

The sun sets later each day too. Aaron is standing at the sink by the bathroom window. He is shaving by the last of the evening light. He has two razors—one in the shower for his legs, and the one now tracing the gaunt parabolas of his jawline and cheekbones. His arms and neck bear tan lines clean enough to be the work of a pencil and ruler. Though he is naked, Aaron appears to wear a pale, ghostly jersey.

Because of his big thighs and his thin arms and because after so much time in the saddle he walks with a stoop and because of the voracity with which he eats, Maria started calling him 'T-Rex.' Later, just 'T.' Pass the pepper, T. Night, T.

When he takes a deep breath his ribs open like a pair of

hands and his chest balloons beyond what seems a necessary capacity for air.

He pulls on boxer shorts and gets into bed with Maria. They have been dating for a year and a half, and living together for half that time. Aaron lies face down while she massages his legs. She kindly kneads the calves, the quads and hamstrings, and then the glutes. It never fails to arouse her to lay hands on him this way. She puts her lips on the velvety skin at the small of his back. Aaron says nothing. She arrives at his neck with her pulse rising and her breath warm in his ear.

I have to ride in the morning, he says quietly.

She reads this as bedroom silliness, Aaron playacting prude. He is still on his belly. She slides her hand between the mattress and his abdomen, inside the elastic of his shorts, only to pull away.

He gets up and retreats into the bathroom. She goes to the door. Taps on it.

It's okay, baby, she says.

Aaron says nothing.

It's probably your bike seat, she says. It's nothing to be ashamed of.

Aaron knows this. That he should feel ashamed. Emasculated. But he can't help asking if the numbness he feels is progress.

When he comes back out she pats his side of the bed. They lay together atop the blanket with the windows open, desert breezes on their skin. They hear thunder and see muted flashes from a storm not far away, on the mountain. Maria waits for Aaron to speak, to apologize so she can reassure him that it's all okay, but words never come. She takes his hand and soon she is asleep. He waits out the wakeful silence, staring up.

In the morning he goes to the kitchen and looks out the window past the aspen trees to the silhouette of the mountain beyond. With knife and thumb he makes change of a banana, the thick coins plunking into a bowl of muesli. He pours the milk and eats, standing at the window. Light spills over the ridge. It colors the boulders and trees on the foothills, endowing the mountain once again with dimension and texture. He tips the bowl to his mouth to sip the last of the milk. It is tinged with honey and banana. He sets the spoon lightly in the sink so as not to wake Maria. She'll be wanting to talk about last night.

From a high shelf he retrieves a tub of protein powder with a screw-off lid. He listens for a moment to be certain of the silence, then reaches into the tub and pulls out a small plastic baggie. The baggie contains five small red pills, given to him in secret by the team doctor two months ago. Aaron has not yet taken any of these pills. He takes one out, re-stashes the baggie and returns the tub to the cabinet. He fills a glass of water at the sink.

He takes the water and the pill with him out the patio door and tiptoes barefoot across the cool concrete. In the corner of the yard there is a wood planter box. He leaps up to it and balances on the edge to get a sense of the wind. The clouds are dissipating, but the air has not yet warmed up. Cold doesn't bother Aaron once his blood is pumping, except for his feet and his hands. Furthest from the heart. Left to fend, to engage handlebars and pedals, and on days when he pushes the big gear into the teeth of the wind and the cold is bitter, it is these—especially the feet, the toes numb and pallid —that ache most when blood returns to them afterward, in the shower. Winter rides have left his knuckles raw and flaking.

He tries for the record once a week. Otherwise he sticks to his regimen. Twice a week he rides the lasso: a one-hundred-and-two mile circuit over three mountain passes, the route forming a ragged 'Q' on the map. Maria calls this route the noose. Sundays he rides it clockwise. Wednesdays counterclockwise. Mondays he rests. During the week he rides three or four times, with teammates or without. In the warm afternoons after work, or in the cool mornings before. Usually in sunlight, but sometimes with rain and sweat plastering his clothes against his skin and his legs sodden with exhaustion.

He sets the pill on his tongue. It sits there long enough to begin dissolving into something bitter before he brings the water to his lips and gulps.

Maria is still in bed when he enters the bedroom. He stands at the foot of the bed and strips naked. Pulls on his riding bib and plucks obsessively at the fabric. It won't sit right today. Today is different, and somehow his body knows it. His jersey knows it. Maria squirms and leans up, squinting at the clock.

T, let's talk, she mumbles. I'll make pancakes...

Already ate, babe, Aaron says.

He zips up his jersey partway and leans over to kiss her forehead.

Aaron goes into the garage. He ducks under bikes that dangle in the dark and sidesteps until he comes to the one he wants and he takes hold of its frame and lifts the wheel off its hook. He pinches the tires and they feel okay. He fetches the pump and adds air all the same.

He guides the bike down the driveway with his hand on the saddle. The cassette ticks quietly. In the back pouch of his jersey are a pair of half-gloves with padded leather palms and breathable rope netting. He slides them on and works his fists to loosen the salty leather.

The chamois built into the groin of his bib gives Aaron a wide-legged saunter. His cleats grate and clack on the concrete sidewalk. His jersey pockets bunch up on his lower back. He is like a scuba diver still on dry land, readying for the moment when his gear can at last afford him the grace of its element.

An old woman on the opposite sidewalk leads a spaniel on a leash. She eyes the young man and when he returns her gaze she frowns and looks back at her dog as if she hasn't been staring. She doesn't allow herself to look again. At the display of him. Muscle and sinew and guts and genitals, all shrink-wrapped in obnoxious primary, corporate colors. The woman cannot remember when it became necessary to take leisure so seriously. He belongs in a loincloth, she thinks, not spandex; he should be fighting for survival, with his face and body painted, his eyes wild. But no: evolution has reduced his exertion to a pastime.

Aaron stamps his cleats into the pedals. Like a film reel, the chain starts with a lurch, soundtrack warbling, then tension takes hold and the movie begins.

The bike gives back what Aaron puts in. The air wraps around him. He glides alongside the morning traffic, picking his way through the grid of streets. The drivers idling beside him at intersections yawn and sip commuter mugs. He hears muffled morning shows and songs inside the cars. Lawn sprinkler mist drifts across the road and glazes his skin and clings like dew to the fine blond hairs on his arm. He is in no hurry yet.

He allows himself to visualize Maria. He guesses she's sitting in her usual spot at the kitchen table by now, reading. One evening not long ago she sat there while he portioned out protein bars and mixed batches of energy drink.

You've got to hear this, she'd said. It's Thoreau. He's climbing this mountain, right? Writing about what it's like to be up there. *Some part of the beholder, even some vital part, seems to escape through the loose grating of his ribs as he ascends. He is more lone than you can imagine.*

Aaron had nodded, noncommittal.

No wait, she'd gone on. *The tops of mountains are among the unfinished parts of the globe, whither it is a slight insult to the gods to climb and pry into their secrets, and try their effect on our humanity. Only daring and insolent men, perchance, go there.*

Perchance, Aaron had said.

Well, insolent you definitely are, she'd replied.

I ride up hills, Maria. There's no poetry in it. Most of the time it's boring, the rest of the time it's work.

Yeah? Then how come I'm jealous of your bike?

Maria, Aaron said. He'd tried making a defusing chuckle.

T, she'd said.

Because he'd lied, of course. Sometimes when he's half a day from home Aaron stops to buy food, and when he comes back to his bike, waiting where he left it like a loyal animal, he admires its lean and nimble lines. Form following function and nothing excessive except the logos. The bike is the one thing that belongs to him as he passes through places that don't, and sometimes when he crests summits or coasts to a final halt in his driveway, he leans over and pats the top tube.

Aaron had yawned.

Go on, Maria had said, looking back at her book. Go to bed. You've got gods to insult in the morning.

Aaron is beyond the city proper now, into the wider expanses. The road is quiet and unpainted and flat. Cows graze in the corner of a muddy pasture tinged with dandelions. He passes under the humming girders of a freeway overpass where the funneled wind tests his pace and makes him shiver. As he reemerges into sunlight he can see the mountain fully. It is a small mountain.

The shoulder of the road has eroded like coastline. The

pavement is pocked. He rides the smooth white line, his tires singing a steady note on the textured rubber. To stay balanced on the line, the mistake is to stare down at the front tire and aim. To concern yourself with position instead of trajectory.

The grade is slight. He passes a yellow warning sign bearing the profile of a wild horse. A crosswind nudges Aaron into the lane. He inches back onto the line just as a dually pickup towing a hay trailer roars by. Loose bits of hay flip about in the tumultuous air and settle over the road.

The first time Aaron met this mountain he felt uneasy and ill-prepared. In the times since he's come to know its shapes and moods and he doesn't feel that way anymore, looking up at it. What he feels is aggravation. A twinge in his gut. Anticipation of imminent, voluntary suffering. Knowing he will never really fly up this road, only slog. Sprinters need flat land. Masochists, mountains.

Aaron feels the familiar pangs of anger as the sweat pricks through his skin and makes him itch. He knows he is angry with himself for choosing to do this thing and that the anger will only go away, or become something useful, once he is doing it. He knows that Maria wishes he devoted less of himself to such a 'silly' sport. She's told him that putting 90 percent of himself into it would be an improvement, from her perspective. But for him, devoting himself entirely, putting all of himself into it, is the only thing that keeps it from being silly. Silly would be giving nearly all of yourself, being nearly great. And he's come to accept that his may be as much of an obsession for greatness as it is an unwillingness to be wrong.

He lets go of the handlebars and pedals upright, fingers on his watch. By lore, the great Greg Lemond once hammered his way to the summit of this mountain in twenty-seven minutes flat, starting from the very 7-Eleven Aaron is just now passing. The timer on the watch lets out a peep.

Two flicks of his finger sends the chain to the familiar gear. Aaron inches back on his saddle and takes air deep into his belly and drapes his hands on the brake hoods. He no longer has to be so mindful of his stroke. No longer has to remind himself again and again to drop his heel. His muscles have learned and they remember. For now. Soon they will ache and dead spots will creep into his stroke and it will take concentration to keep from wasting energy.

He comes to a church with an empty parking lot. Other than a few isolated driveways, this is the last turnoff until Virginia City. At the end of a long straightaway the road curves right.

It isn't until he is midway around this curve that Aaron first glimpses the landslide: a swath fifty yards wide of mud and uprooted sagebrush burying the roadway to a depth of two feet, deeper in places. A bulldozer has cleared a path about half a lane wide—not quite wide enough for a car yet. A man in a hardhat leans against a white pickup. Cars are lined up with their doors open, the drivers standing in clusters.

Aaron does not change his pace. He charges toward the roadblock as if his hard-earned momentum will make him exempt. He has no intention of stopping—he's not sure what he'll do, but the timer is running—and then the man in the hardhat is waving at him and Aaron considers this option—that is, letting the referee call this fight—but only for a moment.

The bulldozer is at the other side of the landslide pushing debris off the down slope. This leaves the path through the slide unblocked. Aaron hears shouting as he passes the crowd but he doesn't so much as slow down and a moment later he is on the other side, nodding at the driver of the bulldozer, who confusedly stares back as Aaron pedals by.

Aaron doesn't look back. The road ties itself in knots. It's a sports-car-commercial of a road, and today, empty. Juniper, sage, pine, and cedar grow on the broad faces and in the canyons, though not in great numbers. Aaron can see half of the sky. The other half is mountain. He comes to the place where the soil is white, with a seam of iron oxide as red and as dark as marrow running through it. Around a hairpin the gradient changes but not Aaron's cadence. Soon he can see sections of road below him, on previous planes.

There are sounds he remembers: the faint clanging of cow bells down in the valleys, the thrum of a peloton on cobblestone. The Tour is a race measured in weeks. There is time to listen.

Aaron's legs push the feet that move the pedals that drive the crank that spins the gears to pull the chain that snakes through the derailleur. Cycling. Road grit crackling under the tires. Aaron's tempo is not hasty nor is it patient and the gears he picks just big enough to sustain. Today the air feels a little cooler to him and the pain almost inviting. He suspects he knows why this is, but he denies this suspicion even as he can't help but wonder if it might just make all the difference.

When he gets to the pine tree draped in bras and beads he is eight seconds slow. Sweat saturates the pads in his helmet and dribbles off the tip of his nose. He looks out over the city in the valley below, alive with tiny motions but as soundless as if seen through glass.

He soon reaches the point at which he doesn't really care to go at all but over the winter he has willed himself into a motor, dispassionate and monotonous. Fuel and oxygen in, torque out.

When snow was still on the mountain he'd asked his coach if he was capable of winning the Tour and his coach wanted to know one thing. A number, measured in watts per kilogram. If it was seven, then yes, the coach had said, Aaron was very capable. But it wasn't seven and so Aaron had stopped eating certain things and acquainted himself with new levels of agony. He'd learned about denial. He'd denied the lactic acid in his legs and the growling in his stomach. He'd simplified things for himself. Motors go or they don't, he'd told Maria. People do the things in between.

People eat my berry cobbler, she'd said, nodding to Aaron's untouched plate.

Exactly, he'd said.

Exactly, she'd said.

Paniagua. That's what the Spanish riders were calling it. *Pan y agua*. Riding on bread and water. No little red pills.

I feel sorry for you, Maria had told him. It never seems like you're having *fun*.

Aaron had smiled, recalling an old French woman he'd passed once on the road to Alpe d'Huez. She too must have seen his pitiful grimace. She'd said a French word he recognized: *Courage*.

Aaron hadn't eaten Maria's cobbler. He'd treated his body like it wasn't even his. That was the way he'd found to let himself torture it. Pain *y agua*. That's what Aaron started calling it. It had gotten him close to where he needed to be. Very close.

One of his earliest attempts on this climb had coincided with a motorcycle rally in Virginia City. The bikers granted him generous berth as they swarmed by, but the angry grumbling of their two-stroke engines started to make Aaron mad. Until there came a lull in their traffic and Aaron heard himself wheezing and his bike creaking. When the next wave roared by he was glad for the noise. Since that day he's grown accustomed to the pained little noises he makes. Each ride becomes a meditation once he feels the rhythm of his heart, his breath, and his pedal stroke.

Seven: that is for his coach. Aaron's number is twenty seven.

There are other Aarons. Of course there are. Lovesick young men with their own mountains to court, in the Pyrenees and in the Alps and in the Andes. What Aaron needs to know—what he refuses to go to France without—is whatever secret this mountain once whispered in Lemond's ear.

Aaron rounds a bend and enters a long canyon, the mountain now on his left. He assesses his reserves, then picks out a highway sign three-hundred yards ahead. He upshifts two gears and rises out of the saddle, legs and arms pistoning. When he passes the sign he sits down again and downshifts, but only by one gear. Some days it is the lungs that hold him back. Other days the legs. The wind. There are days when even a distracted mind can hamper his ascent—an unfinished argument with Maria, or the formulation of a to-do list. Rarest of days are those when he cannot feel the chain.

He can feel the chain today.

He can sense Maria too. He's not blind to the thing he's become. When they met he was still an amateur. His ascension through the ranks has been a journey for her too. In a sport where no one but the rider gets to see the entire race, she has always been there, urging him to go—go!—at the start, then waiting all day at the finish. He has needed her there. But he has also needed her to not be there so many times in between.

Soon, the city and those in it are out of sight. A gust of wind sets the forest trembling and then the branches shake themselves still again. In the canyon below is the abandoned road from the Comstock Lode days. Carrying silver home from Virginia City was once as dangerous as digging it out of the mountain: landslides and highwaymen lay in wait—the getting of treasure and the escaping with it being sometimes separate battles, and unequal ones. Aaron swallows a mouthful of water and tosses the half-empty bottle to the side of the road to pick up later. He's decided nothing is negligible. What isn't man or bike is burden.

Aaron climbs out of the back rim of the canyon. He emerges onto a high plain where road goes flat for half a mile. There is a weather-beaten wooden cross beside the road. On its neck, a lei. Near the intersection with Cartwright Road, Aaron comes upon a highway patrolman chatting with the driver of an idling pickup. The driver looks up the road and says something and together the two men watch the young man grinding toward them on his bicycle. They listen to him panting and notice the dry spittle in the corners of his mouth. Aaron pedals past without a word. The two men watch him.

Up to this point Aaron has been hoarding strength. Comfortable in his suffering. Now, the time has come to pay. The next five minutes will be the worst.

The pickup he's just passed comes up from behind him and veers over the double yellow to give Aaron room. A small boy in the backseat stares out the back window in wonder, pointing past Aaron at some wild horses just off the road. The horses stand with their heads low, lipping the underbrush.

Aaron notices neither the boy nor the horses.

The road once again pitches upward. Aaron comes to terms with what he is inflicting upon himself. He accelerates.

Four minutes later he wants nothing—nothing—but for it to end. Breathing scalds. Pedaling aches. Thinking ceases. He is out of the saddle, swaying, teeth bared. Near collapse. The summit is within sight and seeing it and knowing just how many more seconds remain pushes him to depths of himself he's glimpsed but never delved. The pain scorches everything his mind shifts to.

He counts each stroke, bargaining with himself for just a hundred more. He gets to ten. Twenty. He feels he will collapse. Still there is road above him. He gets to thirty. He is pedaling his bike underwater. His ears are ringing. Forty. Fifty. Like a witching stick the handlebars steer themselves, turning away from the uphill grade. Sixty. Seventy. Eighty. The hills buzz with insects. The white line slips out of focus. Ninety. One hundred. Still there is road left above him.

And then there isn't. Aaron steals a look at his watch. The

numbers are a blur. With quaking hands he stops the timer. He unclips his cleats and brings his leg over the top tube and lays the bike over in the dirt, the front wheel still spinning. Bent double, panting and retching, Aaron feels the sting of welling tears and tastes his own blood.

He hobbles away from the road and sits slumped against the sign that gives the pass' elevation in feet—6,789, like a counting timer: 6-7-8-9…. He feels like a boxer waiting at the decision of a long fight, ready to hear the announcer yell his opponent's name and to feel the referee let go of his wrist. It has been close. He lifts his watch and looks and sees that he's done it.

It's taken a bigger piece of him than he expected. He almost wants to *undo* it. To take more time and, having trained fully, do it right, under control: *Paniagua*. Because this doesn't carry the dignity he's hunted. He kept the motor in the red for a good half mile and now he is clammy and quaking and delirious and alone in the cold sunshine.

Aaron wonders if Lemond felt this way. If he achieved it this way. Aaron has learned no secret here. He knows he will never again attempt this climb like this. But he will inevitably pass this way again. His wish is to come to the bottom of this mountain and see the coiled road rise up to greet him, and feel nothing.

The back of his throat is coated in bile and he misses his water bottle. The cleats are unstable on the loose ground and his muscles are sluggish and he half-rolls his ankle while walking back to his bike. A cloud slides across the sun. The patch of ground Aaron is on darkens. A minute later the air is bright and warm again and Aaron wants to linger here at the summit and await some swell of satisfaction but he has started to shiver. He feels he needs to get moving. He clips in and settles himself on the saddle with his hands in the hooks.

For the first time all morning the bike moves without being pedaled. Momentum accumulates and soon Aaron is descending, leaning through the turns. Sections of road that took minutes to earn are spent in seconds. For Aaron, it's a familiar movie rewinding. But he is exhausted and not as nimble as usual. The descent feels soupy.

He stops to pick up his bottle. The water is warm. He drinks greedily.

Soon he is back in his crouch, wind whipping. Doubt haunts him: is the record truly broken? Can he say he is done with this? The thought makes his gut roil, his grip tighten. He fails to properly set up his turns. Time after time he comes out of them late, drifting across double yellows. On any other day this would be dangerous. But today the road is his alone.

He is approaching a right hairpin when he hears a pop and sets his rear brake in reflex, squeezing too tight, locking the wheel into a skid. He eases off just as the bike starts to fishtail. The front tire wobbles, hissing. Brake pads rubbing in a panicked rhythm. Aaron struggles to stay upright. He glances down at the bike, unwilling to believe that it's betrayed him, and when next he looks up the guardrail is an instant away.

Ants traffic about on Aaron as they would a fallen tree. His eyes flutter and roll around behind the lids.

Soon he will open them. Soon he will become frightened. He will shudder into a state more fully awake and squirm to free himself from the prickly clutch of sagebrush and his mind will light up. A flurry of signals, all arriving at once, will overload the circuitry. He will shut his eyes and suck air. Groan.

Soon he will feel panic and confusion. He will jolt upright, wanting to reclaim a rightful orientation. And rolling in behind a wave of pain—a wave he's seen coming—will be a bigger wave he hasn't. Soundless recollections, surfacing from aquamarine depths, will rise toward him like divers, shedding bubbles, passing him messages. Reminding him what he was, and leaving him to decide if that's what he is.

He will probe himself with his good hand, running it as Maria would up his side. Fingertips gentle and tentative. Cataloguing what's been broken. His tongue will worry jagged new contours inside his mouth. Naked nerve endings in the sockets oozing a mineral taste he will half savor. A tag of bitten cheek flesh dangling, tantalizingly.

He'll be forced to wait. To endure a new kind of pain—a kind he didn't invite. Eventually cars will pass on the road above and he will scream and hear the disturbing timbre of his own desperation, hear the engines as they fade away.

Earlier that morning, he'd imagined Maria sitting at the kitchen table, reading, and he'd been wrong. At that moment she'd been crumpled on the floor against the refrigerator, crying and cursing him and letting herself finally spill over. Before he even reached the summit she'd packed two suitcases and loaded them into her car.

Soon, Aaron will discover the watch tethered to his wrist —the timer displaying 26:52 –and he'll angrily reset the timer, as if doing so might reset everything.

In the middle of the day, three men in a battered sedan will drive up the canyon on the old toll road. They will get out and stand around making jokes while they set up cans on rocks and take turns shooting them. The reports of their pistols will echo on the mountain. One of them will notice bright colors entangled in sagebrush, and they will hike up to the injured young man and call an ambulance.

The young man will ask to borrow a cell phone.

And when Maria's phone buzzes to life on the kitchen counter of her sister's apartment, displaying some unknown number, her sister will turn the phone off.

While the men wait with Aaron they will fetch him some

water and talk to him. They will ask him why he shaves his legs.

The softer orange light of morning will have long bled out. There will only be the bright heat of a high desert midday, the shadows in hiding. The din of insects quelled. Lizards will emerge from cracks in the granite and lay white bellies against warm stone. To the south a thunderhead will mushroom, clumpy and monstrous. A temporary calmness like night will settle over the mountain.

MAYFLY

OUR MAYFLY WRIGGLES UP THROUGH THE SILT of the river bottom and into the water above, savoring the fresh flavors in his gills. Hibernation has left him groggy. With a gentle hop he joins the flowing murk and is carried downstream, glancing against pebbles slick and cool to the touch. He tunes into the murmurs and clicks of the river underworld. The muted colors could use some punching up, he feels, but no matter. *Carpe diem*. Our mayfly is happy enough just to be alive. A mayfly like any other. Except for the oversized cartoon eyes and the recognizable voice of a mildly Jewish comic actor with broad demographic appeal.

He falls in love right away.

She is clinging to a reed. It sways in super slow-mo. Shall he compare her mouth to a mulcher? It art more omnivorous and more economical. He grows to love this mouth. The way it scrapes and sucks fish shit off rocks. But she plays hard to get. She gives him the silent treatment. The cold pronotum.

He waxes anthropomorphic, praising her rock-hard abdomen, her no-nonsense charm. She stares, chewing, into the gloom. Often she just scuttles off. No nod of acknowledgment, no flip of the antenna. It is as if she doesn't know he *exists*.

Worse. It is as if she doesn't know *she* exists.

He names her Jennifer.

After a particularly fruitless afternoon of wooing, he takes three of her claws in three of his and more or less drags her across the riverbed to a sun-warmed shallow near the bank. *This* she seems to respond to. When she sinks her incisors into his mesonotum, it tickles a bit. Jennifer's a feisty one! And he's open to that. He runs his foreleg through her caudal filaments and she curls into a fetal, shrimp-like position, which at least makes her easier to transport. He rolls her to the water's edge and waits. When she uncurls from an O into a C, her view is of a yellow buttercup, lit by a beam of sunlight, with snowy granite domes in the backdrop.

When the hatch happens, he begins, but her blank expression worries him. The hatch, he says. You know about that, right?

No response.

It's okay, he says. So, when everybody starts sprouting wings, we'll have just a few hours to live, and mate. And I guess what I'm asking is, will you do me the honor of—you know…

No response. He thinks perhaps he has offended her.

Not right this minute, of course, he says. When the time comes. I've found the perfect place. The yellow chalice you see before you. Promise me, Jennifer. Promise me you'll meet me there?

Her mouth gapes. He considers this a positive sign. A 'yes'. Maybe.

But it's something else. It's awe. Jennifer has never seen air.

A figure swift and black glides overhead. It lands nearby and starts pecking in the muck.

Jennifer! he cries.

Jennifer curls up. Jennifer is plucked out of the water like a Cheerio. Jennifer is swallowed whole.

Our mayfly crawls under a rock and there he remains for what would be two of our years, or about 10 days. The next night, a large female squeezes in next to him during a thunderstorm. She's a generous listener. He names her Diane.

Diane doesn't seem to fault him for droning on and on about the time he bore witness to the murder and ingestion of his ex, still fresh in his mind. When next the sun brightens the water, she ventures out and he follows. Yapping away, he bumps into her as they navigate a narrow passage between two rocks. He apologizes. Diane doesn't budge. He scrambles up and over her body to find that it ends abruptly. The top third of her has been pulverized by a rogue twig.

A week later, he is at Sheila's side when she quakes, convulses, and explodes after eating some bad decomposed organic matter.

He reconsiders the practice of naming his love interests.

In fact, he wonders if he's just not cut out for romance. But the days grow longer and the water warmer and he knows he can't just give up, so one evening in early June he finds himself back at the shoreline. Different buttercup, same proposal. This time he really has to grapple. He pins her down with all of his legs, leaving his antenna free to point out the flower. Horrific grinding noises come from her hypopharynx.

Listen, he says. *Listen!* I, for one, am not content to be— hold still! Do we have to be opportunistic generalists like everyone else? Let's make a choice. Together. Stop it! I'm not letting go of you. Can I call you Caroline?

She stops squirming.

That's better, he says. We can be *humane* about this.

He eases his grip.

It's my eyes, isn't it? he says. I know: they're *googly*.

She shivs him with two of her claws and disappears into a carpet of moss.

Caroline, he gasps, you heartless nymph.

Our mayfly stops eating and hopes to be eaten. Hour to hour, day to day, very little changes. He spends most days just drifting. One night he is awoken by the dull reverberations of a floating tree banging against boulders. Another time he is nearly stamped flat by a clumsy set of hooves, only to endure gulp after gulp of hot, cascading piss.

When one morning his guts empty out and fill with air, he attributes it to his hunger strike. He's disappointed to see other, healthier mayflies contracting similar symptoms. Newly buoyant, he rises. The river bottom recedes from view. He somehow knows he'll never see it again. This realization elicits an unexpected and embarrassing little onslaught of nostalgia, which ends as soon as he pierces the surface and is blinded by sunlight. The river's murmur is now a roar.

Others pop up all around him. Hundreds of them. Mayflies bobbing on the surface like life-jacketed survivors of some catastrophe.

He watches his neighbors unfurl glistening wings, gorgeous to behold, and stretch them out to dry. Soon the air thrums with takeoffs and landings. Mayflies skitter to and fro upon the water's cellophane-like surface. Some stay aloft long enough to reach drooping willow branches. Others fall back into the river, where they are met by rising bass—a sight that sends panic rippling through the floating multitude. Crowd-fed panic. Save-thyself panic. Hollow-out-thy-mother-to-make-a-canoe panic.

Our mayfly is washed downstream around a bend. He

eddies out over a sandbar and gets carried into a long, shallow riffle between steep banks. Though his shuck has cracked, it is not open wide enough to let him out. He is stuck. As he struggles, he sees, in a meadow beside the river, a passel of buttercups.

The river bends again. The flowers shrink from view. He is overcome with self-pity. His enormous eyes well up.

Exhausted nearly to death, he glances off a boulder in the middle of the stream and is flipped facedown. Once again, the world turns muffled and dim. He struggles to right himself. Looking up through the water, he catches distorted glimpses of glinting gossamer against a cloudy sky, the new wings of those who've taken flight heading sunward like little Icaruses.

He stops fighting and floats. He wants to give up, but as soon as he tries he gets angry, and all of a sudden he's a raving lunatic, muscling free of a straitjacket. His eyes turn bloodshot. He surprises himself with his own strength and the shuck cracks. He takes a deep breath and discovers that he has soiled himself.

He squirms free of his former corpus and finds his bearings. The river here is slow-moving and shaded. His feet make little dents on the water, but don't quite poke through. He starts walking *on* the water. Kind of like Jesus, if Jesus had possessed wings and two penises.

What would Jesus do with wings, two penises and a few hours to live?

Here's what our mayfly does: he darts upstream, hoping against hope that Caroline is still single. He follows the river until he reaches the buttercups. And that's when he first lays googly eyes upon it: a dark, shifting cloud of mayflies, slung low over the water like smog, scattering and rearranging with each passing breeze.

It's a happening scene. He flies right into it. Once inside, he sees the swarm for what it really is—a quasi-consensual gangbang. A female that might be Caroline catches his eye and he tracks her as she zips among the groping throngs. She is approached by a pair of males, both of whom attempt to snatch her out of the air. Both miss. She picks up speed again, only to be nabbed and doubly penetrated by a third male. She goes limp in his clutch as they hover a few feet from the water, her wings no longer beating. He lets her go. Other males make half-hearted grabs for her as she plummets. She plops into the water, squeezes out a gooey cluster of eggs. Dies.

Our mayfly wants to scoop her up and lay her fragile body to rest inside a clamshell jewelry box with white silk lining. A coffin befitting a fallen pixie. But there are too many —far, far too many—too many to count. The river is littered with fucked-to-death Tinkerbells. Fish and birds are gorging themselves. He sees a brown trout vomit up a paste of half-digested FTDTs, then start eating again.

Hovering mid-swarm, pivoting up, down, left, right, our mayfly takes it all in, this godforsaken fuckfest warzone Armageddon. The sun is all but blackened out. He hears the groans of the ecstatic and of the dying. He smells sex and putrefaction. The air is fecund. The river is a moving carpet of carcasses.

Caroline. He knows he is never going to rendezvous with her. He wants to cry out. He can't. His mouth is merely ornamental, a genetic throwback to some classier ancestor— from a time when adults were adults, who wined and dined, then made love.

He feels suicidal, which is awkward because he also has a handsome, matching pair of erections. Like most everything, they have proven to be well beyond his control.

A hefty male rises up out of the frenzy and grabs him, hugging his metathorax. The embrace is a bit constricting but also consoling, somehow. This is all he needed, our mayfly realizes. Just to be held.

The hefty male rapes him for a few seconds, then flies off.

Dusk falls on the river. Starving, but also lacking a working mouth, our mayfly huddles under a slab of bark. He is spent, although his erections have yet to subside. Normally this would embarrass him, but he's too close to death to feel mortified.

Then, out of the deepening blue…what? A light?

Yes. A glorious light. It wakes him as if from a dream. It shines from nearby and it is breathtaking. He feels compelled to make his way toward it.

As he flies, the light gets bigger and brighter and then it separates into two lights. They are the headlights of a 1989 Ford Escort LX parked at a campground near the riverbank. Apparently, he isn't the first to be mesmerized by these lights, judging by the bumper-high pile of dead mayflies accumulating below each one. Our mayfly spends his last few moments deliberating: Is it more meaningful to die in the pile on the left or the pile on the right? He decides upon the left, and there he falls.

Overnight, the two piles get bigger and then merge into one wide heap. The car's battery dies and the headlights go out.

In the morning a snowplow must be called in to scrape the drifts of dead flies off the asphalt so people can park.

Gross, mutters the snowplow driver.

THE CARETAKER

MATT TOOK THE LATE FLIGHT out of LAX. Ana waited for him at the airport in Reno. She had on high-cut shorts, Ugg boots and a hoodie—dressed like a teenager (or another actress), Matt thought, though he pegged her closer to 30. The other men in baggage claim were sneaking peeks at her. It was the legs.

Ana kept her head down, thumbing a message into her cell. When next she looked up, she spotted Matt waiting beside the baggage carousel. Despite the warm summer night, he had on a corduroy sports jacket over a T-shirt, unkempt jeans, and canvas tennis shoes. Block-frame glasses. Gelled tussle of dark hair. Another brooding cynic, she thought, like the others who'd pilgrimaged to Hugh's house since she took the caretaker job. She slid the phone into her front pocket and picked her way through the crowd of weary travelers to where he stood.

Matt? she said.

He nodded, and she held out her hand. She was a good three inches taller than him.

Ana, she said.

Matt realized that people were glancing at him now. He

wondered how she'd known who he was. Ana recognized the need to explain.

Hugh described you, she said.

Oh? Matt said. And what did he say?

He said you'd look like—like this. Like you. She smiled, held up her hands, framing him.

Matt frowned. Ana smiled, relishing his discomfort, if only for a moment.

And, Ana said, he texted me your picture.

Matt followed her outside to the parking garage, where she unlocked a silver Escalade. At Ana's insistence he handed her his duffel, which she loaded into the back while he climbed into the backseat.

You can sit up front if you like, Ana said through the open back hatch.

It's fine, Matt said.

Ana decided to take the Mount Rose highway instead of going back through Truckee, the way she'd come. She stopped once at Matt's request to buy something to eat at a drive-thru. Cheeseburgers. He muttered his order through the back window, then chewed in silence, taking pulls on his soda while she steered through the hairpins. She glanced now and then in the rear view mirror. It was only a matter of time before he hit on her. Already he'd held out longer than most. She'd never had one choose to ride in the backseat after being given the option.

When Matt fell asleep or pretended to, she turned on the radio at low volume. They crested the summit, and Lake Tahoe spread into view. The water was obsidian, with a scalloped swath of moonlight receding to the far shore. She retracted the sunroof and lifted her hand into the cool push of air. She sang under her breath to the songs on the radio.

After following the shoreline around the north side of the

lake, they came to an unmarked gate. Ana keyed in a code. The long beep wakened Matt. She watched him reanimate. The driveway led downhill through pine trees. As they passed the caretaker cottage Ana turned to look at it, then drove on and parked in front of the main house.

The house was built of wood and steel, but more than anything, glass. Ana led Matt inside, where she moved with obvious familiarity, flipping on lights, deactivating alarms. Matt cast his eyes about the cavernous main room. It looked a lot like Hugh's house in LA. Same discomforting art. Same uncomfortable furniture. There was a bearskin rug under a glass cube that served for a coffee table.

Mountain minimalist, Ana said—noticing Matt take it all in.

Is that what Hugh calls it? Matt asked.

Ana pinned her hair up and adjusted the thermostat.

You should be set, she said. I left the number for the cottage next to the phone—call me if you need anything.

Matt thanked her and peeled open his wallet. Pulled out a twenty, then another. Ana turned away.

Take it, Matt said, stepping toward her with the money.

She slipped past his outstretched hand and looped her arms around him in a hug. By the time he could react—he tried to reciprocate the hug, using his one free arm—she'd let go, telling him this wasn't LA.

She left him standing in the foyer amid dissipating perfume. She didn't feel bad about being so abrupt, though she could see the deflating effect it had on her new guest. She was exhausted. She drove back up the hill to the caretaker cottage, with half a mind to take a hot bath. Instead she melted into the oversized couch, her legs entwining a long decorative cushion, and turned on the TV. She didn't watch it, but she liked the noise it made, the voices, the canned laughs. Soon she was asleep.

Matt, meanwhile, had taken a Fiji water from the refrigerator. He'd stared, sipping, out at the dark main room.

He'd felt the wadded twenties in his pocket, pulled them out and straightened them, as if he could unspend the affront back into his wallet, but surprised himself when instead he flung the wallet into the dark. It struck glass.

Matt found the stairs and descended to the basement where there was no glass. The hallway outside the cutting room was lined with pictures of black holes—a tradition started by an editor who, having spent one too many summer days cooped up down there, pinned an illustration of a black hole outside the door. Subsequent editors followed suit. The early pictures were conventional—purchased in planetarium gift shops or torn from the pages of popular magazines, with galaxies swirling down pinhole drains. Compelling versions to look at, if not entirely realistic. As the tradition expanded away from the door, contributors had pushed beyond the cliché into the risqué. The resulting 'black holes' were what could be expected of people deprived of natural light, fresh air and sex.

Matt found a spare duvet in the linen closet and dragged it over to the cutting room couch. It was nearly pitch black in the room with the lights out. Already it was Matt's favorite room in the house. There was comfort in the dim glow of the video equipment.

The next day around 10:30 a.m., after getting no response to the door chime, Ana took out her key just in time to see Matt emerge from the stairwell with his hair flattened to one side of his head. He opened the door and shielded his eyes from the gushing daylight. Ana stepped in, unbidden. The hardwood floors were warm underfoot. She loved that about the place.

She handed Matt a FedEx package. I came by earlier, she said. You didn't answer.

Matt smiled, squinting. Ana could tell it embarrassed him to be caught off guard this

way. Had she misread him as self-absorbed? Now he just seemed garden-variety shy, or even sad.

You painted your fingernails, he said.

Ana held her hand out in such a way that it seemed rude for Matt not to take it. He did.

Too red? she asked.

Matt swallowed. Just the right amount, he said.

This is fun, Ana thought. She hadn't had fun in a while.

Matt thanked her again for the package.

On her walk back through the pines to the cottage, she stopped to pluck a pine needle from her bare foot and glanced back just in time to see Matt ease the door shut.

Matt took the package into the kitchen, cut the tape with a steak knife and sifted through the bits of Styrofoam for a 572-pound man named Curtis Montgomery III.

Curtis seated on toilet in small bathroom.

Curtis: You come up with ways. I got this out of a catalog.

Curtis holds up device with handle on one end and a clip for toilet paper on other. He reaches down, off camera, grimacing.

Matt didn't like to be around during filming any more than a defense attorney likes to be around when a crime is committed. And so by the time Matt first got a look at him, Curtis had already been treated by a small team of junior editors Matt called the triage unit. For weeks they had been cleaning things up as best they could, cutting away the obviously inconsequential, the dead time. They had saved what remained on a pair of 200-gigabyte hard drives and overnighted them to the lake.

Curtis leaning against condiment counter, squinting as he scans menu board. Nearby, a young girl holding tiny paper cup is gawking. Curtis finally notices.
  Curtis: Oh, I'm sorry, darling. Am I blocking the ketchup?
  Girl looks at camera, waves.
  Girl: Are you making a movie?
  Curtis: They are.
  Girl: About Wendy's?
  Curtis shares smile with camera crew (off camera laughter).
  Curtis: About me.
  Long pause. Girl looking around. Curtis turns back to menu board.

For Matt, the next four days became a single, 96-hour period. In the morning of this overgrown day, he watched film and took notes, then went back to the kitchen to eat three bowls of stale Apple Jacks. He watched more film and took more notes, went to the bathroom, watched more film. He sucked his way through a box of Tic Tacs. He fell asleep. Watched more film. Went upstairs. The sun went down, came back up, went back down. The basement stayed dark. Matt ate and slept. Woke up and ate again while he watched film. He filled one notepad and started another.

Hugh called. He told Matt to help himself to whatever he wanted from the wine cellar and the humidor.

Somebody needs to enjoy my things, Hugh said. How's Curtis?

He's a sad tub of shit, Matt said.

So…*you*, Hugh said. Only fat.

Fat*ter*, Matt said.

I was thinking, Hugh went on. Remember that campaign a few years back where they were trying to save the manatees? The boats were cutting them up with their propellers? Well, that's what we've got here. Let's get people to see a victim. So they get to place blame. Blame America. The critics eat that up.

You're out of Apple Jacks, Matt said.

You listening to me?

Apple, Matt said. Jacks.

Tell the caretaker.

Ana, Matt said.

Ana, Hugh agreed. That's another bottle I've never managed to open.

Really? She seems like your type.

Agreed, Hugh said. Problem is, she doesn't want to be an actress and of course she's already got money. Leaves me with no leverage.

Matt didn't respond. He was trying to remember something. After a short silence, Hugh told him to go crawl back into his hole.

Curtis, slumped across couch. Sunlight through vertical blinds. He stares at TV.

Curtis: I have to work at home now so I don't dress up. I've had these on since, like, Monday [tugs on sweatpants]. Work, eat, sit, eat, work. It's not living, I think. I'm breathing, I'm walking around, doing what I gotta do, but that's it. So, to answer your question: Nothing. I have hope for nothing.

Curtis lifts remote control, changes channels, watches for a minute, changes channels. Jiggles straw in his cup.

Curtis: It's like, life's going on in there [nods at television] but I'm out here. I can watch, but I can't be in it. It won't be long, they'll have to tear down a damned wall to get me out.

. . .

On the morning of the fifth day, Matt was startled by sounds in the house. He climbed the stairs in his socks and peeked down the hallway, where a repairman stood in the kitchen, filling out a form against a metal clipboard.

Matt bid the man good morning and opened the refrigerator.

Nice place, said the repairman.

It works, Matt joked. He took a tentative whiff from a jug of orange juice.

Especially that view, the repairman said, motioning toward the wall of glass. Outside, Ana was leaning over the deck railing, shaking out a rug. She wore a strappy blue tank top, her hair pulled back in a thick braid.

You're a lucky man, the repairman said.

Ana opened the sliding glass door and came inside with the rug. She resituated it at the backdoor.

Running fine now, the repairman told her. She came across the main room to stand at the kitchen island. Matt took a long pull of orange juice to keep himself from gawking. Ana smiled at him.

Morning, honey, she said.

The last four days, for Ana, had been four separate days. She had paid bills, done errands, run on the treadmill, cooked dinners. She had thought about Matt.

She handed Matt his wallet, the one he'd thrown across the room in frustration 96 hours ago. You dropped this, she said.

Ana showed the repairman out, and was planning to leave, too, when she heard what sounded like popcorn. She returned to the kitchen to find a bag engorging in the microwave. A brand she didn't recognize. Matt was gone, so she peeked in the pantry and found other things she hadn't stocked (Apple Jacks, Cap'n Crunch, bottles of Fiji water, beef jerky). Noticing that the back door was ajar, she went outside and found Matt on the shaded porch that faced the forest. He was smoking a cigarette.

She bummed one, then stood waiting for Matt to light it.

Oh, Matt said when he realized this. I don't smoke, Matt said. Well, not normally. It's a work habit—or, a break-from-work habit… Anyway, I don't have a lighter. I've been using the burner on the stove.

Ana put the cigarette in her lips and assessed Matt one more time before stepping toward him. He still had his cigarette in his mouth and she put the tip of hers against it until it glowed, then took it out and held it near her hip as she exhaled. Inside the house, popcorn was bursting.

I would have gone shopping for you, she said. That's kind of my job.

I'm sure you have better things to do than buy me Pop Tarts.

I didn't see those, Ana said. How'd you get to the store?

I walked, Matt said, holding back a grin, adding: Well, full disclosure, I hitched a ride back.

Ana laughed. Something was bubbling in her. Here, now, was something that hadn't presented itself in—how long? Long enough that merely contemplating it felt silly, but also a little sinister, in the way housecats can be—napping on an armrest one minute, eviscerating a songbird the next.

She told Matt that the dishwasher was fixed. That he didn't have to pile his dishes in the sink anymore. He nodded, took a drag.

You didn't know it was broken, she said, did you?

Matt shook his head. He said, The repairman thought I was your boyfriend.

Husband, Ana said.

You noticed that too, then.

It's what I told him, Ana said.

Matt turned serious.

With repairmen and cable guys, Ana said, I'll usually tell them my husband's downstairs. Otherwise, guys get ideas.

Wow, Matt said. Yeah. I guess it's a real concern. For someone like you...

Ana didn't respond. She let the moment stew a little.

Matt carried on: I just mean, as a woman, who's...

...alone, Ana said.

...pretty, Matt said at the same moment.

He paused. Sorry, he said. I'm bad at this.

Bad at what? Ana said, savoring his discomfort.

Talking, Matt said.

Talking to you own wife? Ana said. She shoved him, gently. He held his ground. He felt as if his body were pure electricity. Popcorn like gunfire now.

Then I want a divorce, Ana said. You'll be hearing from my lawyer.

Our lawyer, Matt played along.

Not anymore, Ana said.

Shit, Matt said.

But first we should go in the hot tub, Ana said. One last time.

Fine, Matt said.

He started a laugh to break the tension, wrap the scene, but Ana stubbed out her cigarette and took his hand, assuming (correctly) that he had no idea where the hot tub was.

The Tahoe Gal paddle wheeler cruised by on schedule, just after 1 o'clock in the afternoon. Those aboard drank complementary beer and wine while the tour guide clued them in on the shoreline real estate, telling the ladies to keep their eyes peeled in the next cove where they might spot a particular heartthrob sunbathing on a dock...

The people craned their necks and borrowed each other's

binoculars, hoping to get a prurient glimpse, but the heartthrob wasn't there. He didn't own the house, could never have afforded it. It belonged to a producer who occasionally let heartthrobs come to the house to escape Los Angeles. The producer didn't like to leave Los Angeles.

What the passengers saw instead was a naked man and a naked woman. The man had been gifted a Sony Betacam for his 12th birthday—the year: 1982, the place: Omaha, Nebraska —and he'd kept the camera in his hand for the better part of the next three days, spending his nights in his pup tent with the star of his film (GI Joe) and his days shooting footage of a war being waged in a jungle of weeds. That same year—1982, when the woman was six years old, in Halmstad, Sweden— she'd been handed a used Prince Junior tennis racket by her stepfather and told to take it downstairs and across the street to the public courts and hit against the backboard, which she did, for the next three hours.

The man and woman sprinted down a footpath along the side of the house—the man unable to keep up—then out across the lawn onto a long wooden dock. One young passenger on the boat was quick enough to capture a snapshot with his digital camera as the couple leapt into the lake, but when he zoomed in all context was lost, the genitalia just pixilated splotches, too vague to titillate.

Curtis. Same couch, same pajamas, same sunlight through vertical blinds.

    Voice, off camera: Do you have a girlfriend?

    Curtis: No, sir. Haven't for a long time.

    He watches a little more TV.

    Curtis: A real long time.

. . .

Matt slouched in an Adirondack chair and felt about as good as he'd ever felt. In the span of an hour he'd done no less than escape a black hole, only to stumble into an unscripted hot tub scene. Ana had taken off her clothes and tapped a switch on the wall to turn on the bubbles and settled into the churning foam as naturally as if she were alone, so Matt had stripped down and plopped in beside her. The watery kissing and caressing lasted a while, and when sex seemed imminent she'd slipped his embrace and boosted herself over the side of the tub and taken off running. So he'd given chase like some plodding goon.

The cold water of the lake, when Matt hit it, had excited pathways inside him that, he thought, must have fallen dormant. He'd remembered that life could actually feel this way, sometimes, and he'd surfaced with a whoop into the sunlight and climbed up a ladder into a white towel Ana had found inside the ski boat and the towel was intensely warm.

Ana, too, basked in her own Adirondack. Seeing Matt happy warmed her pride in an almost maternal way. She'd seen men like Matt before. They stayed at Hugh's house all the time, but never before had she felt a desire to intervene, if that's what this was. She was happy with herself for bringing a little joy to this one. Joy enough to split, it turned out.

They sat side by side in their chairs, not talking.

Then, feeling outmatched by a moment bigger than he was used to living, Matt started talking. Harmless, giddy chatter at first. But Ana wasn't saying much in reply, and this left Matt desperate to fill the dead air.

It scared Ana a little, the way Matt talked. As if he were arguing. He would ask and then answer his own questions. Then fall silent for a spell. Then start up again.

He apologized for the dirty dishes, and for hiding out in the basement. He wasn't like this in LA, he told her. In LA he was different. For starters, he explained, he was a neat freak on the verge of compulsive. And he wasn't such a vampire. He had routines.

She listened awhile, then gave him an out by offering to fetch the cigarettes. Matt politely declined, and off he went again—about the Venice boardwalk, about smiling and petting dogs even though sometimes it was all he could do not to turn and trudge across the sand out into the surf and just, whatever, keep going until he was underwater. Just get underwater. Away from people. This is when he quoted Sartre, in French.

Hugh thinks you're brilliant, Ana said.

Hugh, Matt said.

Thing was, Ana already knew plenty about capital-L Lonely, about self-inflicted isolation, about forcing yourself out the door to the things normal people do even though when you come home, the walls welcome you back in and remind you that you should never have left. And hearing Matt dissect Lonely in what was clearly an oft-employed, therapist-speak (she'd learned the vocabulary, too, once), she found herself beginning to resent him. She didn't want to resent him. She stood up and rewrapped her towel.

No no no, Matt said, putting his palms together, beseeching. Sorry, he said—smiling. I either don't say enough or I say too much. Please. Sit back down. Stay.

She kissed him and tussled his hair, then walked back across the lawn. He didn't see her again for two days.

Curtis steering grocery store scooter. His mother walking alongside. He rolls up to freezer display. Mother watches as he struggles to pry door open, grunts, rising out of seat to reach in. One at a time he wrestles three frozen pizzas into handlebar basket.

Mother: I know Curtis feels like he woke up one day and there it was, he was this way. But we know it didn't happen overnight. We was ignoring it.

Curtis rolls deeper into freezer aisle. Mother shuffles behind.

Matt could take footage of a man buying a pack of gum and cut it to look like armed robbery. He had good reason to worry how it might play with Ana if he showed up on her doorstep unannounced. Desperate? Presumptuous?

He half-turned around, but, looking back at the big house, he knew that he didn't have it in him to spend any more time with the fat man in the basement. Curtis was eating at him.

He rang the bell at the cottage.

Ana answered. She looked angry, and she was, a little. Matt should have come by a day ago, a Friday, when she was expecting him to. When she'd made herself casually pretty— put in a little effort. Instead, he'd come now, at 10:30 on Saturday morning. And so she opened the door wide, letting Matt take it all in. Might as well. She had her hair up inside an ugly baseball cap. Her baggy sweats did her figure no justice. Behind her was a little boy with a stick horse over his shoulder like a club. A little girl sat coloring at the kitchen table. Both the boy and the girl looked to be about ten years old. Ana crossed her arms and adjusted her stance, advancing one slipper out the door.

Couldn't sleep, Matt explained. Thought I'd see if you were up.

At this, the tension in Ana's face lessoned by a degree only perceptible to someone staring intently into it and dying to see exactly that: Matt.

Ha ha, Ana said.

Whose kids? Matt asked.

Ana patted her breast plate.

Ha ha, Matt said.

Ana said nothing.

Oh, Matt said.

Ana gave a guilty smile. Matt had no choice but start

apologizing about all he'd said at the lake. However, to Ana, that didn't matter anymore. She'd moved on, days ago. She told him that it was okay, but lingered in the doorway with her arms crossed, not inviting him in. She was playing from the baseline. Keeping the ball in play. It was, after all, the first time Matt had come to the net.

Who's that guy? yelled the girl.

That guy is Matt, Ana yelled back.

Is Matt coming with us? yelled the boy.

Ana looked Matt over and asked him if he played peewee golf.

Yes! Matt hollered into the house. Matt is coming!

Golf's on me, he said quietly, so only Ana could hear. That's how we say thank you in LA, he explained.

Matt rode up front while Eliot and Ida sat in back, whispering to each other. Ana drove them all to a family restaurant with a miniature golf course out back.

Inside, a spry Jewish man was resituating pizzas in a brick oven. When he saw Ana and her kids, he leaned his peel against the bricks and came out from behind the counter, wiping his hands on his apron. He gave Ana a long hug and shook Matt's hand, then kneeled to greet the kids.

The owner's wife emerged through another door. She, too, came over to embrace them. She peered conspiratorially over her glasses at Ana for a moment before stepping toward Matt with arms open. Matt stood still, got hugged. Ana could see he was doing his best to be cordial and that it didn't come easy. While Matt was patting the woman's round back, Ana winked to him. The woman took them over to the cashier, where they were issued well-worn putters in four shades of neon. When she turned around to get them a scorecard Matt produced his wallet, but Ana snatched it away and stuffed it in her purse.

I told you I'm paying, Matt said.

Hearing this, the woman frowned and shook her finger at Ana. The husband materialized, making similar gesticulations, prompting Ana to apologize.

Outside, on the first tee Matt asked Ana how she knew the couple. She said she didn't know them very well, really.

How come they're so enamored with you? he asked.

Eliot dropped a pinecone on the bright green turf and hit it hard with his putter. It banged against a concrete windmill. He asked what *enamored* meant. Matt told him.

Oh, Eliot said. They're enamored because Mom beat Steffi Graf.

Twice, added Ida, heading into the trees to gather more pinecones for her brother.

Matt looked at Ana.

Let's not hit the pinecones, guys, she said.

Matt stared at Ana. She set her ball down and putted it. It rolled into a little tube protruding from the tentacle of an octopus, then out another tentacle as her cell phone started chirping. She looked at Matt, gaging whether it would be impolite if she answered it, but Matt was nodding: go ahead. She took the call, and Matt turned away, grateful for the time it afforded him to try and regain his bearings. Over the last half hour his compass had done nothing but spin.

It's for you, Ana said, handing Matt her phone.

Matt took it. Ana said nothing. Matt said, Hello?

Red handed! said Hugh.

Why are you calling me on Ana's phone? Matt asked.

Why aren't you working on my movie? Hugh replied.

Ana is Ana *Bruun*, Matt said, looking straight at Ana Bruun while she poked at the turf with her putter.

You knew that, Hugh laughed.

No, Hugh. I didn't.

. . .

Here's what Matt knew about Ana Bruun, because it was what most everyone knew, even those who didn't follow tennis, because she'd been on Entertainment Tonight as often as SportsCenter: she'd grown up in Sweden; her stepfather was a prick—he had a mustache if Matt remembered correctly —and a shabby old visor he wore all the time, and he'd taught Ana a nasty two-handed forehand and they'd traveled all over, sharing hotel rooms and winnings. Because Ana was good. Great, actually. But then it got tabloid. Something about her stepfather telling her not to have her baby? Right, that was it. But she hadn't listened, had she, and it was actually *babies*—twins—*his* twins!—but she left him in Stockholm and had the babies in (where else?) Los Angeles.

During dinner, the twins got in an argument about who got the last video-game quarter. The argument became a hitting match. Matt stood by as they were separated, and did his best to sustain the disciplinary atmosphere Ana seemed to want during the ride home. Everybody quiet in their own ways, for their own reasons. As soon as they got home Ana put the twins to bed. They had expected curt little kisses, but she stayed in their room awhile, chatting with them. They didn't realize how much she'd welcomed their misbehavior, how it had provided a welcome distraction from the upheaval. She asked them if they liked Matt and they looked at each other, agreeing: they did. He was fine. She kissed them both again.

She came back downstairs to find Matt on the porch swing. She sat on the chaise lounge, but pulled her legs up and hugged them. They sat in shared silence for a moment, listening to the traffic on the main road.

Hey, Ana said at last.

Nice to meet you, Matt said.

Ana smiled. She hadn't tried to hide anything from Matt, but she couldn't help but feel she owed him some *clarification.*

I don't make a big deal about that part of my life, she said.

But, it kind of *was* a big deal, Matt said.

Is it still? she asked.

Matt shrugged.

I assume you know the story, then? she said.

Some, he said.

She nodded.

When I came out of the hospital, she said, after they were born, there were cameras and reporters everywhere. I was a mess.

Cue Hugh, Matt said.

Exactly, Ana said. That's right when I met him. He convinced me to do the documentary. He said I should be telling *my* side.

I saw it, Matt told her. Years ago.

It *was* years ago.

Matt remembered the shaky home video footage (*girl hugs racket to breast, smiles proudly, leans racket against net, begins running line drills*) sentimentally spliced with fading tabloid covers, the personal interviews with ancillary family members who said more than they knew, the blonde phenom grunting at serves, a teenager who'd never been a little girl.

I watched it again not long ago, Ana said. It felt different. It made me into...I don't know.

Matt knew.

How'd you end up here? he asked.

Here? she said, tossing her head toward the cottage door, and Matt nodded, and she told him that one morning, as the dust from her ordeal was starting to settle, she was nursing the twins in a hotel room when it struck her that her father was probably looking for her, and though she didn't fear him, she also never wanted to see him again and she didn't want her babies growing up in LA, and what struck her next was that she knew only one person, really, who might do something for her. Hugh. And she was right: he gave her a house to take care of.

Your hair used to be short, Matt said after a while. You look totally different.

Ana nodded kindly, allowing Matt this chance to explain his oversight to himself.

I *am* different, she said.

Really? Matt asked. You think people can just…change?

Well, not overnight, Ana said. That's just in the movies.

Matt raised his brow. Yeah? he asked.

He got up from the swing. Walked across the porch toward the open front door of the cottage.

May I use your phone, Ana Bruun?

You may, Matthew…

Matt waited—knowing she didn't know his last name. Enjoying that.

Curtis in pajamas, leaning face down against bedroom dresser, hands folded in prayer. Room is dark. Prayer is inaudible, except for 'amen.' He steps away from dresser and tugs at duvet on bed and sits on mattress.

Curtis: I wake up in the middle of the night and I'm surprised I'm still alive. I figure I only have a few months left of actual life. But when I wake up and it's all pitch black in here, I always say to myself, I say out loud: well Curtis, you're still alive.

Hugh? Hi. No—no, it's Matt.

What's wrong? Hugh said.

Nothing. Where do you keep the wine up here?

The wine cellar.

Right. Where do you keep the wine cellar?

HILLBILLY

A TENNIS COURT FENCED IN IVY. A man in a white hat and matching warm-ups feeding volleys to an eager, sunkissed blonde. A gazebo as the centerpiece of a garden, and behind it a swimming pool, flat as glass.

The pictures were of a place called Stewart's Tennis Ranch. The brochure came to me in the mail when I turned 12. Across the front someone had written simply, "Enjoy!" There was no return address, nor was it signed, but we knew who'd sent it.

Grandma Jane found ways to pepper our lives with flavors of a lifestyle just beyond our grasp. Tickets to plays in San Francisco, weekend getaways to wine country. Grandma's benevolence often came by just such 'anonymous' means.

Dad had recently lost his job. The bank he'd worked for had pulled out of Nevada. They offered him a job managing home loans at a branch in Utah—a promotion in all but the geographic sense—but Todd and I cried for hours at the prospect of relocating. Life as we knew it in Reno would be different (over) in Ogden. Dad selflessly declined the offer. The Reno loan department he oversaw was phased out, but he stayed with his branch, working as an account manager and finally as a teller supervisor until at last the sign on the door changed.

That was a few months ago. He was still looking for a job. He resented his mother-in-law's charity, and I think Mom did too, but how could they argue? I argued though. The tennis camp was three weeks long.

My friends will be *here*, I said. (This was going to be a crucial summer for me and my friends: ten weeks to transform ourselves, by all mischief necessary, into middle schoolers, pedaling our bikes over hill and dale to whichever of our homes lacked parental supervision.)

You'll make friends at camp, Mom said.

You better, Dad tacked on. For what your grandmother's spending...

Stewart's Ranch was outside Carmel. Dad drove me there. We made our way down from Nevada's hills into California's long central valley, then over to the coast. We arrived around sunset and splurged at a Sizzler. After dinner we turned inland and drove to a little two-story motel that was the only place to stay near the camp. As we were waiting to be issued our key, I noticed a doughy, freckled boy availing himself of the complimentary coffee. He polished off the pot into two Styrofoam cups. I noticed the tennis camp logo on his hat and hoped Dad wouldn't. No luck.

Hey, maybe you and Toby will be bunkmates! Dad said to the boy. There was nowhere to hide from Dad's enthusiasm.

You drink coffee? Dad asked the boy.

Everybody drinks coffee, I said, turning my head.

You don't, Dad said.

Susan and I have a cup of decaf at night, said the boy. His name was Jean-Philippe Sassoli. Later I learned that Susan was his mother. Later still, I learned that he was from Switzerland, but had recently moved to New York City, after his father died (after wrapping his BMW around an overpass support column, drunk driving). Jean-Philippe asked if I'd like to come up to his room. Dad told me to go on ahead while he parked the car. He tossed me our room key, which I dropped.

Jean-Philippe's sister, Zoe, answered the door to his room. She was dressed all in black and her hair was blood red, parted up the middle. She looked at me then fell back onto one of the two beds. Susan! she yelled.

Susan emerged from the bathroom in a robe and slippers, smoking a menthol. A hairdryer droned. Jean-Philippe handed her a coffee.

She said, If I'm not back before the morning, you kids get yourselves ready for camp. I left a few hundreds on top of the TV.

Jean-Philippe slipped away to the corner of the room, where he was rooting through his gear. Stacks of folded white tennis clothes rose from his footlocker like baking dough. He pulled out a plastic baggie. A novice might have mistaken its contents for golf tees. But not a boy who'd tossed whippersnappers at all forms of domestic wildlife, ridden over long lines of them with his bike to simulate machine gun fire, and Scotch-taped bunches into softball-sized bombs. Jean-Philippe pinched one from the bag and threw it at his mom.

That, I had never done, or even considered doing. It popped on the vanity mirror.

Goddamn it, Jean-Philippe!

Perhaps expecting one in her direction, Zoe just said, Don't.

You like firecrackers? I asked. Jean-Philippe held up the bag as Exhibit A. I mean real ones, I said.

He set the bag down. You got some?

A few, I whispered. Some Roman candles, black cats, bottle rockets, M-88s, M-90s...

M-90s! he said. I heard those are illegal!

M-80s are.

Isn't an M-90 bigger than an M-80?

I wish, I said.

Jean-Philippe was already at the door. I looked back to see his mother wink at me in the bathroom mirror. She was puckering up to a tube of lipstick. Zoe didn't move. We ran downstairs, where Jean-Philippe chatted with Dad about the details of his mother's relationship with Donny, the owner of the tennis camp. Meanwhile I slipped across the room to get into my backpack. I reached in, feeling around. I could tell the 90s from the 88s by touch. I grabbed one of each and a couple bottle rockets, then pulled up the cuff of my jeans and stuffed everything into my sock. Jean-Philippe suggested we go buy some candy at a 7-Eleven up the road.

Dad looked at me and hugged my head to his chest. I stood still lest the wrappers in my sock crackle. He took out his wallet and thumbed through the bills. He handed me a five.

Then he teased out another five and, with a mischievous wiggle of his brow, handed it to Jean-Philippe. Here, he said. You stock up too.

Thanks, Jean-Philippe said.

Jean-Philippe loved to prod me about bands and movies, just to see if I'd heard of them. I didn't know what a 747 was and this shook him to the core. Having attended camp since he was 11, he knew the juicy backstory of most of the campers and counselors and, of course, Donny, the owner. This knowledge went both ways though. At the welcoming barbeque, a boy named Gavin Dell—whose hair was so fair even his eyelashes were blonde and whose father owned the New England Patriots—held his racket handle between his legs like a cock when Jean-Philippe walked by. Apparently, Jean-Philippe had never lived down a poorly timed arousal in the boy's shower a few summer's earlier. And, apparently, anything Gavin said was funny to the other boys, even when it wasn't, really. In a pack of Richie Rich's, Gavin was Richie Richest.

The camp sat on 25 acres beside the Carmel River. A full-time squad of gardeners tended to the grounds, cringing each time a shanked ball tore through a flowerbed. The ranch's borders were hedged and fenced to such a degree that we soon lost awareness of car traffic or commerce or the outside world in general. My sense of security was hardly diminished even when Jean-Philippe told me about the hillbillies who lived on the ramshackle ranches that abutted the camp and sometimes played pranks on the tennis brats: a skunk trapped in the stringing room, holes poked in an entire shed full of tennis balls, a turd drifting in the hot tub.

I had glimpsed some boys playing stickball in the road on the other side of the fence by Dorm 3. They didn't look all that devious, or poor. They were dressed like the guys I hung out with in Reno. I said as much to Jean-Philippe.

Those're them, he said. The hillbillies are white trash. They fuck their cousins and their dogs.

Each morning we woke up at 7 a.m. to sweep the patios or blow leaves off the courts. To some of the campers, chores were a novelty, like an affected accent; to others chores were a complete mystery. I had to teach the heir to *Banco de Mexico* how to operate a push broom.

The camp director was Gordy Stewart. A tour in Vietnam had ruined his knees and his chance at the pro tour, but legend had it he could still bounce his kick serve over the back fence and that his backhand was prettier than Ken Rosewall's. To Gordy, tennis was tantamount to religion, only with less singing. He made lazy campers cry. His palms were wooden. Though I'd never seen him play tennis, I *had* seen him hit a ping-pong ball ninety degrees around a tree trunk and into play on the table, where it aced a very perplexed boy from Chevy Chase, Maryland.

When we weren't on the court we'd lounge in our dorms, listening to music and lighting our farts. Farts burn blue. Natural gas, I called it. This made a few kids laugh.

I was just getting warmed up.

As incentive for us to get settled into our bunks without a fuss, our dorm's head counselor, Jason, read aloud to us from *Penthouse*. While my bunkmates reached down in their sleeping bags to tuck erections behind elastic waistbands, my hands were also deep in my bag, sorting through my stash. The days on the tennis court, to me, were an absolute bore, and I loathed the sport of tennis more and more, even as my game improved. At night however, I became cooler than I'd ever been in my life. My popularity was nocturnal.

About an hour after lights-out, I would climb down from my bunk and slip outside. The grass was wet. I saw owls. Jean-Philippe would make his break a few minutes later, and we'd rendezvous behind a shed with kids from other dorms. George from Hong Kong was usually there, and the Chase triplets, and Billy Tracy, and Fernando and Guillermo—cousins from Mexico. Under moonlight we'd follow a dirt road that meandered through camp, beyond the greenhouse, through a fence and across a meadow. We moved as an amorphous little herd, complete with stragglers and zigzaggers and frontrunners, but it felt as though I was in charge. I was the nucleus. It's hard to explain. I just knew that if I veered into a thicket, everyone would have followed. I'd never felt that way.

We'd walk for a mile or so down the hill to a small canyon where a creek joined the river. Jean-Philippe said we looked like ghosts in our tennis whites. So we adopted that as our official name: *The Ghosts*.

The first night I brought some Roman candles. The next, a Tijuana Tremor fountain. Then George convinced me to throw a couple M-90s into the river, so I did. Each explosion made a crowd-pleasing splash. River rocks clattered. We lit a whole package of sparklers in celebration and ran wild under a canopy of oak trees, trails of light lingering in our wakes.

That night we snuck back into our dorm sometime after 3 a.m. The cold nylon skin of my sleeping bag raised the hair on my neck as I snuggled in, waiting as my warmth multiplied inside the down. I drifted off. The next thing I knew, the dorm's screen door creaked. My drowsiness evaporated. I caught a glimpse of a boy moving across the room.

Jason rolled over in his bed and grabbed a watch out of his shoe. The watch's phosphorescent face lit up Jason's.

Gavin? he said in a groggy whisper. Where the hell were you?

Out.

Don't give me that shit, Jason said, sitting up. Who were you with?

Jean-Philippe and I looked at each other. The air in the dorm was clammy, overbreathed.

Zoe, Gavin said.

That freaky vampire girl? Jason said. She's older than you.

A little.

Did you kiss her? Jason asked.

Gavin nodded. I saw Jean-Philippe stir in his bed.

Jason persisted. Tongue? he asked.

A smile from Gavin.

C'mon, Jason said. *Details*, or I report your ass. Did she bite you? Suck your blood?

Smell my finger, Gavin said.

I heard Jean-Philippe's bedsprings coil. I expected at any moment to see him lunge from his top bunk and wrap his meaty hands around Gavin's throat. He didn't.

Jason told Gavin to get in bed. All went still again.

. . .

The next morning Jean-Philippe and I were zombies with mops. It was Sunday and we had a white glove inspection. The guest inspector was Lloyd Bentsen, U.S. Vice Presidential nominee from the year before. Jean-Philippe dragged a bucket across the tile floor, wheels clacking, suds sloshing out. In an abrupt rage, he javelined his mop into the shower room. I hurried to pick it up.

Leave it! he said.

He'd cracked a couple shower tiles. A counselor rushed in, wondering what the ruckus was. I told him I'd dropped the mop. The counselor looked at Jean-Philippe, who'd taken out a can of Comet and some paper towels to distractedly rub a faucet. The broken tiles went unnoticed.

Later, we did a skit for Lloyd and his entourage and they asked us if we were enjoying camp and we told them what they wanted to hear. A woman with her white hair in a taut bun wore the ceremonial glove. She got a kick out of caressing the undersides of things. Her face was stern but it was an act, just like our skit. Having deemed our dorm immaculate, the inspectress awarded us first place. Gavin had been elected dorm captain and was asked to pose with her and Lloyd in a photo commemorating our win to be framed and hung in the tennis shop. The inspectress held up her gloved finger to show off its spotlessness. The photographer thought it would be cute for Gavin to hold up his finger too.

Lloyd had his arm around Gavin but kept his eyes on the camera. He said, Tell your father I haven't forgotten about that box of Montecristos I owe him.

Of course, Gavin said as the camera flashed, his teeth the whitest of whites.

That was the afternoon I stole five big boxes of Diamond strike-anywhere matches from the charcoal cabinet beside the barbeques and buried them in my footlocker.

When I returned to the common area I found everyone at the hot tub. Ghosts and girls alike dangled their legs in the swirling jets, sneaking peeks at each other between wisecracks. Gavin was there with his hand on Zoe's knee. She was rubbing Carmex on her lips. The circle of backs at water's edge seemed impenetrable so I sat on the pump box. I asked Zoe where Jean-Philippe was.

Who cares, Gavin said, prompting the usual sycophantic laughter.

Hasty disrobing had left shoes and warm-ups strewn about the pool deck. It was no secret that the tub served as the sexual hub of the camp. Counselors took their dips, too. Whoops, giggles, and even the occasional moan issued from the gazebo after lights out.

Outside the circle, my ear caught only fragments of conversations. Soon a spot opened up. One of Zoe's friends, a girl named Jessica from Long Island, looked over at me, then to Zoe. Smiling. Jessica was knotting a friendship bracelet, one end safety pinned to her skirt.

There's room, said Jessica.

I was staring at a tenacious gob of foam revolving near the middle of the tub—the flotsam of suntan lotion, sweat, secretions—and doing the math. Five boxes times two-hundred-and-fifty matches per box equalled...enough.

Oh, I said, realizing Jessica was still looking at me. My feet aren't cold.

There was a ball machine at the far end of camp that campers could reserve by the hour. The sign-up sheet hung outside the snack shack. On the day Gavin Dell's name graced the noon timeslot, I went to the dining hall in search of Jean-Philippe. I found him eating alone, dredging steak fries through barbeque sauce. I told him I had something to show him.

We walked together out to the meadow courts, then cut through a row of trees. I told Jean-Philippe to keep quiet, which irritated him because he was the kind with rash-prone skin and we had to trudge through tall brush. We got on our hands and knees to slip under a hedge and he almost turned back, but I insisted. We stalked up to a wood fence and peered between the slats. Before us was a row of bushes, then a sloping lawn that gave way to the red concrete of a tennis court, which was empty save for a ball machine.

Why had I chosen to inherit Jean-Philippe's vendetta? To collect on a debt not mine? For one thing, Gavin Dell had it coming. Leonardo Da Vinci invented all sorts of bombs and flame-throwers and things to earn favor with wealthy heads of state, people with enemies. I don't think I was quite so in tune with my ambitions. I will tell you this, Leo: with a good pair of scissors you can snip the heads off half a dozen matches at a time. The strike-anywhere variety have little white yarmulkes. These are *critical*. They lend spontaneity to the combustion.

Gavin walked onto the court. Jean-Philippe let out a dismissive, *pfft*. I held a finger over my lips.

Watch, I said.

Gavin did some calf stretches against the fence, then flipped on the machine. With a whir, it began spitting balls into the empty court. Gavin got in position. Forehand, backhand. He lunged back and forth, punching with his racket. Grunting.

Okay, that's pretty funny, said Jean-Philippe. He stepped away from the fence.

Keep watching, I said.

Kids, write this down: First you get a tennis ball. Punch a small hole in it, about as big around as a pencil eraser. There are 250 matches in the big box. It takes roughly 800 match heads and a little over an hour of your time to fill the ball to a volatile density. Certain kinds of water coolers (coincidentally including the type often found on tennis courts) dispense small paper cones instead of cups. If you cut the point off one of these cones, you can use it as a funnel to get all the match heads in. I recommend cotton to plug the hole.

A pod of girls materialized courtside. It was the girls' hour off before lunch. Zoe was among them. Gavin said something to her and she said something back.

Jean-Philippe put his ear to the fence. Damn it, he whispered. Can *you* hear what they're saying?

A few of the girls were giggling. One of them was braiding Zoe's hair. Gavin took a few more volleys, then stepped out of the oncoming barrage. I held my breath. He walked around the net while balls were wasted on an empty court. He crouched out of view behind the machine, adjusting its controls. Suddenly the trajectory changed. With about a third of the balls left in the hopper, Gavin Dell, bless his heart, decided to practice his overhead. Big, juicy lobs rained out of a blue sky.

A man standing on a moving rail car tosses a ball in the air. To him, the ball goes up and down in a straight line. But to the man watching the rail car go by, the ball travels in an arc. It's relative. Gavin, and Jean-Philippe too, saw normal lobs. But, for me, the balls oozed through a syrupy space-time continuum.

The girls pretended not to be watching. Gavin pretended not to be affected by their presence, though he swung hard enough to make a few balls stick in the diamond mesh of the back fence. The steady thwacking entranced me, but then it happened. He swung at a ball just like all the others, though this ball made a dull sound against his strings.

Then it burst into a white fucking supernova and made an insane hissing sound,

loud and evil, just above Gavin's head. The thing consumed itself within a second, and when it had disintegrated, singed particles of rubber and fuzz carried on the breeze. The smell was *fantastic*.

Better yet though, Gavin lost his mind. He shrieked. His Prince Profile fell from his hand and as it clattered to rest on the court, he started running in place, thrashing his arms as if to defend himself from a swarm of wasps. The girls backed away. Balls continued to plummet, one after another, bouncing all around him. He looked to the sky. He looked to the horizon. The girls started laughing. He looked right at the wood fence.

Eat fuck! Jean-Philippe hollered, then we bolted. Jean-Philippe was laughing and snorting as he ran. I gave a whoop.

We circled around the back of camp behind the maintenance shed and re-emerged by the pool, where counselors were sunning themselves on the deck. Jean-Philippe jumped into the pool with his tennis clothes on, so I followed suit. We plunged without hesitation into the deep end and sank to the bottom, howling and laughing until our lungs were empty. I watched the bubbles float up to the glassy surface. They made it roil.

When Gavin showed up behind the shed a few nights later with his cronies, Laird and Kristof, in tow, I feared my number was up. But he didn't even know my name. Feeling more at ease, I started down the moonlit road. Eleven boys fell in behind me and we headed toward the edge of camp. Gavin stopped in the middle of the road.

You ever set off anything in camp? he asked.

I laughed. I kept walking. But Gavin hung back. Laird and Kristof did too. So did George from Hong Kong, and the Chase triplets, and Billy, and Fernando, and Guillermo. Even Jean-Philippe. Gavin's gravity was lunar. I felt the tide sucking at my toes.

Gavin was grinning. Everyone'll think it's the hillbillies, he said.

I appreciated better than any of them what this meant, what it entailed. If firecrackers were to be set off *in* camp, then those responsible would need to have already made themselves scarce before the firecrackers went off. Which was to say I needed to make a fuse.

The importance of a reliable fuse cannot be overstated. An older brother of one of my friends had shown us how to make them by soaking shoelaces in lawn fertilizer and smashed-up vitamin C pills. But in the middle of the night at tennis camp, one must improvise.

A candle, I said. We need a candle.

Kristof asked if the birthday variety would work. His mother had made him bring some to camp to celebrate his upcoming 13th birthday. I nodded, and he snuck off to the dorm to fetch them. Meanwhile, everyone huddled over me as I rigged our device. After considerable debate, we decided upon the rear gate, the one delivery trucks used, as the best location for detonation. It was across the street from a few hillbilly houses, out of the way enough that we'd most likely go unnoticed as we set it up, but close enough to the dorms that everyone would hear it.

As a test I lay one candle on the ground and lit it, checking the second hand on my watch as the flame inched along. It took about three minutes to go the whole length of the candle. That would be all the time we had to scurry back to our dorms and pretend to wake up, just as shocked as everyone else. I considered stringing candles together to make a longer fuse, but it was too risky. I didn't have time to experimentally verify the candle-to-candle transition. I positioned the candle between some rocks to keep it from rolling. I had a full magazine of firecrackers—bangers—each about the size of a AA battery. All of them were braided into a common Bickford fuse that ran up the center of the pack. I arranged the end of this fuse just above the butt end of the candle so that the flame would slide right under. Then I lit it.

Run, I whispered.

· · ·

Sprinting in utter silence, our footfalls quieted by tube socks, we made for our respective dorms. When you can't see the fuse, it's always the same. At first you expect to hear the bang at any moment, but when it doesn't come, you second-guess. Is it still lit? Was it a dud? This is when idiots go back and end up losing fingers. Jean-Philippe, Gavin, and I made it back together. We slipped in through the bathroom. I scaled my bunk's metal frame in one motion and fell on my sleeping bag, forcing breath through my nose in an effort to calm down. The fuse would reach its end any second. Jean-Philippe climbed into his bed. Gavin had a bottom bunk, but he had yet to get in it. The fool! He was just standing there, staring at his sleeping bag as if a corpse was in it. Then I saw the body too. It moved.

Mr. Dell, Jason said. I see you took some friends along this time. Well, I want details, gentlemen. What was it, some sort of gang—

Bang! Bang...Bang!! B-B-B-b-B-b-b-Bang! BANG!!!!! Bang! Bang! Upon bursting, a single banger releases five kilojoules of energy and forms a pocket of overpressure, creating waves that propagate through the air at the speed of sound. Bang! Bang. Bang, Bang! One hundred and sixty decibels, unless the factory worker responsible felt frisky and added an extra pinch of aluminum. BANG, bang, BANG!!!!!!!!!!!!!! Bangers always sound louder in the middle of the night.

One of my dorm mates screeched. Others rushed to the windows, rubbing sleep from their eyes. Everyone used their best swear words. Were we under attack?

Jason ordered us to stay put and ran into the night wearing only tennis shorts and running shoes. While he was gone I gathered my remaining M-90s and flushed them down the toilet. We had no idea if any of our cohorts had been nabbed, or what commotion might have been stirred up in the other dorms. (A few days earlier, a girl had been rushed to the camp doctor when her lily white bloomers suddenly flushed crimson. If a footwork drill can induce a girl's first period, what about a few dozen firecrackers in the middle of the night?) When Jason returned he said not a word, except to tell us to go back to sleep. His calmness put me on edge. They *knew*.

I bet it was the fucking hillbillies, Gavin said.

Jason wasn't in the mood. Shut up, Dell, he muttered.

In the morning after the flag ceremony, the boys were dismissed to breakfast. On the path to the dining hall, Gavin, Jean-Philippe, and I were pulled aside and asked to return to our dorm, unfed, and await further instruction. We were right back in our bunks.

They're treating us like criminals, Gavin said. I should call my dad. He could get Gordy canned for this.

No one cares about your dad, Jean-Philippe said.

Guys! I said. We've gotta get our stories ironed out. If I get kicked out of this camp, my dad—Jesus… (This was the first time it had struck me that this was a possibility, and suddenly I needed to urinate.)

They don't know shit, Gavin said. The evidence exploded!

They know we snuck out, I said.

Jean-Philippe shook his head. This is no big deal, he said.

Are we still going to say we saw someone by the back gate? I asked.

But neither of them answered because we heard footsteps on the path. The creak of the door. Sunshine framed Jason as we shielded our eyes. He demanded to see our footlockers.

The lighter inside my dopp kit was soon confiscated. Meanwhile, Gavin was sent to the office. Our instructions were reiterated—stay put—and Jason was gone again.

Later, he returned to fetch Jean-Philippe. I was left alone. I retreated into a lonely pocket of my mind where all I could see was myself, and my predicament. I wanted to travel back in time to when Gavin suggested we set off the fireworks in camp. Or maybe further back, to when I was packing for camp and I tapped into my stash—no, let me go all the way back to the family trip to San Francisco, the Chinatown alleyway I searched out when I was supposed to be at the arcade, the collapsible street booth bursting with all things pyrotechnic. Give me back three months of squandered allowance.

I'd never said a word to Gordy and had never been to his office. It was tough to visualize our impending encounter. Both Jean-Philippe and Gavin went to prep schools. They were accustomed to living under the thumb of a headmaster. Gordy was a headmaster in his own right. Unmarried. Enigmatic. And I, lacking backbone and pedigree, was a Chef Boyardee noodle of a boy.

Jason came and ushered me without a word through camp. I either sensed or imagined the false indifference of my fellow campers we passed, all of whom must have known something by now. I could feel their eyes on my back. I was a dead boy. I'd become a ghost during the daylight hours.

While I was forced to wait on a bench outside Gordy's office, I noticed a Jaguar parked under an oak tree. Some small leaves and twigs dappled its otherwise spotless red paint. The leaping cat hood ornament glinted regally. The front tires were left casually turned, like in an advertisement —the car at ease. The windshield was a slice of sunlight, a gilded mirror I couldn't see through. A woman's arm emerged from the passenger side to ash a cigarette.

A man came out of the tennis center. He looked at me. His silver hair was slicked back. He wore powder-blue tennis warm-ups, a clunky gold watch, and loafers without socks. He walked across the grass to the Jaguar, slipped in, and started the engine. The woman flicked the butt of her cigarette into the roots of the big oak. They drove up the hill out of camp and I saw her lean across and plant a kiss on his cheek, and I remembered where I'd seen that car before.

Jean-Philippe came through the door. His eyes were glassy and red. He saw me and tried to tighten his upper lip.

I think I just saw your mom, I said. What kind of car does Donny drive?

Just tell Gordy everything, he said.

I started to ask what he meant, but the door opened and Gordy came out. I stole one last look at Jean-Philippe. He wouldn't look at me.

Mr. Brooks, Gordy said.

Your grandmother calls, Gordy said, every few days.

He looked at me, registering my reaction. I sat with my hands in the taut pockets of my tennis shorts. In the corner there was an old couch and a television with a VCR. I'd been told Gordy brought the best players here to analyze video footage and find flaws in their form.

She likes to know how you're progressing, he said. I suppose she has that right. I told her you've got a decent serve. Maybe some potential. What I haven't told her is that you're unmotivated and undisciplined. You could be an A2 if you worked at it.

Bastard was flanking me. I hadn't expected to come under fire for my tennis game. The psychological bunkers I'd built were facing the wrong direction.

He pulled out a notebook. Its pages were thick with pencil entries. He looked through it, then shut it. Leaned back.

You've played about half as many challenge matches as everyone else, he said. It seems someone in your position ought to feel fortunate to be here. Make the most of it.

I bit my lip. I realized I was crying.

Gordy picked up my lucky Bic lighter. Rubbed his

calloused hands over the flint finger wheel, the red gas trigger.

You smoke, Toby?

I shrugged. Gordy was going to crack me. Wouldn't take long. I was a frightened boy and he'd killed Viet Cong and he wasn't married and it was hard to believe he'd ever been a boy himself. But I held out for as long as I physically could, like a fuse.

Mr. Brooks, I'm not asking you these things because I need to know the answers. Your cohorts Mr. Dell and Mr. Sassoli were quite *cooperative*.

Are Gavin and Jean-Philippe in trouble? I asked.

You'd be wise to worry about yourself, son. Those two will have their own arrangements.

Am *I* in trouble?

Give me your parents' phone number, Gordy said.

Don't tell them about the fireworks, Mr. Stewart. *Please*.

He was shaking his head already. He sat back. I stared at his mustache.

See that picture? he said. He flicked his head, directing my gaze over his shoulder to a framed photograph in which everything—the jungle, the mud, the tents, the fatigues—was some shade of green. Except the horse. The horse was white. Straddling it were three young men. I recognized the one facing backward on the saddle.

Fella in the middle, Gordy said, that's Todd Diaponte. Our Ammunition Chief. Smart kid. Taught me trigonometry. I used to help him inventory the rockets and landmines and grenades—whatever came off the trucks.

Had I misread Gordy? Was this man reaching out to me? Did he know the difference between gun-cotton and picric acid? I couldn't be sure. I asked a stupid question.

Whose horse is that?

Gordy pointed at the picture again, this time jabbing his finger as he spoke: Todd can't see anymore, Toby. And he can't read Braille because he lost his hands. Not because he was careless. Because explosives are *unpredictable*.

We just had some firecrackers, I said.

I know what you had.

Are you going to tell my parents?

He uncradled the phone and looked at me, waiting.

I relayed the ten digits, the combination of a lock.

Dad drove down from Reno early the next morning. My footlocker packed, my sleeping bag stuffed, I sat in street clothes on my bunk. A maid came and stripped my sheets. Everyone was gathered at the other side of the ranch to watch the finals of the mid-session tourney. I heard only birds. Their stupid singsong, their rhetorical questions.

I *know*, I nearly told them.

It was another beautiful day in the Carmel Valley, the fog having burned off late in the morning. The dorm was surrounded by evergreens. I felt the breeze through the screen door and the shadows on my skin and I was shivering. Gordy told my mother that I had left camp property without permission, repeatedly violated curfew, and coerced others into doing the same. Made me sound like some cult leader (but a *leader* nonetheless). While I was away, Dad had found a job selling insurance. He had to skip a training seminar and burn a vacation day in order to come get me.

I heard the Wagoneer roll along the dirt road. The engine died and a door opened. Footsteps.

He said my name through the mesh of the screen door.

Yeah, I said.

Let's go, he said. Now.

Footsteps. I heard the car door open again, shut again. The engine start up. I lugged my footlocker down the steps and loaded it by myself into the back of the idling Wagoneer.

When our eyes finally met it was in the rearview mirror. Dad looked tired. More tired than I was.

You should be ashamed of yourself, he said.

I hung my head and kept my mouth shut, but I wasn't ashamed. I was angry beyond words.

The road out of camp led past the center courts. I slunk down in my seat. Jean-Philippe and Gavin and all the other Ghosts were sprawled on a knoll overlooking the matches. Jean-Philippe stood up and came over to Dad's side of the car. There was a tiny polo player embroidered on Jean-Philippe's white shirt, galloping off the fabric right at us, mallet poised to strike.

Hi Stan, Jean-Philippe said. Dad's expression softened a little. Jean-Philippe wasn't looking at me, which was just as well because I couldn't look at him.

We'll all miss your son, Jean-Philippe said.

There came a sudden roar from the crowd. Then another, even louder. Jean-Philippe turned away for a moment. Then he looked back at us, sitting there in what suddenly felt like a windshield-less, clattering Oldsmobile overburdened with furniture and footlockers and frying pans, and he patted the roof of the car twice, as New Yorkers do to dismiss a taxi.

THE UNBRIDLED UNDERESTIMATION
OF RACEHORSES

I ALWAYS WANTED to be a racehorse. You probably won't understand. Maybe when you were in elementary school you used to dream of being a cheetah. Seventy miles an hour and all that. Only in bursts, my friend, only in bursts.

I don't do bursts. I'm 290 pounds.

Racehorses go the distance. Forty-five miles an hour for a mile. The whole time. Cheetah's sitting over there on the sidelines, unzipping his warm-ups, doing calisthenics in front of the crowd. Sure, sprinters get the shoe sponsorships, the photo ops. Racehorses, they only pose for photo-finishes. That's because they have heart. When Secretariat died they cut him open. He had the heart of a whale.

Cheetahs, they got spots. Oh, super!

My penis is twenty inches long, lady. Well, not my penis, per se. I'm not a racehorse. And maybe you're not a lady.

I just think, wouldn't it be grand to be out in a big pasture? Finish up a distinguished racing career and be put out to stud? I'd fill fillies till the day I fell over dead. I'd rub the tastiest hay around on my huge teeth. Apples. Sugar cubes. All that. Not to mention all the running. All the big fields squared off with split-rail fences. I'd make up stories for the rookies in the barn. Tell them about the time my buddy broke a leg on that clubhouse turn and they put a pistol in his ear and *bang*, glue. Racehorses are only kept around to pay other people's bills.

I got bills. So I go to work. But lately there's a better reason to go. To see Julie. Julie is smarter than me, I think. I know she's better looking. If I'm a 7, she's definitely a 10. But I'm a 3½. I love it when she walks next to me in the hall. Her perfume smells like flowers and I really like it, even though my favorite smells are gasoline, rain, and food. One time she put her hand on my arm and it was warm because she was holding copies fresh off the machine and it made me aroused and I had to sneak away.

Her perfume makes me wish I had horse nostrils. I see her and just peel back my lips and show her my teeth, gums and all. I used to think she didn't like me one bit. She's a cat person. Got like a dozen of 'em. Knows 'em all by name. None are cheetahs as far as I know.

Last night my supervisor had this barbecue for our department. Pretty fun. We all went over to his house and drank alcohol. Everyone seemed kind of nervous at first. That's the impression I got. But pretty soon people stopped complaining about work and started laughing about it. This one guy, Peterson, he barfed while he was in the pool. I helped him climb out and I got him a towel and I let him hang over my shoulders all wet and we went into the bathroom where, in exchange for my loyalty in his darkest of hours, he passed along an interesting tidbit: Julie had asked about me. Specifically, she had asked whether or not I had a girlfriend. More specifically, whether I was quote-unquote gay. I told Peterson I didn't, wasn't. I told him I liked Julie. Everyone did.

I felt sixteen hands high. I felt *giddy*.

I went back outside. Julie was out there talking with a couple fellow staffers, so I waited for her to notice me while I sipped on a beer. Pretty soon I'd finished the whole bottle and had nothing left to occupy myself and she still hadn't noticed me so I started to walk away and she said, Where are you going, Bernie?

My name is Ernie. But *still*. Either way.

Okay, so that was last night. Now I'm back at my desk. I've got two hours' worth of work left to do and it's 4:00. I don't care, I'm leaving at 5:00. I'm no workhorse. Peterson, he's a Clydesdale. Works so hard, poor guy's got to party even harder just to stay balanced. That's why he puked in the pool. You know the type. I go to his office. I ask him: how much you want to bet I can land a date with Julie before quitting time? Hundred bucks? Well, that's pretty steep. Fifty, you say? Sure. I'll take that bet. Fifty. We shake on it.

Let's go, he says.

Now?

Now.

I envision myself at the track. I'm drinking mint juleps in the shade. I'm betting on Me, that beautiful racehorse down there with the stand-in jockey on his back. (The original jockey refused to ride longshots.) They call jockeys that fill in for other jockeys 'bugs' because there's an asterisk next to their name in the program. The asterisk looks like a squashed bug. My horse, Me, he's 100 to 1 odds. I grin to myself. No one sees me because I'm in the back row. Plus, I have on Ray Ban sunglasses and a hat.

Julie works on the second floor. Person and I work on the fifth. I don't want to take the stairs because I get all sweaty. I think I mentioned my weight. My mom tells me I'm just big-boned, but she hasn't seen me with my shirt off in a decade. I have full-blown tits, Mom.

When we get off the elevator, no one is around. All the cubicles are empty. We can hear voices coming from the conference room. We wander over there together. Everyone who works on the second floor—accounting, mostly—is in the conference room. There's balloons and cake. Everyone is wearing cone hats and the guys have loosened their ties. One lady has her shoes off. She's wiggling her toes inside her nylons. There's a pyramid of plastic champagne glasses on the table. We better come back, I tell Peterson, but he says we should try and get our hands on some of that cake, and I'm not against that idea.

But still, it's not our cake, you know? There's just something that feels wrong about barging into this party when we don't even know what it's for. But Peterson just heads in there anyway, so I follow him, and nobody really takes notice and that's what makes me feel more comfortable about the whole thing, even though I still don't feel as comfortable as Peterson must feel because he's already slicing himself some of the cake. It looks like ice cream cake.

Julie is right there. She is so close I can taste her and I'm pretending like I haven't seen her. I pretend like there's something really important I've got going for me and I'm distracted by it. I make that distracted face as long as I can. Everyone is swallowing cake. There's a banner strung up: HAPPY BIRTHDAY! It helps me figure out what the party is for.

My stomach begins to feel like I drank too much soda. Girls have always done that to me. Girls seem to go for more of a cheetah physique. But: twenty inches, I keep reminding myself. Heart. The little bug on my back starts whipping me like crazy. Faster! Eventually Julie is going to see me.

Eventually she's going to see me.

But Peterson gets to me first. Gotta try this cake, he tells me. Here, hold this.

He hands me his paper plate. His piece of cake—what's left of it—looks like someone put a firecracker in it. I feel guilty and embarrassed holding it. One of the head accountants sees me, which is good because he's talking to Julie. Wilson's his name. He looks over at me.

Like that cake, big guy? he asks.

Some of the other accountants laugh, but I don't see the humor. Like I said, I don't always agree with people about what is funny.

All of a sudden, Peterson's nowhere to be found. It's just me and a bunch of second floor people, including Julie. I tap her on the shoulder and she turns away from the group she's with. She takes her hand off the arm of another guy and puts it on *my* arm. That's the way Julie talks to people. Even other girls.

Aren't you gonna wish me happy birthday? she wants to know.

No problem, I say, and I do.

Now we've all seen the movies where two guys make some bet about scoring with a girl and we all know what happens. The guy ends up falling in love with her and she finds out about the bet, and he spends half the movie apologizing. I figure I'll just tell Julie right up front about my wager. I'm glad, too, because she's flattered. She gets up on her tiptoes and puts a kiss right in the middle of my big, smooth cheek. I'm standing there, letting the feeling of her lips on my skin last as long as I can, and when I come out of my little trance the crowd has gobbled her back up.

Eventually, she looks back at me. I peel back my lips and show her my teeth. She takes her hand and, with her thumb and her pinky extended, holds it up against her head like it's a phone. I know *exactly* what that means. That's easy. She means it's time to go back upstairs and collect fifty bucks. I eat what's left of Peterson's cake in the elevator. It tastes as awesome as you'd expect at a moment like this.

. . .

You should see me. There are so many people to get around but I steer clear. All the way back to our little spot outside without spilling a drop. Julie's is a Mai Tai, with a pineapple triangle and a Maraschino cherry and a lime wedge all shish-kebabbed on a little red sword. It even has a toothpick umbrella, and we all know that a cocktail with that much stuff on it costs a lot more than a beer, so I just get a beer, which is fine by me.

It's Julie's decision to blow my winnings at her favorite restaurant. I can understand why it's her favorite. Everybody there is tan. And slim. Tan and slim and chatty. They all like to stand at the bar and drink and I bet if the hostess never calls their names, they'll forget they even came to sit and eat. We're standing outside on the patio. Our arms are bent at the elbow. Our hands hold our drinks. The sun is going down over the parking lot and everything starts looking pink.

Thanks! she says when I hand her the fancy drink.

You really should see me. I'm wearing an awesome shirt. It's black. That way she won't be able to notice if my armpits get sweaty. She's wearing a dress. Her armpits are not covered and neither is anything above them.

I ask her how old she is and she says, Twenty-seven.

Now... I say—meaning, now that her birthday has just come and gone.

Yes, she laughs. Now.

Talking with her is not as hard as you'd expect. I don't know why I expected it to be hard. Actually, that's not true. I know. Anyway, we talk about work at first. I have a lot of funny 'takes' on the characters in our office—ones I'm sure the accountants she's always hanging out with don't have. I make fun of some people and she laughs really hard. One time she has to set her drink down so it doesn't spill while she's laughing. When they say my name over the intercom, we meet up with the hostess, and then we walk in single file to a table. I see the people at the tables seeing us.

Then there's a menu in my face and I'm imagining all the amazing things in my mouth when I see Julie's hand grab the top of my menu and pull it down so she can see me. I get the feeling she's been looking at me for a while.

Being with you is refreshing, she says. You're a special one, Ernie. You're all the things my mother keeps telling me to look for.

That's what she tells me, word for word. She looks at me, really deep, and I feel like a mirror. I'm sure she's about to cry but she doesn't, and I can tell it's tickling her behind her face like a sneeze. She smiles and puts her hand over my hand on the table. Then she looks around the restaurant.

I see myself at the racetrack, somewhere in the back row, setting down the julep as I bring my binoculars up against my Ray Bans. I'm standing now. I look kind of stupid because my mouth is open. All the horses are running. My horse, Me, is running. He is *really running*.

Julie scoots her chair out and says she has to pee. She takes her purse with her and puts her hand on my shoulder when she passes me. The waiter comes by a little later and asks if we need a little more time to decide. He refills my water. The angles on the bottom half of the glass are cold and wet and they feel like a good fit in my hand. I sit there and think and smile at the other happy couples who are eating around me.

Me, a racehorse. Giving that bug the ride of its life. Moving in along the rail, homestretching. The track is muddy, cuppy, but Me gets a grip somehow. Somehow. That's how long shots win. Somehow.

When the waiter comes back, he asks if my friend is planning to stay for dinner.

She went to the bathroom, I say.

He smiles and refills my water. I drink it and pretty soon I have to pee, too. I get up and follow the signs to the bathroom, where I use the hand dryer to blow air up my sleeves at my armpits.

When I get back to the table, she's still not there. The waiter doesn't come back for a long time, but when he finally does I tell him, Thank you, but I don't need any more water.

He nods in that way waiters do sometimes, like The Customer Is Always Right.

I see myself taking a final sip of my julep and letting the ticket flutter to the ground.

I say, Longshot, under my breath because it's not something I want other people to hear.

The check comes to eleven bucks because of the fancy drink. I pay. I leave.

One time I took this fat girl on a date. I can call her fat because she was actually fatter than me. She told me that if she could be any animal, any animal at all, she'd be a goddamned duck. They can fly, she said. They can swim. They can walk. Not many animals have it so good, she said.

Well they just have it all, don't they?

When I get back to my house, I'm thinking about that girl. I can see how well thought out her duck had been. I appreciate her duck. I didn't at the time, but now I do. The reason I say this is I got the same feeling about Julie before she got up and went to the bathroom. I felt like I was everything she wanted and needed, except one thing.

My answering machine light is blinking. It's Peterson. He wants all the juicy details, especially since he paid for the whole thing. His message is still playing when I go into the other room and get in bed with my clothes still on. I smell like the restaurant. I'm starving. There's a full moon, so I have to shut the blinds or it feels like noon. I want to be a baby about the whole thing and call my mom.

I wait there for a long time with my eyes closed and then I

start crying even though I don't want to. I dry the tears as fast as they come out—get them off my face. My fingers get all wet.

I work up the courage to call her. I get her answering machine, which is a relief. It says something funny like, Hey, this is Julie, the cats and I are busy so leave a message. I guess it wasn't so much the message that was funny as it was the way she said it. A lot of times I think a thing is funny or great while other people consider the same thing neither funny nor great. I don't leave a message.

The next day is Sunday. I eat breakfast, lunch, and dinner by myself, then go to sleep. Monday, I go to work. At my desk there's an envelope. It's not an office kind of envelope. It's not an eight-and-a-half-by-eleven manila one and it doesn't have typing on it. It's handwritten, pretty letters, curly. I rip into it.

Dear Ernie, it says. Then there's a bunch of personal stuff she probably would prefer I not share with everyone, although I think it's safe to say it deals mostly with her luck with men in the past. Or, her lack thereof. And sorry. She says she is very, very sorry about leaving me at the restaurant. Love Julie, it says. PS: She wants to meet for lunch.

The building's got a pretty okay cafeteria and outside are tables in the shade where people like to sit. That's where we go. I buy an egg salad sandwich, sour-cream-and-onion chips, and a Coke. And a couple chocolate chip cookies. They're only a quarter.

I'm so sorry, she says.

It's okay, I say, which isn't easy.

Wanna take a walk?

Yes and no, I think. Yes, because, of course. No, because, I'm going to get sweaty.

We start walking. We keep walking. We keep talking, her hand always on some part of my body. There's this concrete path and we pretty much stay on it. The path meanders through corporate lawns with trees. The grass has just been mowed and there's clippings on the path and loads of it in the garbage cans.

The grass smells nice, she says. Then she's taking off her shoes. She steps onto it. I follow, but I don't take my shoes off. We sit down by this big manmade pond with a fountain in the middle. Some ducks are waddling around on the shore.

You're the sweetest, she says.

You're the sexiest. That's what I say back.

She laughs and I sort of turn away smiling and when I turn back she leans over and kisses me. Gently at first, but then she opens her mouth up and we're really going at it. It tastes like a spoonful of warm vanilla pudding and the spoon never glances my teeth. The ground swells and I can feel a pressure rising from the ground. The lawn seems to come alive. There's a hiss sound. A sprinkler by the pond pops up. Then another. They're those little ones that spray knee high. The ducks are just standing there like imbeciles getting soaked. But we're still kissing but then Julie pulls away and laughs and says, I can't get all wet! I have to go back to work!

We stand up. The sprinklers near us are starting to hiss. We take off running but there's too much grass to cover. Hell, a cheetah couldn't make it back to the path dry.

I watch myself grab Julie and boost her onto my back. She wraps her arms and her legs around me and I dash for the concrete path where it's dry. The sprinklers splatter my khakis but my stride is steady. My stride is steady. She is mostly dry. And me, the one sitting in the back row at the race, well he nearly wets his pants. There's mint julep all over the guy in front of him, who's muttering something about odds. Me, I'm picking the ticket back up off the ground putting it in my pocket, ready to be cashed in...

But I don't actually do any of that. I pretty much just run

to the concrete path as fast as I can, and still Julie beats me there. I'm soaked. Which is funny. Right? It's kind of funny.

Julie thinks so. When I catch up to her she's tossing her head, laughing.

Later, I tell her a little about racehorses, just to kind of see what she might say, and she smiles a certain way while I'm talking so I can tell she doesn't like racehorses the way I do, but I can also tell she really likes how much I like them, or that she thinks I'm funny. So, either way, you know?

Either way.

NUCLEAR WINTER

December, 1942

FERMI HAD ME ON the graveyard shift. We did as we were told. This was, after all, the project he was born to lead. There was profound purpose in it. But the camaraderie of shared discovery can warm the world only to a degree. It was fifteen below zero that night.

Our laboratory, if it can be called that, was tucked under the western bleachers of Chicago's old Stagg Field, inside a brick building with Gothic windows and crenellated towers that looked like a castle. The university no longer used the stadium. There was little reason to head out there that winter, unless you were one of us.

It hadn't snowed in days, but the stuff never melted. The roads were icy. Gasoline rationing had everyone taking streetcars and elevated trains, but my shift started after the last train, and ended before the first. Fermi paid for my gas.

The night guard had on a raccoon jacket. We'd found a closet full of fur jackets in an old locker room and passed them out to our dedicated sentries.

Evening, professor, he said.

By then I'd stopped insisting he call me Andy. I offered him a cigarette. We smoked with our gloves on, staring into the night.

He said, I hope they're paying you well, with the hours you work.

I took a drag.

Now *Fermi*, he went on. *He's* got it figured. I see him here in the mornings, but he's gone before lunch. *Italians…*

He has an office on campus, I explained.

I'm sure he does, the guard said. And I'm sure he's at home right now. Sleeping.

I toed the dirty snow. Yawned. Stubbed out my cigarette.

In you go, the guard said, holding the door open for me.

Inside, the hallway was like a mine shaft. Shiny black dust had settled on every surface. The walls and floors were slick with it. It was in our hair. Our teeth glowed white against our carbonized faces. To fight the cold we'd tried burning charcoal inside barrels but the smoke was intolerable. We'd tried gas fireplaces, the kind with false logs, but those contraptions stole our oxygen and gave us back only fumes to breathe. So we just kept our coats on while we worked.

The heavy lifting was done. I'd told my crew to stay home that night, get some sleep. They'd want to be wide awake come tomorrow, when the thing we'd built awoke from its slumber. Long, long ago, man gained dominion over fire. Tomorrow he would graduate to fission.

I reached the end of the hallway and climbed a narrow flight of stairs to a balcony that overlooked a squash court. It no longer looked anything like a squash court. The white walls were caked with soot. The wood floorboards were warped and scraped. Extra doorways had been added. The restless little black ball that once ricocheted inside had been replaced by a much, much larger, motionless black sphere.

Some said it was ugly, but I say they were blind to the thing's elegance. Fermi had given it a name. He called it a pile. We'd been building it for months, layer by layer, out of graphite blocks. The blocks weighed 20 pounds and were the size of two bricks held end to end. The pile was 57 layers high. It weighed 30 tons. Interspersed throughout the graphite blocks were chunks of uranium.

It was the most well-designed and elegant experiment I've ever seen. Through each stage in its development Fermi lorded over us with humble curiosity and fatalistic confidence. Not only did the pile give him joy, it behaved exactly the way he asked it to.

Send one neutron into the uranium atom, two neutrons can come out. This is fission. Now consider a lot of uranium. Send a neutron into the first atom, it sends out two, which in turn shoot out into two other uranium atoms. The energy doubles once, then twice. Carry this out a few trillion times. It's a nontrivial amount of energy.

Fermi had been waiting to reach layer 57 for weeks. He'd done the math, plotting our progress on a graph in his notebook. With each new layer, the data points began to follow an inevitable progression. He connected these points with a line. Extrapolated. The line went out and up. It crossed the critical threshold on the vertical axis near 57 on the horizontal axis. All that was left to do was seed the pile with neutrons, Fermi assured us, and the thing would go critical.

There had been the matter of whether to inform the university president of our experiment. There was a legitimate fear of a very large explosion. By this I mean an explosion that decimated the university, or the city of Chicago. We had no way of knowing. There were those who feared we might unleash an energy so violent it would feed upon everything it touched, propagating indefinitely, devouring the whole country, boiling the oceans, liquefying the Earth—a planet where men brimming with hubris once flourished. Men like Enrico Fermi.

Fermi chose not to alert the university president. The most pressing question in all of physics could not be left unanswered because of a bureaucrat. We were at war. At such times, you choose a side.

There had been talk of a fission bomb. In Europe, carpet bombing was knocking down buildings, but a fission bomb would be something else entirely. It wouldn't knock things down, it would erase them.

The choice I made that night had little to do with any of that. Better bombs are inevitable. Mankind went critical long before Fermi's pile. The thing I did was personal, and petty to its core.

Fermi's first life had been in Italy. He wasn't Jewish, but his wife was, and when the Nazi's stranglehold there tightened, citizens wishing to permanently leave the country had been allowed to take with them the equivalent of fifty dollars in cash. In winning the Nobel Prize, Fermi had earned a sizable sum of money which he was allowed to claim outside Italy's borders. It was enough money to relocate his family to America and start a new life. Max von Laue and James Frank also left Europe, entrusting *their* golden Nobel medals to another Laureate, Niels Bohr, who chose to stay behind. Fearing the medals would be swiped by soldiers, Bohr dissolved them in a jar of acid. Science's highest honor disperses easily into an innocuous black liquid. And so it was in this state that these medals remained, in hopes that after the war the dissolved gold could be recast, into new medals.

I was a grad student at Columbia when Fermi accepted a

professorship there in 1939. I wanted nothing more than to work at his side. Fermi was a genius. I use that word so very sparingly. I have met Bohr and Einstein. Those two alone share the distinction.

Fermi saw the world as, perhaps, a boy king does—with a child's untrammeled curiosity and a king's immense authority. He taught me this: knowing the magician hides doves in a secret compartment in his sleeve doesn't make the trick less magic.

Fermi and I coauthored many papers in those early years. He was my kind of physicist: an experimentalist. There was grease under his fingernails. He built things with his own hands to test his own ideas. To test limits. His ideas kept coming. The limits kept moving.

In time, *I* became his greasy hands.

Please understand: if you were working in science in 1942 and you weren't in physics then you were merely collecting butterflies. And if you were in physics and you weren't working to unlock the atomic nucleus, you were a bystander. That's how I felt, at least. I was happy to get my hands dirty.

I worked very hard. I did not receive, nor was I nominated for, the 1942 Nobel Prize in Marriage. Marriage was an equation I'd already solved. I assumed that it—that *she* —Elaine—would *stay* solved in 1943 and in 1944 and in 1945, but I was wrong about that.

Elaine taught me that neglect is a choice. Each of us get a finite amount of time and energy. We decide, each of us, how to allocate these. We cannot split ourselves, as we do atoms. We cannot be two places at once—not at a dinner table *and* a laboratory. The Heisenberg Uncertainty Principle teaches us that the harder we look at something, the more we change it. It's dead true of subatomic particles. It's not true, in my experience, of the past.

I worked incredibly hard to become the physicist that I did. I strived to be meticulous. Fermi had every reason to trust me to oversee the nightly stacking of his graphite blocks. Each layer more volatile than the last. But the harder I worked, the less inspired I became. I became derivative.

The balcony was crowded with control equipment that gave off a dim green light and even a little heat. I made routine checks of the boron trifluoride counters and the ionization chambers. Someone had left a hammer on top of the pile. The final neutron count was still on the chalkboard. I picked my way down the stairs and walked through a passageway onto the court, ignoring the switch for the big lights. I left the room dark. I crossed the floor and took a cargo elevator to the top of the wooden scaffold. At the topmost layer, I stepped out onto the pile. The graphite had a sheen to it, like a lacquered wood stage. I had it all to myself. The old building windows were shuddering in the wind.

Throughout the pile were wooden rods covered in cadmium. These kept the pile from reacting by absorbing the neutrons before they could reach the uranium. I set about removing some of these rods, one at a time. I removed all but one. Such had been Fermi's instructions. I took a neutron tally, the instrument clicking as it counted. I didn't write the number on the chalkboard, but it was clear that once the final rod was removed, the pile would go critical.

The atom is a little cage. In the morning, Fermi planned to let the energy out of the cage, watch it rampage a little, then usher it back into captivity. I thought of the people who would come, dapper in their suits and hats, to bear witness. If the first tiger you ever see is jumping through hoops in a circus, you might conclude that tigers make fine pets.

The day before, Fermi had pulled me aside. So we're agreed? he'd said—looking past me at the pile. You'll take your measurements, reinsert the rods, and go home?

Yes, I'd said.

I could not have done this without you, he'd said.

Words meant to stoke the pride of a sidekick. Did Fermi pity me? Could he tell the toll of so many midnight trudges through the snow? Did my bloodshot eyes betray more than sleep deprivation? I was too tired that December to accept anything so genuine as appreciation. It all sounded like pandering.

Because he *could* have done it without me. Meticulous physicists abound.

Maybe, instead of what I did do that night, I should have just yanked out the final rod and gone home to bed as the pile awoke, the frenzied swarm of neutrons melting Fermi's beautiful experiment and so much more.

What I did instead was ride the elevator down and find a wood box—the biggest I could carry. Returning to the top of the pile, I began plucking warm uranium spheres out of their graphite dens. I did not take them from the topmost layer, where the empty holes would be noticed. I removed about a dozen spheres from all over the pile, then put the graphite blocks back where they had been. I carried my crate of spheres to the back door. I unlocked it and set the box outside like a basket of Easter eggs. It was the darkest hour of the night.

Stepping back inside, I granted myself one last look at the pile, then exited through the main door. I nodded to the guard but did not stop to smoke with him.

I warmed up my car and drove around to the back of the building and picked up the uranium. On my way through the city I stopped behind a restaurant and tossed it all in a trash bin. It wasn't enough to hurt anyone. It would end up in a landfill, radiating, unnoticed and unacknowledged.

I drove home. The city was dead. I got back to my apartment and poured myself a drink. I'd taken to bourbon to help me get to sleep before sunrise each morning. My mind felt out of shape. It hadn't been pushed for a while, but now it had come to life. It played through vivid scenarios and seeded doubts. I drank more than usual. I didn't *want* to think. I didn't need to look for root causes of my insubordination. I needed help, actually, sorting through it all. I missed Elaine. She had been so good at talking me through things because she had, over time, lost her bias. She became impartial about me.

I suppose if an explanation must be provided, it's this: I knew I wasn't going to stop anything for too long. When the pile didn't react, Fermi would just tell me to add another layer. I just wanted to see him standing at the switch in the morning, puzzled as to how his math had failed him. To experience just once how lonely it feels to be wrong.

When I woke up I still had on my boots. The sun was up. It wasn't any warmer. I got in my car and drove back to Stagg Field. We all drank coffee together, all 40 or so of us, and then we pulled the control rods out in succession and made our measurements. We pulled the last rod out six inches at a time. The neutron intensity spiked just as we were about to remove it completely. And, standing on the crowded balcony, watching Fermi direct the show, I realized that the math wouldn't fail him at all. The critical layer wasn't 57. It was 56½. Since we couldn't build half-layers, Fermi's goal had been a safe overshot. The measurements were coming in lower than expected—lower than his calculations said they would—but the pile was still progressing to criticality. The chain reaction was inches away.

Fermi looked over at me. I turned away for a moment. When I turned back he was still looking at me. The look on his face was one I'd not seen before, nor one I want to see again. He knew the math had not betrayed him. Math is not capable of the things a man is.

I'm hungry, he said, and then he took everyone to lunch.

Italians.

Later that afternoon Fermi controlled the release of energy from the atomic nucleus, and as the celebrations began he sent me away to buy enough Chianti for everyone who'd helped make it possible.

MAN OF LETTERS

VIRGINIA CITY, NEVADA
AUGUST 15, 1867

Szilard,

Arrived this forenoon well battered by the coach, only
to be battered further by Tanner. To those we encounter
about town he announces, 'Here's my big brother, The
Professor.' A one-two punchline. (T. is the taller.) The
menfolk pinch a brim or offer a handshake with
palpable restraint of grip as if I were a lady. None
hazard a laugh. Nor would I, were I in their boots.
They know, as I do, and everyone else surely does in
this City, that Tanner Stewart is not to be taken lightly.
My 'little' brother keeps a most sober countenance, &
his big beard obscures all manner of smirk, & his eyes
twinkle (with rascality? malice?—only a brother could
discern). No. Safest bet is to take the Stewart Bros. at
face value. 'Assistant Professor,' I offer the
dumbstruck. One lie piled upon another, as you well
know.

Remain a stranger to this town, as I was when I knew
most everyone in it. Folks here still equate professor-
hood with similarly irreversible conditions,
circumcision coming first to mind. (No offense.) So be
it. Reputation precedes me. Shall therefore proceed
from it. To them I shall play The Professor, while to
you I shall continue in my role as The Confessor.

Assistant! Anyway, what would I call myself instead:
The Starving (Con) Artist? The Writer (of Bad Checks)?
Ought I take pains to clarify that, academically
speaking, I do in fact assist a certain professor in the
'tutoring' of his delectable daughter? (Have yet to
mention Orelia to T. She's a painting I'll keep in my
attic, safe from his critical gaze.) Thank you in advance
for calling on her while I'm away. She so enjoys your
company. Tires quickly of her lady friends. They do not
make her laugh until her sides ache as you and I can
once we get going. Wonder though, can you 'duo'
without me?

My damn brother. I suppose I should make
allowances. He's remained here, after all. Of course
this cannot be all too great a sacrifice, or he would've
flown the coop like I did. Nothing's changed, Szilard.
Still cannot do right by him. He'll bite off a plug of
chew and, gnawing away, offer me some, only to step
back in holy judgment if I decline. Or if I accept, he'll
laugh at how much I bit off, or of the way I bit it, or of
the volume or velocity of spit I produce. Were criticism
spittle, I'd be T's trustiest spittoon.

Yet. Finding myself eye to eye with the bastard as I
alighted the coach, I got the feeling these six some
years had changed things betwixt us. The relentless

elbowing for rank and attendant cruelties of our
boyhood finally behind us. I offered out my hand, he
took it. Shook. Only to twist my arm so as to read my
palm, as it were. Seems he found what he sought,
judging by the way he dropped my hand. He is most
callous to those of us lacking calluses.

You et? he asked.

We broke bread in a new restaurant downtown. Water
chalky, steak overpriced, bill obscene. T. insisted on
paying, I'll grant him that. Had much to catch up on,
but also v. little—being brothers, etc. I filled him in on
our various recent adventures. He slurped clam broth,
and with it dripping from his beard, articulated
disgust for: the 'opportunists' who've overrun our
town; the striking Celestial tunnel diggers; the General
State of Things.

I see you're still full of piss, I said.

And you of shit, he said.

More than once during the meal we heard the reports
of firearms in the thoroughfare, T. making no
comment. (As a boy he once happened upon a man
stumbling down an alley; thinking the man half-
stewed, T. passed him up, only to see that the
impediment to the man's locomotion was occasioned
not by whiskey but by a ball of lead recently
established in the man's gut. The man was trying to
fish the ball out of its bloody hole when he died right
there in the alley, T. attending, dying a little too I'm
convinced.) I asked after our father.

He's a fuckin ghost, T. said.

Do you think he'll know me when he sees me? I asked.

Oh, he'll know <u>you</u>, T. said.

Couldn't tell if he meant to reassure or impugn me.
Dropped the subject.

How queer to be back here, Szilard! To raise the very
hill that built up my young legs and find the goat path
now a bonafide road through The Suburbs. Wood
houses by the hundred where there used to be only
sage-brush. And yet, right where I left it, the humble
homestead, the same tendril of juniper smoke curling
from its chimney as was curling out the day I left.
Father's forge adjacent. All those pine logs held fast by
nails and hinges Father made. The man can transform
a bucket of horseshoe nails into a rifle barrel truer than
the gospel, I've seen it. I, who transform food and
everything else into shit.

As T. and I drew upon the place the quiet disquieted.
No hammer ringing. My earliest memory was forged
in that shop. (See me approach the anvil, feel a prick on
my bare heel—a shard of white-hot metal lurking in
the dirt. Hear me shriek. Watch as Father whisks me
up, dunks my foot in the slack tub. Too late! Soul
already blistered. Have I shown you that scar, Szilard?
Is that what I've just done?) Anyway, with my eyes on
home and my head in the past, my boot struck horse
manure. So I ask you—whose delightful race stomps
fine stemware to get the bad luck out of the way—does
my misstep bode well?

Mother came out to intercept us in her garden. She looks to have aged 20 years. Embraced me like the prodigal son while T. stood by and toed the dirt, averting his eyes from our Pieta pose. Do I exaggerate? (Tourjours.) But is it not rather biblical? Might we recall the New Testament (no offense): Brother A comes in from the field to find Brother B's returned home from squandering the family fortune on whores; watches as Brother B is lavished with robes and fed the fatted calf... Trope as old as time—though Mother cooked us only swine (no offense).

Am as much my Mother's son as T. is my Father's. Both of us should by now be reconciled to this. Still, mother heaped as much praise on me in our first minute together as she probably has on T. all year...

We take what we can get in this life. Or, is that just me?

Do please allow me to show you around: kitchen, parlor, bed chamber. A few rugs, a few mirrors, a few lamps. Privy's out back. Thus ends our tour.

Teasing! I know how you enjoy walks at dusk, before folks think to draw their blinds, their apartments lit up like store displays. Or, is that also just me?

It is hard to see our house from the street, actually, for the height of the tomatoes and corn and other vegetables in mother's garden. It's a wood house, painted the dark green of an Irish moor. A stone path bisects the garden and leads to an iron-hinged door flanked by matching windows.

Step inside, you find a heavy wood table and benches.

Cast iron stove to the right, doorway leading away to the bed chambers on the left. Two of the walls hung in a fine blue wallpaper, the others whitewashed. Two rocking chairs at conversational angles before the fireplace. Venture down the hall, you pass a framed seascape Mother painted ages ago. Two bed chambers. Both contain only what furniture is necessary, some heavy drapes for fending off drafts, and precious little in the way of ostentation except an occasional doily.

In summary: as plush a home as folks discomforted by comfort can stand.

Oh, but here and there dangle all manner of implement! Firedog and andiron. Ladle. Spit. Unconventional in appearance, one might even say grotesque, yet ingenious in design. Father once fashioned Mother a set of metal curlers with which she piously primped for church every Sunday. (See T. and I bowing our tow heads in time with the other unwashed sinners, Mother & Father thanking God for sparing us from the famine that devoured their homeland entire…)

Sorry. How is all this history and histrionics striking you, dear friend? It occurs to me that you know me better than anyone in San Francisco but that no one on the isthmus knows me as well as, say, little Tommy Drager—one of the half dozen urchins with whom I shared a schoolhouse when Virginia City still had her Virginity. Long before The Great Emancipator dressed us up to look the part of full-grown, voting Republicans, Lil' Tommy suffered my jokes and my brother's blows, stuffed his dirty mouth with Mother's hot bread (his own mother long dead), and feared my father as one fears the Father of the Old Testament. Which is to say, having known me back then, Tommy'd know me just as well now. However: I met an old neighbor of ours in town today. Charles. A bit younger than Tommy, used to run with him. I asked after Tommy, only to learn he and another of the aforementioned urchins were killed years ago in a mishap involving black powder and a chicken, also killed. As a kid, Charles curated a stirring collection of female paraphernalia—mostly undergarments and lewd drawings. He is now a constable.

Worst for last. Arrived at the right hand of the Father. He is poorly, as advertised. Here on this hillside, in this humble house, in the meager light of a tallow candle, reposes what remains of the man that, to me, means <u>A Man</u>. Trembling like a mouse despite the noon heat. His red mustaches now a grayish beard draped over the blanket. The stroke left him speaking out one corner of his mouth, drooling out the other. He's in the grips of some unholy fever. To see your father laid so low… Perhaps it is an inevitability. Still it throws you.

Knelt beside the bed. Took his hand. We talked. Or, I did. Prattled on and on, and damn if he didn't smile, Szilard. The ghost grinned right at me.

Was reacquainted at that moment with a couple old chums I <u>wish</u> had perished: Anxiety & Self-Loathing. Father smiles at me because I am his hope incarnate, the basket into which he has placed his eggs. He is wont to say, 'One does not waste his best iron to make nails.' (And, no, it is not lost on me that similar hopes ride on you, S. But trust you'd agree, installing you at Santa Clara cost your old man a few strokes of a pen, not a few million with a hammer. More exaggeration, you say? Au contraire, mon frère! Father once did the maths: 100 strokes a day, 300 days a year, for 35 years.) As for my old man, I am his Man of Letters. He smiles when he looks at me because I am just another of the many things he's forged, or is still forging. What can I say to him on his death bed when his dying wish is...me? What choice have I but to smile back? To pretend all is as he hoped it would be for me.

As I sat there at the bedside, T. barged in and, without so much as a glance my way, whispered for a bit into Father's good ear. Father grunted. Their exchange like some deep ocean current (while my stories seem only to ruffle the sea's surface). Their tête-à-tête over, Tanner tipped his hat, took his leave. Father returned his attention to me, and shortly to the back of his eyelids.

I'd always expected that before I returned here I'd have risen to some higher station, high enough at least to look my old man square in the eye. At 26, he had a forge and a family. My baby brother has a mill and holds elected office (Recorder of Claims, Flowery Mining District). I hold a carpetbag.

Was not ready to come home.

Blame you for paying my ticket.

Sincerely,
Eugene

P.S. Have you yet summoned the chutzpah to venture down the carpeted hall and broach The Topic with The

Man in the corner office? What if he surprises you?
Had a thought, actually: is not a free press a shining
example of free enterprise? Magazines make money, or
can. Paint yourself the intrepid entrepreneur, & he'll
look at you and see himself. Might that get <u>your</u> father
to smile at <u>you</u>?

VIRGINIA CITY, NEVADA
AUGUST 16, 1867

Dear Orelia,

Miss you terribly, San Francisco some. Am exhausted
by my travels, though have walked little more than up
some stairs at a lodge in Strawberry, and across a
thoroughfare to reach a barstool in Genoa. The snow-
bound summits of the Sierra are something to behold
up close. Carson City's a wind-scoured and stunted
little place. Sacramento—albeit verdant—is drab too, in
its own special way. How do such lackluster locales
come to be 'capitals'? Maybe it's to do with their
equidistance to everywhere else, some geographical
average-ness. Middle ground. Or, the map upon which
these cities are well situated is not at all geographical,
but political. They flourish along the banks of gerry-
meandering rivers of power. The confluence of
influence!

I digress. You are well aware of this. Oh, O.! Can
practically see you reading this. You are smiling. Am I
right? Wait…shaking your head? Some comely
combination, I'm sure. Your sugary kiss at the station
lingers upon my lips. (Or is it the macarons you
slipped in my bag, you she-devil?) Three days without
you feel like thirty. You would tell me I'm in need of a
bath and a laundered shirt, and right you'd be.

Promise I will introduce you to this place someday,
now that it's polished itself up enough to deserve such
acquaintance. Certainly it has more to recommend it
than when last I was here. Change comes fast with
energetic injection of capital. No longer answers to

Virginia 'Town', insists it's 'City' now (as Nevada
dropped its maiden name, 'Territory'). There's a
theater where I'm told the Westwoods play on
occasion. Would wager the Union Street here was
livelier this afternoon than the Union Street there.

Tanner kindly met me at the coach. Removed us to a
restaurant off the main. Fancy: brass railings, lacquered
booths, bowtied bartender. T. generously paid for our
steaks and whiskies. Through the window the
boardwalks teemed. All manner of man, darling! Your
wild cat miners, of course. Your teamsters,
horsetraders, nabobs, bummers, cowpunchers. Your
deadbeats, murderers, cardsharks, crooks,
counterfeiters, bigamists. Your tycoons. Vocations
discernable by hat, though I can't always tell The Rich
from The Poor. The ore to which the former hold claim
is so often still un-dug; the latter strut from saloon to
saloon with chins cocked, acting flush on account of a
few specks of color in their tailings.

Some things are just as I remember. Everything's
coated in alkali, everyone's armed. It's the scale that's
new—a bigger energy to the place. Palpable. Literal.
Dynamite rattling the bedrock every few minutes. A
mill up every alleyway. Din's so steady you forget it's
there, only to find yourself hoarse from shouting at
everyone. Place is an ant hill, teeming aboveground,
but just as many ants—more!—below. If I'm to believe
what I'm told, it's some 5,000 souls in the tunnels,
night and day (though no different down there).

Still feel under- or over-qualified for every job here.
Will stick to what I know: Observation & Ostentation.
You'll be pleased to know I jot furiously in the

notebook you gave me. Descriptions, snatches of dialogue. Today I saw a girl making her toilet behind a church in full view of a priest.

Tanner's changed not a lick, bless his heart. Pretends to loathe what our town's become. A complaint, I suspect, to heap guilt upon me for absquatulating to sunnier shores (as if San Francisco can claim sun). So be it. We live our lots, we wear our hats.

A joy to see Mother again, despite circumstances. Looks unwell, though her letters made no mention of her state, as you know. Irish pride. Manifests as masochism, masquerades as humility. We Hibernians can suffer with the best. I say 'we,' when truly this apple fell far from the tree, rolled all the way to the Bay, bumped into a sweet Georgia peach…

As for Father. Prostrate. Cannot tell you how strange this is. Cannot recall ever seeing the man down. He only ever sat at the dinner table and in church pews. Ergo, that's not Father in that bed. The doctor comes weekly to drench and bleed him. Has declared Father to be of fine constitution, considering. Mother, ever the helpmeet, gives Father vapor baths. But make no mistake. Father is v. sick.

Mother refused to let me stay with them and help with the caretaking. Insisted I stay with Tanner. I insisted back. She refused. Was adamant. Is Irish.

Alors, here I sit, chez frère. Suffice it to say I am not writing at a mahogany escritoire. Tanner's cabin slumps in a canyon in the eastern part of town—a spot I still think of as east of town. The structure is drafty

and cramped, the abode of a hermit. But the larder is
well stocked.

One of the town's many tramp dogs has attached itself
to T., or vice versa. The runty bitch materialized in the
doorway the moment we arrived and sat with
practiced patience as T. filled a bowl with scraps. It is
mangy and walks with a limp and its dry tongue lolls
out the side of its jaw. 'Bella,' T. calls it.

It clung at his heels as he toured me through the mill
he leases up the road. A 10-stamp affair. Took that
many teams of oxen to lug it all up from Sacramento.
Digests that many tons of ore a day, for which T.
charges $500 regardless of what the ore yields (it taking
a gold mine to run a silver one, as they say). Stood by
as T. harangued a dozen dreary men in his employ.
Held a gob of quicksilver in my hand. Queer stuff.
Cool to the touch, heavier than it looks. Saw my
reflection quiver in it.

T. showed me the product of a week's work. Just a dull
metal hunk the size of a horse head. The whole point
of this damn place, these poor people. Paused in
contemplation of the thing's cost: the time and toil, the
life and limb. Saw it ain't quicksilver washes the silver
from the rock, it's blood.

Lingered at the mill into the evening. Careful not to ask
too many questions. Dare not provoke the brother's
belligerousness. Ignorance in such matters has always
amounted to an affront to him, if not to all of
Christendom: how in God's name can a man not know
from whence comes his metal and his meat? Such is
T.'s contention. Ashamed to say T. & RWE occupy

common ground: 'A man is no worse metaphysician for knowing how to drive a nail...' Thank God he doesn't read: he'd use my own books against me.

My retort (which I make to you, not to T., and never to Ralph!) remains: Isn't it all just too much for one man to know? Mustn't some men be bankers and others butchers for just this reason?

Leaves me to wonder if I'm not cut out to be a writer. For aren't we expected to somehow know it all, or a little of it all? Or maybe writers only ever see the surfaces of things, and even then, only our own quivering reflections. Again, I say 'we.' When I'm penning only letters these days. Long ones at least. There's a novel in me, somewhere, O. Can feel it rising in me and wanting out, like a burp!

Szilard shall be stopping by to tap as he might upon your funny bone. Quite the fellow. A fine friend to the both of us. I'll keep nagging him about the magazine, but you ought put in a word, too. Better yet: skip Szilard the Jr. and go straight to Sr.! Alight upon <u>his</u> bony lap! Whisper like a muse in his ear, seduce the miser into benefaction!

Gone v. late, and this line fills up my sheet. Write me. Meantime I remain,

Faithfully yours,
Eugene

VIRGINIA CITY
AUGUST 18, 1867

Szilard,

Gone nearly midnight. Hunched again at the candle. A
bit thick-tongued. Wind howling against the planks.

This morning Tanner left for the mill before I woke.
Found my way to the homestead, where Mother
cooked me a breakfast of eggs and potatoes, no meat.
Read to Father from Gulliver's Travels. (Back in Cork,
Mother had books aplenty, but few worth their weight,
apparently: she shed most somewheres between St.
Louis and Salt Lake. Never re-stocked. Kept the King
James and the Jonathan Swift, the latter the more
canonical to Father.) Thought he'd fallen asleep as I
read, only to hear him grunt at the line, 'every man
desires to live long, but no man wishes to be old.'

Supped with T. in town. Afterward he bid me follow
him through the backdoor of a hurdy gurdy house,
past a pantry where dancing girls were powdering up
pre-show, down steep stairs to a private parlor. Dusty
chandelier dangling over a felted table. Chairs
fashioned from whiskey barrels. Men standing about,
shoulder-striking. One plucked a pipe from his fat lips
so as to point at me with it: 'And this must be The
Professor…' I curtseyed. T. shot me a look.

A barmaid came down bearing brandy and rumor of a
stage robbery. The men shrugged at the news, but I
snagged the girl on her way back upstairs. Pumped her
for specifics. She said the robbers realized some $14,000
in cash money. Further, she claimed the coach between

Bodie and Carson City is robbed so frequently that, upon reaching the particular bend in the road where thieves keep halting it, the horses stop by force of habit and remain at a standstill despite the exhortations of the driver! Naturally I gave this report little credit, but multiple of the men assured me it was genuine.

We sat. Cards were dealt. Taunts slung. Gossip spilled. I started calling T. 'The Poker' for how he jabbed fun at everyone. He teased one man for his rheumy eyes, accused two others—both widowers—of finding sexual relief in the other's hindquarters. Meantime, quite the grand jollification upstairs, the patrons dancing or fighting, hard to tell despite the accompanying accordion. The bootfalls loosed a fine dust from the ceiling that snowed upon our game.

Stakes started high, got higher. Held my cards close to the vest. Won a few small pots, stayed out of most. These were men who no longer play for sugar plums. Real muck-a-mucks: an editor, a mine superintendent, a banker, a veterinary surgeon, a lawyer, plus the saloon keeper in whose establishment we'd established ourselves. He's the only one I already knew. His saloon's been lodged in this hillside as long as the silver.

T. was gay. One time thought he was choking but he was laughing. These men could sit in with him, could themselves weave insult and innuendo into the mere calling of a bet. Pioneer Californians to a man; well, save the lawman—an Arkansawyer and Mexican war vet, but above all a runner of the mouth. He went bust first.

T. bade him buy back in. Suggested he put up as
collateral the Blue Tick coondogs whose wiliness and
obedience the man had earlier extolled. T. said, 'Them
dogs are wasted here. Hardly any coons about.' 'Nor
trees to put em up,' the man agreed. 'There's plenty of
Chinamen!' someone suggested. T. said, 'Supposing
we tree all the Chinamen, who'll wash our clothes?' I
pointed around the table and asked: 'You call those
clothes washed?' Perhaps because I'd been so quiet up
to that point, or because my insult was taken to
impugn the entire Celestial race and not, as I'd
intended, the griminess abided by this town and its
citizenry, I took in the night's biggest pot of laughter.
Even T. chuckled like a black-bearded Santa Claus.

Considered myself flush for the night & made no
further bets.

Same cannot be said of T., who delved time and again
into his coat for specie to stay in the game. He lost
more money at that table than I spend in a month.
Speaking of: enclosed are most my winnings, in partial
repayment for the coach fare. More soon.

Gone to see Orelia yet? I'm haunting the post office,
but have yet a letter from her. Dying to know how she
fairs. Write back when next your hands are idle, see
what words the devil finds for them.

Sincerely,
E.S.

VIRGINIA CITY
AUGUST 29, 1867

Dear Orelia,

In receipt of yours of Aug 23. Sat savoring it at my
mother's table, prompting a string of inquiries from
her as to my 'intentions.' From your letter I know this
makes two of us now lobbying on my behalf. Told her I
am the gentleman she raised me to be. (How's that for
reassigning authorship! What fault can she find in me
under such a premise?) If your mother did indeed
'beam' at mention of me, I can only assume you're
slandering my bad name. Careful: you'll leave me
forever digging out from under the praise you've
heaped on me. If only the rest of the world saw me
through those sky blue eyes of yours...

Little change to report in Father. I read to him, he
listens, drifts off. Breathes without rhythm. Withers.
Don't know what more I can do. I am here. Maybe
that's all I can be.

Your recent envelope was quite the Trojan Horse, dear!
The article nestled inside your letter caught me off
guard, & has me at a loss. Am I to assume by its
inclusion that you believe, as this C. McNamara
contends, that 'conceptualizing the penis as a
specifically male anatomical organ is fallacious and in
critical need of discursive revision'? Was this
something meant to make me laugh? To think? It's
certainly the thing to rile the chauvinists should
Szilard's magazine ever see a press, my pretty little
provocateur! Bully for you!

Need I add: this McNamara (he? she?) has a point.
Some men <u>do</u> answer to such a vile description. But
you've never heard <u>me</u> refer to my 'Mr. Morning' as a
'beaver basher' or a 'cranny axe'! Still, if it be
necessary, do allow me to herein and henceforth
renounce this most troublesome organ, which 'serves
as duct for the transfer of sperm but equally so the
dissemination of so much poisonous masculinity.'
Lord. To think all my life I've been lugging such a
weapon betwixt my legs! When last we shared a bed
and you tugged me to tumescence, am I to understand
you were actually trying to uproot the root of all evil?
Do tell...

In all seriousness, and for the record, I miss your laugh
more than your moan. Also—and risking further
offense—I am compelled to point out that, the selfsame
discrimination which bars young ladies like yourself
from your father's beloved university is what enabled
us to meet, and eventually to edify one another behind
'classroom' doors.

Believe I shall take lunch in town today. Enjoy a shave,
get my boots blacked. Am running the risk of looking
local. There is to be a hanging this afternoon. Tanner
insists we attend. He's always cottoned to such things
—the beheading of chickens, the gutting of trout, the
dowsing of brothers attempting conversation with the
fairer sex...

Back from the execution. Reading over the start of this
letter I considered crumpling it, so struck was I by its
stupidity. Have you ever seen a man hanged, dearest? I
had not, nor do I believe I care to again. Or, perhaps

it's just the momento mori we ought be prescribed with greater frequency.

The gallows was in a ravine north of town. Can't remember ever seeing such numbers gathered in one place. Women in their Sunday dresses, boys in little hats. A man peddling cider. A pretzel booth. C Street must have looked a ghost town.

The condemned was one Pierre Molyneux. French. Sentenced to die for the strangling of his wife, whom nobody in town much liked, I gather—victimhood her sole redeeming quality. Molyneux arrived via closed carriage. Priest met him at the steps of the scaffold and bestowed some final blessing. M. alighted the platform. Took opportunity to read from a prepared statement, the paper quivering in his hands. Crowd listening best we could, save the occasional outburst. M. said he wished life had turned out different, but that death might be the place he'd finally get some peace and quiet, neither of which his wife had afforded him. (Smattered laughter, whooping & hissing.)

He spoke well of his treatment by the Sheriff. Begged a drink. A jar of whiskey was produced by some humanitarian and passed hand to hand up to the platform. M. eyed it with some contempt. (Preferring vin rouge, monsieur? Champagne?) But the sheriff compelled the communion, tilting the jar to M.'s mouth to force a generous gulp, whiskey dribbling off his chin. M. gritted his teeth, nodded his appreciation. The sheriff wiped his charge's mouth with the same black pillowcase he then used to hood him.

A deputy stepped forward and fit the noose, taking

time to arrange the knot under the ear. M.'s knees
buckled under the weight of the moment. He began to
strangle (wishing perhaps to do himself as he'd done
the late Mrs. Molyneux?). Sheriff and deputy
shouldered him back up. M. stood there, teetering
upon the trap and time itself, looking out across
thousands hushed to the point you could hear birds
chatter. A mother clucked at a little boy tugging at her
dress. A shadow across the sun brought a sudden chill
to the air. My heart galloping.

Then—!—Molyneux plummeted six feet through the
scaffold, reaching rope's end. Snap. And there he
dangled, pendulating, convulsing. This went on for
minutes. (I hope this is not upsetting you?) Finally a
shudder and he was overtaken. Stilled. A physician
manifested, felt for a pulse. Nodded. M.'s toes left
pointing straight to hell, his neck cocked at an unholy
angle, his soul launched God knows where. The crowd
dispersed. Back to schoolyards, stockyards, pulpits. To
writing desks, such as they are.

I lied. I said you could hear the birds in the long
seconds before the trap opened. Pure embellishment.
Can't say I heard birds. Can only say I noticed their
singsong as T. and I made our way back into town.
Saw the green of the leaves and the blue of the sky
because suddenly one of our number no longer
could.

And here I thought last night's wind left me feeling
feeble! Such a fickle thing this life, a candle flame like
the one I shall presently snuff betwixt wetted
fingertips. Damn it, dearest: regret to leave you on a
melancholy note. Were you here, you'd make a joke,

and I'd be grateful for it. I need some of your sweet
sunshine.

Faithfully yours,
Eugene

P.S. As if on cue, T. has in his slumber just now passed
a most ignoble wind, the audibility or aroma of which
rousted both he and Bella! He muttered 'cocksacks!',
the bitch growled, and now both've resumed their
snoring. Thank you, dearest brother, you repulsive
clown.

VIRGINIA CITY
SEPTEMBER 9, 1867

Szilard,

Appreciate yours of Sep. 1 and 3, and your visits to
Orelia. She writes: 'he's no substitute for you, but a
salve to be sure.'

Have taken up an afternoon post at T.'s mill in
exchange for a wage. The wage is meager. (What is the
opposite of nepotistism?) I was only after a few
greenbacks so that I could buy my own supper and
Sozodont, square my debt to you. Instead have been
shown how the sausage is made, I being said sausage.

It is not overstatement to say I was floored by certain
of T.'s revelations, which he shouted in my ear as the
mill pounded away, its clamor providing a privacy of
sorts. Felt the ground rise to meet me. Plunked down
on the dingy floorboards. T. stood over me, shaking his
head.

Comes down to this: I've never been much for the
maths of money. You know this. Figures bore me. And
figure themselves out, eventually, do they not? Perhaps
this is how the fiscal irregularities of my family have
for so long eluded me. T. set me straight though. It's
his favorite thing to do. Figures.

Care for some sausage, Szilard?

Starts when T. and I were young, and Father was
taking home $3/day as an underground blacksmith.
This wage set him a rung above the Cornish brutes

with whom he shared a dungeon, but wasn't nearly enough to send a son away to university. Studious though I was, this simple calculus was apparently beyond my capabilities, certainly my curiosity. Never occurred to me to wonder how I was afforded the chance to rub shoulders with the likes of you and other appendages with the likes of Orelia. I suppose I figured Father for a squirrel—he'd sacked away the nuts. My diploma might have been of some use had I flipped it over to scratch some calculations on its backside. For years I've held my chin high, poised upon the yet-earned accolades of my future self. Like a caterpillar I have overindulged, sure in the knowledge I would metamorphose into an iridescent papillon.

Dear Eugene,

You're no butterfly, you're a fattening maggot.
All this time you've been eating shit.

Sincerely,
Life

The things T. describes put to shame the petty schemes you and I've cooked up (with the possible exception of your fated tussle with the late dowager O'Rourke). We are but pickpockets, shaking down baronesses and scalping forgeries for the kick of it. Meanwhile my family has been running the most lucrative laundry in all Nevada.

Another sausage, sir?

You see, the Wells, Fargo & Co. stages that travel daily from here to all petals of the compass carry not only the rich but their riches: silver bullion. The peons left standing in the dust have come to believe that these coaches' extortionate fares and general haughtiness more than justify the habitual 'reacquisition' of said riches. The thieves are often the selfsame men who wrested the precious stuff from the ground in the first place. They welcome comparisons to Robin Hood, but philanthropists these men are not. Philistines, more like. The bullion bricks are big as a pig of lead and stamped with identifying digits, special seals, etc. Hence, they needs be melted and re-molded if they are to be safely reintroduced to the open market. For years, Stewart & Son have been providing this valuable cleaning service.

It started small, I'm told. Years ago, Father helped a petty thief—his brogue as thick as Father's—by melting down some purloined coins in the forge. Soon enough, Father was being sought out by a spidery network of holduppers. As with his above-table dealings, Father established himself as loyal and fair. Honor among thieves, etc. He became the city's go-to middle man, brokering the terms by which his faithful son—i.e., not me—would come to comingle the silver extracted by pick with the silver extracted by pistol. This is how ore processed by T.'s mill occasionally yields upward of $300/ton instead of the typical $40. It is how Father, humble though his means appear, has managed to make ends more than meet. It is how Tanner affords to hobnob with nabobs and suckle top-shelf titties. And it is how I've been afforded the luxury of a prolonged latency in San Francisco.

So there it is. Behind every family fortune, a crime.

Asked T. point blank if he's partaken in road agentry.
He made no reply.

Growing up, T. regularly asked after my grades. He
once delivered a brutal whipping when I admitted
they'd faltered. Hadn't known until today it was
Father put T. up to that.

I have been trying for years to stalk the shady side of
the street so that I might capture it in words, when
come to find out I was sent away to be spared exactly
such darkness. I was put out upon the wider world to
escape the world my family lives in.

Seems we three Stewart men are Father, Son, and Holy
Ghost. I've been kept high and dry on my lofty
pedestal. My being away only enabled my mythology:
I was never around, so Father could never see that I am
a turd. T. knew though. He's always seen right through
me. To him I'm not holy, just full of holes.

From the embers of my father's forge a flame has
today leapt out to burn me…a memory that in this
new light reflects all too bright. See a young Eugene,
tasked with manning Father's bellows. Three tear-
shaped boards sheathed in leather, forming, 'like
Congress, an upper and a lower chamber, which
together dispense a constant stream of air.' Father's
joke. Watch as I pump away—then, suddenly, 'bop!,' a
sound like a cork leaving a bottle of Veuve Clicquot,
muffled by the sommelier's towel. (I make myself
thirsty for a visit to Josephine's…) Watch Tanner, still
in full possession of his baby teeth, shove me aside and
lever at the bellows vigorously while Father looks on,
vigilant but no longer fearful, for I have been

supplanted. You see, a bellows will occasionally suck in flammable vapours, which can explode within. This can happen when the bellows is manned by a bookworm mama's boy.

Wasn't long after this that Tanner was appointed Father's apprentice. He rose each morning before dawn to scrape the forge clean of ash and slag. While I lazed in bed with a dawn-lit book, T.'d start a new fire so it'd be hot enough to melt metal by the time Father finished his morning tea.

All of this to say, it should come as no surprise to me that my soft hands were kept clear of my family's mechanisms. Still, I'm haunted by a derivative question: did Father believe I <u>couldn't</u> or that I <u>wouldn't</u> handle the Stewart Secret? That is, did he find me lacking in mettle, or devotion?

E.S.

P.S. This letter notwithstanding, I remain so v. curious. How fare your efforts to melt the iceberg? Will the old man buy in, become a magazine magnate?

Next hardest task be naming the thing, but leave that to me! Believe I may've solved that riddle:

<u>LEFT BANK</u>

We'd of course justify the title as such (against the cover's left edge). Meanwhile, allow me to justify the title itself. It's a triple entrendre! Can you find them all?

1. The obvious tip of the beret to the Rive Gauche & its writers, philosophers, bohemians, etc.

2. It separates us, see? Draws distinction, as you've rightly insisted, between we of the west, at the frontier, and those in the east. We are budding Portland, Oregon & they are dying Portland, Maine, with its intolerable temperance and fucking liquor law. We are wet, & they are dry!

3. A wink and a nap of the nose, in that you 'left the bank' to found the thing—with any luck, using some of that selfsame bank's holdings as foundation!

How say you, partner?

One more thing. Obvious though this may be, I ask that the revelations of this letter not be shared with Orelia, no matter how she bats her lashes. Merci!

VIRGINIA CITY
SEPTEMBER 15, 1867

Dear Orelia,

Up with the dawn. A heinous wind blew last night. Feared my brother's roof would peel away and I would be sucked out of this cabin into the night sky. Sat for a spell at the window, huddled in a buffalo robe, peering into the maelstrom. A whimpering Bella kept me company, her master sleeping straight through. The air so thick with dust I could scarcely make out the cabin across the road.

The dust infiltrated the room, as did backdrafts of smoke from the buffeted stovepipe. As I sat sneezing and coughing into my robe, it struck me that habitation runs both ways: we live in a place, but it lives in us, too. The sounds spill into our ears, the dust and smoke fill our lungs. We eat from the soil, drink from the well. We've no choice but to take it all in, and in so doing, it becomes us. Virginia City lives in me. San Francisco too. Some salt in me is from that air.

Anyway morning finds T.'s cabin intact, if repainted in ashy alkali. People up and down the road digging out, dusting off. Getting on with it. Down the road, a Jew's mercantile in the process of erection was blown bodily out of place by more than a foot!

Have fallen into something of a routine. Rise as near dawn as the prior evening's pursuits permit, make the walk to the homestead, chop wood for Mother. Fetch and heat her water for tea. Make Father a cup too, help him to sup it. He takes it with honey now. This, to him, constitutes indulgence. He is best to sit with mid-morning, once he's propped against his headboard and his coughing is subsided. He asks about San Francisco. I read to him from the local rag and he huffs in approval or disgust.

Once he drifts off again, I rejoin Mother. Sit the same wooden bench I did as a boy. We chitchat. She cooks. T. will stop in sometimes. Mother still piles food on any plate within her ladle's reach, except her own. Her appetites have always been artistic. She's starved for libraries, museums. Her eyes are red, her hands are raw. This town mined her of her youth. Left her sallow and anemic and prone to cave-ins.

She tells me Tanner's taken up with the wrong type of folk. Says I ought to be getting back to San Francisco, back to you. I assure her that everyone is where they need to be for the time being. She piles more salty food on my plate. I wolf it down, then tend her garden, run errands for her in town. 'A man is fed, not that he may be fed, but that he may work.'

How stands the City? Strange how unmoored I've begun to feel from the place. Not from you, of course, mon petite chou. You are steadfast Polaris when all the other stars wheel. Am just this very minute pressing to my face the perfumed paper of yours of Sep. 1, breathing you in. You needn't worry so about my 'state,' dearest. Am content to toil for now alongside my brother in the mill. Mind too occupied for preoccupation. I continue my usual weight. Father can make neither claim. Of course he makes no complaint. Were we all of such constitution.

There's a negligee in a shop window downtown. Crepe
de chine. Pause every time I pass it. One of precious
few reminders here that women exist at all, what
female specimens there are providing lesser proof.
Something about the mannequin moves me, though
you needn't be jealous: while she shares your perky
bust and swan neck, poor thing lacks a head—my
favorite private part of you.

Tanner takes every opportunity to scoff at my
ignorance—in matters of metallurgy, plumbing, steam,
screwdrivers. Dare I remind him that he is all but
illiterate? That I know more about <u>his</u> work than he
<u>mine</u>? Should I—as I make a mess of his amalgamating
machine—expound for him upon the philosophies of
Pythagoras, the tenants of natural selection? He'd eat
me alive & digest me & extrude me into his slag pile.

We're by this point adapted to v. separate worlds,
simple as that. I'm a peacock amongst porcupines.
Haven't seen a library since San Francisco, but have
seen 1 dog fight, 1 cock fight, and too many man fights
to enumerate. As if I've returned to Ireland. Best to
keep my head down. Tuck pants into boots, lips into
teeth. Work! My hands begrudge me the fresh cuts and
blisters.

Mother finds no fault in me, of course. Enjoys having
someone to chew the fat with. The burrs on the pines
have begun to open. Gathered a basketful and bashed
them to get out the nuts, which are fine and sweet like
chestnuts. Mother's favorite.

For his part, Father was never much the
conversationalist, but ever a first-rate listener. Now

catatonic, his eyes on that far shore, his ear is still here for me. So I prattle on. It's not a conversation, really. It's the incessant chirping of a cricket in the dark.

I hear myself, and wonder: What of all that we mutter every day matters in the end?

'Hello' & 'Goodbye.' Probably.

'I Love You.' Surely.

'I'm Sorry.' Hopefully.

Here I'd set out in this letter to convince you of my cheery disposition! How about this, then: everything you say matters to me. This is irrefutable.

How fairs your family? Am learning things about mine I never knew. Being away so long, I've not been privy to certain particulars of their lives & livelihoods. Will share the details with you in due course. The mill in my mind operates day and night, refining raw life into letters, for you.

Here's something! A story Mother told me. From soon after she and Father first crossed paths... (Father at full run, late for supper after an afternoon at the pub; Mother accompanied by her sister, lugging warm basketfuls of baked goods to sell in town... I've heard that story, from Mother: how Father was all in a lather and stunk of beer, but had impeccable manners and blue eyes to match. From Father, how the sweet smells wafted from the baskets, how Mother's cheeks flushed at his attentions. Father claims to have all but ignored my aunt; Mother insists he doted on both sisters in

equal measure—that in fact this was the thing that
quite touched her: my aunt, you see, much resembled a
man, and not a handsome one. With a tap of his brim
Father was off, promising to search out the ladies in
town some future evening and sample their wares. A
simple encounter. Retold here because my life depends
on it, and our love, therefore, too! For Father was true
to his word, and later sampled Mother's buns...)

As for the part I hadn't heard. For reasons of faith and
finance, they lived in a one-church township. Mother's
family were newcomers to the flock and took up a pew
at the back. Father's clan, devotees for decades,
gathered nearer the front. This proved a torturous
arrangement. The lovebirds could only sneak glimpses
at one another. They dared not court openly within
Christ's house. (I can't believe she never told me this
story!) Ever the problem solver, Father devised a
means of unholy communion. Using hand signals,
they'd indicate verses from the Bibles piously open in
their respective laps. They limited themselves to the
page being preached so as not to draw eyes with a
flurry of page turning. Which restricted the vocabulary
of their covert conversations, but do not such pressures
(iambic pentameter, haiku, etc.) squeeze the sweetest
juice from poets in love?

Mother could not (would not?) recall for me a
particular phrase thusly conveyed across that stuffy
nave. I asked if an error in transcription ever led Father
to inadvertently call her a whore (say, during the
sermon on Hosea) or to propose an orgy—the Bible
providing as lewd as lexicon as any text yet compiled
by man. Made Mother blush.

Precious, yes? Strange to picture as scheming lovebirds those two, who are now at such remove from romance. Their love was biblical before they knew each other biblically. While ours was sacrilegious from the start!

Tanner still has the Bible we shared as boys. Have it here. Go ahead, see for yourself: Deuteronomy decrees that he who seizes and lies with a virgin must pay the deflowered's father fifty shekels of silver. Alors, pray we are not found out! Still, I shall start scraping together shekels...

More seriously, I can expect to soon be called upon to help steward the Stewart name and finances, modest though both may be by San Francisco standards. Am therefore getting to know all the ins and outs. As Adam knew Eve's,

And I yours.

Piously,
Eugene

VIRGINIA CITY
SEPTEMBER 22, 1867

Szilard,

Am in receipt of yours of Sep. 15. Answers to your questions are, respectively: of course, and no. Now do allow me to skip the pleasantries.

I—we—robbed a stage. It's true. Two, actually. God! Tingling still. To my accomplices the whole thing seemed but a whim, an evening's entertainment. For me: a strong cocktail of fright and exhilaration, with a dash of guilt. Feel I've lost my virginity again.

Already ahead of myself. Might we start over? Yesterday evening. Yes. The night progressing inconspicuously, or perhaps that was only then, in that present tense. Seen now, in past tense, I can say the night progressed suspiciously.

Tanner had me along to a watering hole he prefers— one Father, too, used to frequent—well removed from beaten paths. The men with whom we imbibed were, on this occasion, not muck-a-mucks. These were employees, not 'ers. The whiskey cheap and harsh, to say nothing of the whores. (Tanner will tell you: there are prostitutes, and there are destitutes. Can assure you these were the latter—not that I partook.)

I think it apropos to admit here that, in the company of such people—or, truly, the company of people in general—I cannot help but hear an inner voice, forever whispering, 'imposter'... Amongst San Francisco's gentry, it tells me I'm just a heathen, that I'm only pretending to have pretensions. But here, amongst my kinfolk, it makes jokes at my companion's expenses. It is a voice of obnoxious, unjustifiable superiority. How dare it?

I've the same grime under my fingernails as these folks do, the same red in my blood. I'm fluent in their filthy tongue. Anyway, I concentrate hard here to keep my nose low, for fear I'll be caught looking down it. I let the tanglefoot whiskey do its worst, let it numb and dumb the voice in my head, and hope no one will recognize me for what I actually am. Which is…what? Something akin to a newspaperman installed with an army regiment—at the battle, but to write, not fight. To blend in. I suppress so much. And to what end? (This end, I suppose—another stack of secrets folded into an envelope and mailed off to poor Szilard! Please tell me you feel similarly afflicted? You, whose blood is half blue, half Jew, when you wish it were pure red. We are purple-blooded, you and me.) I mention this voice in my head because it figures in what happened next.

Believe I mentioned a stage robbery? Call it the calling of a bluff. Had worked shoulder to shoulder with two men from T.'s mill all day. Was similarly arranged with them at the bar. Together we drank our daily wages. Tanner on an adjacent stool. Had just begun to feel that lovely defiance one gets after a couple droughts, rising in one's own estimation, conscious there is more in you than anyone is yet aware of, when an argument arose. The topic: yours truly. I stood like a sculpture while they—one with a toothless Squaw on his arm, the other with a Senorita on his—hemmed me in, assessing.

Their question: was The Professor yellow? Or, more specifically: did he have it in him to commit crime?

Pled the fifth. Whores stared off into oblivion, bored. The verdict: The Professor <u>was</u> capable of <u>certain</u> transgressions. Tax evasion. Forgery (which is at least a variant of 'forge,' Father!). Extortion. Blackmail. To wit: a jury of my peers finds me a lowly conniver. Felt it necessary to take the stand. Defend my dishonor. To fucking <u>fit in</u>.

I'm capable of more than you think, I said.

Assault? one asked.

If provoked, I said. Sure.

Battery? probed the other.

I asked, What's the difference?, prompting a gentlemanly debate over definitions, ended the moment one of the whores muttered, Murder? (She <u>had</u> been paying attention!)

Depends, I said. She spit on the floor.

Robbery? Tanner asked. He'd kept quiet up to this point, but now I can see the look on his face was that of a man admiring a raccoon his dogs have treed.

Two hours later I'm stone sober, standing at a hairpin curve along the Geiger Grade, a good three miles from the bar where the whole thing was hatched. (Implying it was first <u>laid</u>. Which came first? the man called

chicken or the stage he robs to prove otherwise?) We—
there were four of us by then—donned hoods of glazed
oilcloth. Holes only for our eyes. T. brandished a bone-
handled .44. A Navy revolver on his hip. We three
flankers had Henry rifles and shotguns. Barrels of mine
crudely sawed off. The guns and masks had
materialized somewhere between the barroom and the
highway. We'd stopped once behind a row of houses so
Tanner could speak in low tones over a fence with a
man I'd never seen before. Later, a different man on a
horse exchanged something with T. before dashing off.
I was in the dark. Swept along by a fast-flowing river
toward a cataract.

Standing there beside the road, I felt it worth
mentioning to my nearest associate that I wasn't much
use with a scattergun, having last fired one as a boy,
my aim the salvation of innumerable chipmunks.

Point it at people like you mean to use it, he said. And
you won't need to.

Just don't fuckin shoot it, Tanner said.

We crouched in moonshade behind a stand of
juniper. T. out in the middle of the road in the full
moonlight. We heard a pair of 'up' stages
approaching. Horses huffing around the switchback
below ours. Then they were upon us. T. stood his
ground, raised his weapon. Calm as can be, said,
'Hold up.' Stage driver stamped the brake, halted his
team. Horses sucking at the thin air, chests heaving
in their bellybands, wet hides shimmering. T.
ordered the passengers down.

Leveled my twin barrels in the general direction of the
second coach. Guns are heavier than I remember.

Eleven passengers spilled out and were presently
arrayed roadside. I watched in awe as T. and his gang
separated money from man as systematically as his
mill separates silver from soil. We left the females and
the mails unmolested—thereby avoiding both general
and Federal offenses. The ladies clutched their hoop
skirts up off the dirt and shifted about. One of them
wore a hat from which protruded a feather longer than
a man's arm. T. pulled some cushions and buffalo
robes from the coaches. Arraigned them upon what
level ground there was, invited the ladies to sit, which
they did, looking more irritated than frightened.

Valises were tossed from the coach and rifled. We took
greenbacks, watches, specie. A sack of oranges. A
stubby Chinaman had nearly $300 in his waistcoat!
One of our detainees was a judge of some repute,
who's sat the bench here since it was just a bench. A
friend of Father's, actually. Feared he'd recognize T. or
me. He begged permission to light his pipe even as he
did just that. He stood off to the side and gazed
regularly at a gold-chained timepiece as if timing us. I
thought to mention this watch to my cohorts, but was
distracted by the sight of T. as he clambered onto the
front coach and attacked the hasp of the iron express
box with hammer and chisel. I kept my gun up.

T. lashed two cans of blasting powder to the box's
padlock. Lit a long fuse. All present watched in awe,
fixated by the sparkling, crackling progression,
until......BOOM! Night flashed to day. My ears left
ringing. Hadn't covered them up as others had known

to. In the dissipating smoke saw the box successfully rent. Also, the coach afire. T. threw dirt on the flames, extinguished them.

Unsettling to know how quickly a small fortune can slip from a safe to a sack. Neighborhood of two-thousand dollars! Poof.

Loaded down with loot, we bid the coach parties a pleasant remainder to their evening and let them carry on—of lightened load, if burdened mind—to Virginia City.

We hustled over a rise to where some horses were tied. T. redistributed the haul amongst five gunny sacks. Not sure what he sought to balance (or imbalance)— volume? value?—but the men made no complaint. All hands accepted from T. a sack and a firm handshake.

They all mounted and rode down the very grade the coaches had just ascended, traveling opposite the news of our robbery, whereas T. and I circumvented it, circling east round Virginia City on foot. Favoring rocky routes where our footfalls left no trace. Navigating by starlight and memory the rocky hillsides we ran as boys. Still I stumbled, spilling specie into crevices. With each such slip I expected rebuke from T. but found myself instead on some heretofore unknown positive side of his ledger. Usually when he turns quiet it is to shun me, but there was a patience to him last night. He wasn't inflicting a silence on me, he was sharing one.

Just read back over this account... Trust me, I'm only scraping the surface of what may well be a gold mine.

Pay dirt, Szilard! These hills crawl with pro- and antagonists, the likes of which are not to be found in your Martin Chuzzlewitts, your Bleak Houses. 'Let the words be gazetted and ridiculous henceforward.' Let them indeed. May've tapped a vein here. Praying the lode widens as it deepens. All my years spent seeking out stories in San Francisco & they were up here all along! Ridiculousness here in spades. Robberies as research. Trick'll be to tell a story that doesn't smell of the lamp.

Where were we? Yes. Six-Mile Canyon. Straight to the mill T. and I went. The moon was set. Place was empty, eerie. No pounding. No shouting. (T.'d called off the night shift, claiming a lack of material to process. Horseshit: here was material galore!) We emptied it all into a safe under the floorboards in T.'s office. And that was that. I made no inquest as to what my share of the booty might be. Nor did T. see fit to mention it. Perhaps I am further in arrears with him and/or with my family than I'd imagined.

Locking the mill door behind us, T. looked me in the eye as square as I can ever recall. I half wished Father'd been there to see.

By the way. Father took a turn for the delirious yesterday. Started shouting. Mother and I hurried to his room. He stared at me, demanded to know what I was doing there. 'You're neglecting the mill!' he said. Demanded I return there immediately. Kept calling me Tanner. Mother tried to soothe him. 'This is Eugene, darling,' she said. Which only further confounded Father. 'Eugene,' he said. 'Eugene?' My heart broke where I stood. Father might as well have been dead already, or I. He didn't <u>know</u> me, Szilard. The delirious old man in that bed was not my Father, who knows me from my brother. In fact, I'd submit it is the telling of us two apart that is Father's greatest source of pride. Or maybe it's just <u>mine</u>.

In the end, nothing would pacify Father, save 'Tanner' taking his leave, so that's what I did, feeling the weight of a mantle I'd never before donned. They say to know a man you need walk a mile in his boots. I walked three, all the way to the mill. Encountered T. in the flesh—huddled over figures at his desk, inventing invectives. I left his boots and mantle in an invisible heap on his floor. Lingered, taking new measure of the man behind the desk. Who looked up, bid me 'fuck off and get to work.' 'Yes, sir,' I said, without irony.

When next I returned to the house, Father's eyes had softened, as if the whole episode never occurred. Mother says he has no memory of it!

It should come as little surprise to you that last night I tossed in my cot, so tumultuous were my thoughts. Awoke to find the sun high, T. gone.

I'm hardly man enough to walk in my own boots: last night's skedaddle left my heels blistered, my stockings stiff with dried blood.

Anyway—like I said, there's a decent yarn in here somewheres, one worthy of the publication you keep threatening to establish, and I to name. Apologies for such a rough draft as this. You've been such a gracious first set of eyes all these years. Choking on my chaff as I grind my way to what wheat there may be.

Finger still tingles which last night curled against a trigger. I feel different all over. Carnivorous. The way one does at the first bite of a juicy steak. I feel alive. I feel like….

a Man,

E.S.

VIRGINIA CITY
SEPTEMBER 24, 1867

Szilard,

Pardon this dispatch on the heels of my last. The intervening day…where to even begin? It rained, it poured. Will start with the letter I've just received from O., which shocking revelations may trump mine. She is <u>late</u>.

Perhaps that is all she is. Taking, as we do, the customary precautions. What's the rule of thumb for how long a lady ought await the arrival of menstruation before concluding she's no longer being patient, but become one? There seems a corollary here to our policy re: tardy lecturers—full professors deserving 15 minutes, assistants 5… O. waited two weeks. Assures me I am the father.

Dear god, I shudder even writing the 'f' word. I believe her, of course. She has not yet told her mother. Let alone her father…who trusted me to plant <u>ideas</u> in her <u>mind</u>…and not, well… God willing, there's a letter on the heels of her last, apologizing for raising false alarm. Such a repugnant thing I pray on—Dear Lord, let blood runneth as the Nile from my lover's fertile crescent, amen.

I am as qualified to be a f-f-father as I am to be a fucking fish.

'Tis but one of my troubles! Listen further. Ventured home with Tanner today for supper as a rainstorm swept our way over the hills to the west. Mother'd prepared a spread, all Father's favorites. We dragged chairs into his room and arraigned ourselves around his bed. Tucked into a Thanksgiving of sorts. Sardines, a thick stew, soda bread. Mother slipped spoonfuls of canned peaches over Father's purple lip, tore for him bits of breadwhite. Man can hardly summon strength to swallow. Seemed an insult to dig in as he looked on, but a greater one to mother if I abstained. Ate what I could.

Storm arrived. Drops pattering the shingles. We sat on ceremony. T. took seconds, then thirds, the rest of us watching in awe as he sopped his plate clean with a slab of crust nabbed off Father's plate. Between bites he tallied for Father the mill's accounts. Father nodding. His appetite for information sharkish as ever.

Mother and I cleared the table. T. fetched Father's pipe from a drawer. Packed and lit it for him. Mother clucked her tongue at this development while she and I crouched together over the washbasin. The coolness of the rain crept in. From the bedroom issued pipe smoke and manly mutterings, even chuckles. Mother noticed me flushing green. Insisted I rejoin them in the bedroom. Did so, sensing as I entered a straitening of T.'s back, a clearing of F.'s throat.

Our conversation stepped around on stilts. Excused myself to the parlor, took a dusty demijohn of whiskey down from the shelf. Mother shook her head, emptied the coalscuttle into the stove to stoke the flames, then brushed me aside to fetch 4 tin cups, make the pours. Together we 3 delivered this communion to the bedside, raised our drams to our prostrate paterfamilias, toasting his good name & long life. He who'd hammered out both the cups and the sons raised his cup back, in thanks.

I lamented that the whiskey wasn't Irish, to which Father replied, 'All whiskey's Irish,' and down the hatch it went. Candlelight in our eyes, we beheld one another across the room, our little family, dry and warm as the storm outside intensified. Mother winked at her husband. He closed his eyes and was at peace. T. bowed his head. Thought the old man'd leave us right then and there. Tears welling, I beat a hasty retreat to the kitchen, feigning some task there. 'Bring the bottle,' Father called after me.

Dried my eyes. Did as told. Upon my return to the room, Mother—sensing as only a mother can the need for a Manly Moment—claimed further work in the kitchen and made herself scarce. Father tapped his cup. I filled it. Then T.'s. Lofting our libations, T. shot me a wink. I savored it. Finally had a secret worthy of his vouchsafing. Until he spilled it all over the goddamn place.

To Eugene, he said, who on Tuesday joined the family [perceptible pause]...business.

The stench of his revelation permeating the room like a fart, T. tossed back his whiskey. Father suddenly staring at me as if I were a stranger in his house. Tanner told me later that he, T., had only been trying to welcome me into the fold, that I'd earned his respect for what I'd done, and deserved Father's, too. Well.

Paternal pride is not what I saw in Father's milky eyes. Saw heartbreak. His frail features quivering.

What's this, son? he asked.

I didn't know which of us he'd addressed. T. did. He explained to Father that I could now be counted on to provide cover during the proper fleecing of a stage. Must admit, part of me rejoiced, hearing this. Holding up a stage was holding up the family. I wanted Father to know that I knew the truth about us. Then I wondered, what if he'd never seen something 'special' in me when I was a boy? Would he've engaged in this whole wicked enterprise in the first place?

They say in death a man's life flashes before his eyes. While T. and I looked on, Father's focus fell betwixt us, to the wall, but it was not upon the whitewashed slats he gazed. The distance of his fathoming was profound. Across a continent and an ocean, to the verdant island he'd fled. But to what end? To raise thieves in this barbarous swath of yellow and brown?

I wish you'd of told me, I said.

He looked through me, his eyes not yet refocused.

Mm, he said after a moment.

T.'s chair creaked. He crossed his arms. Through the open doorway we could see Mother toweling a dish, humming some dirge.

She mustn't know, Father told us, sotto voce.

We nodded. He looked at me. Said, Just because
you've been exposed, that doesn't make you infected.
You understand? Things haven't changed, not a bit. Yer
to return home at yer earliest opportunity and leave all
this hard-scrabblin behind ya.

This is home, I said.

Eugene, he said, as if he pitied me. Do ya honestly
believe that?

(This stung.) What about the three of you? I asked.

Us? Father said, as if they weren't a question worth
asking. We fend for ourselves.

As can I, I said.

We don't want you to fend, Father said. A bird's meant
to fly.

And pigs are content down in the mud, T. said.

Well, Father said, they needn't be contented about it.
Not always. And discontent isn't what gets a bird off
the ground, now is it?

No sir, T. said. It ain't. Which I suppose explains how
come Eugene here can't seem to grip a hammer, on
account of his having feathers instead of fuckin fingers.

A trout could have swum through the room, the air
having assumed the chill and density of water. Mother
in her omniscience saw fit just then to rejoin us,
bearing a plate of chocolate truffles dusted in

powdered sugar. We chewed and swallowed these
sweet offerings, the storm lashing the windowpane,
the men smiling as wolves smile. Father drifted off.
Mother pulled his sheets up under his chin. We left
him be.

Mother insisted T. and I stay out the storm, but we
could neither of us remain there another minute. We
pulled on our hats and kissed her separate cheeks
goodnight and took our leave. Were back on the road
when T. shouted to me that I needn't accompany him
on foot, that I should feel free to fly back to the cabin.

Punched him. Right in the foul-smelling gap in his
beard from which such filth has for too long issued. Or,
could be I was swinging at something larger and more
upsetting than his mouth. Hard to put a finger on it—
easier a fist!—but my rage at that moment seemed to
want only for connection. To fly across this stupid
separation we've for so long sustained betwixt us, if
only to prove—to us both—it isn't so wide a gap. I can
reach the bastard. Make him bleed.

We set upon each other, right there in the mud. Blows
raining down. The both of us top heavy from the
whiskey. It's been ages since we scrapped, but
nothing's changed. I struck the first blow, but was right
away on my back, taking a pummeling. Blood gushing
from my nose, my lip. Still have a tooth ajar.

Taste it, Eugene! T. said. Same blood as mine! You ain't
some special breed!

Never said I was!

T. stopped swinging, held me pinned. Dabbed his finger below my nostrils and drew with my blood two lines across his cheekbones. Stared down at me like some war-bent savage about to take my scalp.

You want to kill me, I said, go ahead!

Mother's worried voice carried across the dark. Boys? she called. Is that you?

We peered up the hill to the little homestead, front window glowing. Neither of us called back. We peered into each other's souls long enough to recognize, if nothing else, consanguinity. Mother went back inside. T. took his weight off me. Stood up. Wiped his hands on his pants. I stayed in the mud.

Sometimes I hate you, he said, like I ain't never hated anyone. But I ain't gonna kill you, brother. I'd die for you.

I studied him. He spit, then stumbled off toward town.

I walked back to T.'s cabin and licked my wounds. The rain had washed off most of the blood and mud, but my conscience could not get clean. Now here I sit, finally dry, warming myself at T.'s fire. Getting all this to paper while the cuts are fresh.

So, can you now grasp my pickle? (Sorry. Don't.) My predicaments, plural. The impossibility of my being both the son my father wants and the brother my brother wants? Coupled with the possibility of my being a goddamn father?

How can I be a father? I'm penniless! In my present state, I am only of sentimental value to Orelia. I must write her now. Been putting it off. I've no idea what to write—a state altogether foreign to

Your faithful correspondent,
E.S.

VIRGINIA CITY
SEPTEMBER 26, 1867

Dear Orelia,

What news! What news. Been sitting here at Tanner's
little table long enough to watch the sky turn from
black to orange to pink. Now it's baby blue. Saw a 'V'
of wild geese pass over, the first of the season. Seems
an omen, but of what?

The strangest thing. My pen all but refuses to prattle.
Never have I been struck down with such a case of ink
constipation, and in a letter to you, no less. But—here!
—my pen is moving! Perhaps logorrhea is the
counterintuitive cure. Write about not being able to
write. The Description Prescription.

Enough, Eugene! Stop beating about the bush. Let us
address said bush directly. Yes. You, my dear—we, We
—have managed, it appears, if not the immaculate,
then certainly the miraculous. It is hard for me to
conceive of how we did just that, considering the care
with which we copulate.

Nonetheless. Nonetheless! I recognize it is a feat far
from impossible. On the contrary, quite mundane.
Couples the world over managing it by the million,
no? In the time I spent sitting here this morning,
willing my pen to stand, many a pen was stood, many
an exclamation point dotted! Why, then, did it seem
impossible until the moment your letter arrived? Oh, I
know. Because I am an idiot.

Forgive me. For this and other transgressions. I am most out of sorts. But, no: it is you who are the more out of sorts! You, whose body has been usurped, whereas only my pen is in revolt. You, who accommodate this unexpected (but not wholly uninvited) guest. Certainly not an unwelcome one. Might I inquire, then, as to how you feel about its arrival? A silver mine for your thoughts…

I have to tell you: Father is so near to death that were there not an urgency to address your amazing news I'd have held off writing for another day in order to say with finality that the thing I've come here to see through has run its natural course. But he lives on. Not that I would wish otherwise, any more than I would wish your current condition anything other than what it's meant to be. Come what may. Know this: I will take care of us. There is money to be made here by those willing to rise to the occasion.

We must savor life's comings and its goings, don't you agree? How else to say it? Were photographs capable of color, I'd capture for you the view now framed in T.'s window. Autumn leaves quaking in sunlight. A patchwork of life and death.

Can't shake this feeling that everything big in my life has yet to take place. That I hang in the balance. But how to tip it? Can life be steered, like a coach? Or are we just passengers, shouting directions up to a driver who can't hear us? Is there even a driver? Or are our fates just the collective whim of the harnessed horses, who obey only their stomachs and their balls (or ovaries)?

Our baby will need a name. If it's a boy, I hereby
submit for consideration: Harold. Father shan't be
needing it much longer, and it's a decent one.

Faithfully yours,
Eugene

VIRGINIA CITY
OCTOBER 4, 1867

Szilard,

Summer's over, that much is clear. Is San Francisco
now enjoying its allotted month of sunshine?

At the homestead I'm more spectator than savior, at
the mill I'm just another thing for Tanner to grind, so I
spend many an hour wandering the hills. Purchased a
Panama hat for the purpose. My legs seem to find their
own way, leaving my mind free to sift the musty
corners of its attic—all those half-carved busts and
collected correspondences, the heirlooms and trinkets,
my painting of O. (a semi-nude). Climbed to the
summit of Mt. Lincoln, took in the length and breadth
of the land. Carson, Empire City, Genoa, Silver City,
Gold Hill, Virginia City, Como, Fort Churchill, the
sinks of the Carson and Walker rivers, the saw-tooth
Sierra. From such a height this can look a calm and
civilized country.

Sometimes get clarity during my ambulations. Always
get thirsty. There's a watering hole I've taken to. The
shelves above the bar stocked with books and bottles,
both. Barkeep reads between dispassionate pours.
Loaned me out his Count of Monte Cristo. Like a dog
with a bone I take it to the corner to gnaw in private.
Sip my drafts, confront myself in the besooted mirror.
What bright notions I may've borne 'en plein air' tend
to suffocate in that dim barroom. Yet, what notions <u>do</u>
survive—those which I can still believe whilst looking
my reflection in the eye—deserve due attention, do
they not? Such notions have been v. rare.

Singular, in fact.

Here it is, Szilard: there have been no such notions. That is, I am unable to look myself in the eye. That is the conclusion I have come to.

Lied. There is <u>one</u> realization: Father may be high priest of The Church Of The Son Who Would Fly, but I am at least a member of its choir. I did not spark my own myth, but certainly share blame for sheltering its flame and tossing on fuel. Bullshit burns.

OCTOBER 6

Stopped in at the homestead this forenoon. Found the doctor beside Father's bed, Mother beside herself. Father'd suffered another stroke in the night. The doc demonstrated for me its severity, lifting and letting fall Father's lifeless arm, pinching his skin here and there, with me the only one to react.

Enough! I said. Doc took his leave with promises to look in again after his rounds. A hush fell over the house. The clock in the hall ticking, ticking. Were we down to the final seconds? I offered to fetch Tanner from the mill but Mother insisted she'd go, said she needed to take the air. Ordered me like a dog: sit, stay. Tell him stories. Then she absconded.

See the dutiful son settle into a chair his father wrought. See the father's chest rise and fall, rise and fall, half his face twitching, his eyes rolled back. Hear the gurgling, rattling noises that accompany his every breath. What compels a body so ruined to persist?

I took his bony hand. Decided in that instant to come clean. Selfish really. But knew I'd be shirking mirrors the rest of my days were he to pass on still believing I'm on my path when in fact I'm utterly lost. Perhaps I thought he might somehow show me my way again.

Told him everything.

Well. The damn Catholics are on to something! Confession's as cathartic and gratifying as a prodigious visit to the outhouse. Forgive me Father, for I have shit my life away. What is a confession, really, but a juicy story? Spun him mine. He already knew Act I, so moved quickly to Act II, in which the Special Son flies off to Santa Clara, only to find he's but a bird of a feather, another flocking asshole.

There's hundreds of Special Sons. The books he's not read fill libraries. He knows neither the proper way to wield a fork nor to condescend wait staff. He has nowhere to Get Away on weekends.

Father gaped at the rafters. No effect in him discernible. Not I. Was back in those drafty dorm rooms. Remember how homesick I was that first semester? Of course I never mentioned it in my letters home. Making them, I suppose, my first cracks at fiction: 'I've plenty of mates, I'm making great marks….' You saved me, Szilard. Never thanked you properly for that. You whose disdain for your own privilege was to me such a revelation. The way you blew smoke, how your dress shoes went forever unpolished. I'd yearned for all the things you sought to cast off. Meeting you changed my life.

Father flinched, or maybe I imagined it. Told him how you and I became fast friends, with nothing in common save our contempt for the show ponies with whom we'd been corralled. You hating them because you'd always been taken for one; me, because I would never be mistaken for one. How we graduated at the bottom of our class. How smug that made us. How you were offered cush jobs in the city, turned them down. How I wasn't, didn't. All the mischief we made, back doors we slipped out, the novels we started and never finished. My characters always caricature, my heroes forever seeing through everything and everyone. Nothing new under the sun to this narrator.

Until, of course, Orelia. Let there be light.

Father, I said, I am bankrupt. By every conceivable definition of the word. I trust in Emerson more than Christ. (The former at that moment seemed to whisper, 'Always do what you are afraid to do.' Did.) Father, I said, I'm no professor. Told him that, if my education has counted for anything, it was to qualify me for employment as a tutor, which opened Orelia's door to me. In that way, then, all has been worth it. I'm in love, I said. Then, overcome by some foreign (fatherly?) pride, I told him he was to be a grandfather.

Sensed a subtle uptick in the register of his gasping. Heard a prattle on the floorboards. Peered under his bed. Saw the mattress soaked through and dripping. Father'd wet the bed.

The smell of it filled the room. Half expected Mother at any moment to come rushing in to deal with the matter. Peeled back the blankets. Father—alive—was a skeleton in long johns, groin soaked, hands and feet bone white. Mouth agape.

I covered him back up and left to search out some solution. Found some canvas sacks in the foundry. Removed the things they'd held for decades. Back inside, levered Father's body about, managed to get the bedsheet out from under him. Used it to sop up what I could of the puddle on the floor. Undressed him. Averting my eyes. Swaddled him. Father grunting, moaning, drooling. Covered him back over with blankets.

Mother returned, trailing Tanner. They saw me in the chair, the pile of soiled sheets in the corner.

We gazed upon my handiwork. Had a laugh. Father would've put a pistol to his ear before letting his son diaper him. Still, felt I'd done something right.

E.S.

VIRGINIA CITY
OCTOBER 7, 1867

Dear Orelia,

Father has departed us. His suffering is over, ours begins in earnest. There is some relief in his passing. A second stroke had rendered him an invalid—an infant, really. The doctor worthless.

Am busy making arrangements. Much was settled beforehand, of course. Asked Father some weeks ago if he wished to be laid to rest in the green fields of his native Ireland.

God no, he said. Let me push up something green here, where it won't just blend in.

He asked only that his name and birthplace be etched upon his gravestone and that he occupy the westernmost available plot in the city cemetery.

Let folks see how far I got, he said.

Will be forever grateful that in his final days I was able to be v. honest with him. Not that I had been dishonest before. Nothing's pure black or pure white, though, is it? Fathers & sons…what books could be written. Won't bore you with the particulars, only say that we gushed to one another.

Father was a man who always knew how to be of best use. There is comfort in the thought that he was needed elsewhere, that he is already, again, lending his strong hands to some lofty purpose. Perhaps spelling

Hephaestus. (By which I mean stepping in for the blacksmith God, although spelling that name is also no small task.) There, I managed a joke.

This world can be sad beyond reckoning. Were it not also surprising, then...well, the surprises sustain us, don't you agree? So much talk of death has me craving <u>life</u>. Birth! There grows in your belly a fresh witness to all this world has to offer. What a welcome gift. For us & from us. Might I inquire as to whether you've informed your charming parents of our wee 'development'? Or are you waiting to attain greater surety in the matter? I leave it, of course, at your discretion.

I ought append an extra stamp to this letter, which bears so much weight. Apologies for my brevity, my lack of levity. You understand.

Thank you for your letters of late. The city you describe sounds, from this dusty vantage, like an imaginary place—as if I've never seen it myself. The quips you relay make English sound a foreign language. Wish I could be there, escape all this for a bit, be of use to you. Soon enough. Let me first lay Father properly to rest and tie off some loose ends. Then I shall be on my way.

It was good I came back here. It took a couple months to understand that. But some things are better late than never. You included.

Was that another joke? My taste in wordplay remains lowbrow. (But not my taste in pudendas...) I'm absolutely shameless. (Don't read too far into the plural within those last parentheses, love. There is but one pudenda—one ( )—for me!) Oh, O., this is helping…thank you. I see Father's ghost sitting up in his coffin at his own wake to point at me, huddled in the back of the room, whispering in your ear—something I will do until the day of my own wake, so long as it continues to make you giggle.

<u>Eugene</u>, the ghost admonishes. <u>Enough!</u>

Yes, Father, I say. Forgive me. And I glare at you, my love, mock blame in my teary eyes, as if to say: Why do you let me carry on so?

Eugene

VIRGINIA CITY
OCTOBER 7, 1867

Szilard,

Father has died. He went in the night.

Spent the morning at his bedside. Tanner wandered in,
removed his hat, sat in the chair on the opposite side of
the bed. His hull of a forehead wrinkled in
contemplation. He shirked my gaze. I think because
there was a tear in his eye. Couldn't help but to pry at
this rare crack in his defenses. Asked what final
expression he saw in Father's face.

T. started to speak. Couldn't. Cleared his throat. He
looks dead, he said.

I see a man at peace, I said.

T. harrumphed. Said, Then I'll have what he's having.

Mother's green eyes are sunk deeper than ever. A face
long past pain. Grief incarnate. Wish the three of us
would all just have it out and wail together at the sky,
but we all pretend to hold fast and sit holding our
cooling cups of tea and call it composure.

Feel some part of me has died, too. The world feels an
arctic place today, despite the earnest efforts of the sun.

Have here a bit of whiskey. Want for something
stronger. Irony is, Father'd not have tolerated this
mood. If he were here he'd be standing cross-armed,

nodding toward the door, saying, Get on with it, Eugene. Make something of the day.

I will, sir. I will. Starting on the morrow.

Eugene

VIRGINIA CITY
OCTOBER 12, 1867

Dear Orelia,

Your correspondent has been a busy beaver. Keeps him
from wallowing too deeply. Sorrow being a syrup my
family indulges in only by the teaspoon. We'd
expected the Reaper to pay his visit for months now,
and yet when he darkened our door he was an
unexpected and uninvited guest. The first of many, it
turns out. Been playing host for days. Mother's front
room trafficked like the lobby of The Regent. Dam it all
to hell, say we beavers. Lose thyself in thy labor!

Speaking of labor: how progresses The Peanut, as
you're calling it? Can you yet detect its protrusion in
your handsome belly? If so, our guts are
complementary—convex and concave (never
remember which is which)…stood on a scale yesterday
at the mill and weighed just 150 pounds. Are you still
nauseous in the mornings? I've not shared our news
with anyone, save a booklender/bartender. Had to tell
<u>someone</u> and he seemed qualified. It goes without
saying—though I shall say—that, while you've never
once asked anything remotely financial of me, The
Peanut changes everything. Trust me: I understand.
Children cost money. It falls to the father—me!—to
cushion what shall soon fall from you.

The outpouring of grief has been something to see. On
the morning Father died there came floating up our hill
a trio of women—two Mother's age, one mine—to help
with the laying out of Father's body and other tasks.
Mother'd already changed Father out of his bedclothes

and into his Sunday suit. I escaped out back, split wood enough for weeks. Built up a raging fire in the stove, made Mother and her helpers a pot of tea. Went into town to locate the priest and arrange the burial.

The womenfolk dusted and polished spots Mother'd already tended to. Straightened portraits. Lit votives. Calm before the zephyr, really. By sundown, seemed every man, woman, and child in town had blown through. Father's body on a board spanning his own sawhorses. A table beside spread with whiskey and sandwiches.

There are dozens of women here who've also outlived their husbands. Each meets Mother head on with an empathic embrace, a sad smile welcoming her to their guild.

I'm getting to know Father anew through his lore. Folks have big things to say about him, even if they speak small. This isn't ignorance, it's parsimony. In San Francisco, words tow around their syllables like so many empty train cars. Words here carry their weight. A woman who used to live just down the hill from us told me, Your father had a good and kind soul, didn't he. Yes, I said.

A man I'd never met but who'd known Father for decades summarized him thus: He was a hard worker.

A neighbor boy said, He made me this!, and he held up a miniature train engine. The boy's father nodding at this verity.

He built everything, I said.

The boy's face twisted up at his father. (Both perhaps baffled by my casual contradiction of the book of Genesis.) The father looked at me as if finally registering the cause of some heretofore inexplicable defect, then ushered his boy along.

Let's just leave it at this: None of us will ever measure up to the man.

Sunday we walked in procession to the church. Heard a fine sermon. Proceeded en masse up the hill to the cemetery. Tanner and I each bearing a pall along with four others. The coffin draped in black velvet, trimmed in gimp. Bella scampered ahead and frightened from our path any jay, chipmunk, or drunkard who dared chatter. We gathered amongst the gravestones and quaked in the autumn wind. T. and I flanking Mother, bracing her up. Bella seemed to sense our mood. She sat as solemnly as a dog (or a man) is capable. Priest said a prayer as my mind wandered up and over the mountain and down to the sea, to you…

I can say I've seen Father properly returned to the ground. Doubt his body will return to dust, though. More likely to a band of iron.

Today is Mother's birthday, of all things. The man with whom she shared bed and bread is forever gone. What gift do you get the woman who has nothing? I believe I will buy her something from the German bakery she used to take me to on <u>my</u> birthday. A chocolate cake, I think. A delicacy like life: dark, bittersweet, gone before you're done.

Eugene

VIRGINIA CITY
OCTOBER 13, 1867

Szilard,

Able to rest myself now that Father's been properly
laid to it. He had a good death. In his final hours he
summoned strength enough to speak his mind. He was
under a roof he built, surrounded by a family he also
did. Weeks ago he turned down a visit from the pastor.
Reckon his conscience was clean as any other Christian
who's had to scrape a living from these hills. Let those
whose fortunes are already made stand on virtue, the
rest of us don't have the luxury. My Father, who art
now in heaven, hallowed be his name.

You'll forgive me if I've come down with a case of
religion. It's contagious in such crowded rooms as I've
been of late, cloistered amongst the devout. Don't
know where else to look, though. Don't know where to
find my Father. I watched with mine own eyes as his
body was lowered into the ground, so why do I keep
looking everywhere for him?

Actually, when we lowered the coffin into the rocky
crust that passes for soil here, the grave was too
narrow at the bottom. Coffin wouldn't rest squarely.
All of us in our Sunday finery, staring down in stunned
silence. I spied a pick leaning on a nearby fence—left
there, no doubt, by the negligent grave digger himself.
Rolled up my sleeves. Demanded the coffin be hoisted
back out.

Jumped into the grave. Picked at the problem like a
man possessed. Was soon drenched in sweat. Sensed

some jealousy in Tanner, that I'd be the son whose hard labor would provide for Father a proper resting place, but there was only room in that grave for one man to work. Noticed at that moment that my hands and I have hardened. The pick felt not so natural as a pen in my grip, mind you, but nonetheless.

Tanner slipped away, returned with a spade. I asked him to hand it down, was refused. Next I knew we stood face to face in the grave, the assemblage pretending not to watch as we nearly came to blows again. Tanner was not about to let go, so I climbed out. I'd sweated through my linen shirt. Leaned on my pick as Tanner lay into the spade. Realized it was possible Father'd wrought both tools.

Realized also that Tanner in his role as mill boss rarely handles handles these days. Fancies himself a laborer and probably always will, but what leverage he lately exerts is mostly financial (or familial) (or filial). Wonder if I've hardened as much as he's softened?

When I pray, it's that wherever Father is now he has it easier than us, who're left behind to grieve and question. Hopefully from the other side it's all quite hilarious to watch—a play steeped in dramatic irony, the characters never privy to the plot's true arc. (Bella had a tussle with a skunk the other night. Got herself so bedewed T. had to tie her up away from the house for two days. He tells me it's happened before, that he ought dose the bitch with strychnine, save himself her hassle—but I know he's soft on her. A dog has no idea why it does what it does, but do <u>we</u>? Seems profound stupidity all around.)

Placed an obituary in the Territorial Enterprise. Wanted to effuse, you know me. Editor insisted on brevity, as did his price per column inch. Humbling to see what a man can be reduced to in newsprint. A couple dates, some places, a few names. Where's the story in that? The rag circulated widely, but rumor of Father's passing had already spread like syphilis. Suspect this to be the doctor's doing. Satchel full of tonics useless against what ails us, the man's capable of curing only our nosiness. Gossip's the infection and remedy, both. Quite the racket he runs.

Must mention: on the morning Father passed—his body not yet gone cold—Tanner slipped off and returned not twenty minutes later in a two-horse wagon with a white pine coffin in the bed. A fine coffin, truly. Lined in white muslin.

Seems I arrive late at every such conclusion. Never Tanner. He handles the mechanical, leaving me the mystical, I suppose. Doesn't seem to begrudge me this disparity, though I envy him. In trying times, wrestling with the actual world, the use of one's hands, the digging of graves, etc., is preferable to wrestling with the heavier stuff inside one's head, wouldn't you agree? Dragging a pen around on paper doesn't quite do the trick.

Take that end, Tanner said, sliding the thing halfway out of the wagon bed. We hefted it toward the house. Waddling backwards, was thinking how I'd never have engaged a carpenter whilst Father breathed air. Would have been an affront to the man. Might've even hastened his decline were he to learn of it. That's when

I noticed the coffin's fine pewter screws and iron hinges.

Father made this, I said. T. grinned. I asked him when. T. said a couple years ago. I asked him to what purpose. The usual, he said. Right, I said. Was losing my grip. Begged a spell to set the thing down. Told T. that, to my knowledge, Father'd been in fine shape two years ago.

There's three more just like it, he said. Back at the mill.

Well I've not seen them, I said.

Don't suppose you would've, he said. Seeing as they're in the tool crib.

Ignored the dig. Three? I confirmed.

A wink from Tanner—grim reaper of all things material & mortifying. And why was I surprised? Father'd built our homes in this life, why not the next? We leaned the coffin against the house and stood for a moment in the sun. T. turned to piss on some sage-brush.

Father and me, he said over his shoulder, we did a couple jobs, a wee riskier'n usual. Suppose that's about the time he saw fit to make 'em.

I asked T. if Mother knew. He took his time stuffing himself back in his trousers. If not the particulars, he said, I'd say she's got a rough idea.

Rough idea indeed.

It fell to Tanner and me to heft Father from his death bed into his casket. The body lighter than I'd expected, like a bird that's struck a window, a bony little thing, belied by plumage. Mother smoothed back his hair, knotted his tie, interlaced his big hands on his hollow belly. Tied his chin up with twine. As such he greeted his many guests. Whole families, widows, and many a grimy, solitary miner. Everyone lingering a few solemn moments over him. The men seem the more devastated, the women attending more to Mother in her black veil. I worry for her. Have not seen her eat in days.

The men use both their hands to shake mine, then my brother's, looking us dead in the eye, conveying heartfelt condolences. With T. that's all they do. With me—'the San Francisco son,' one called me, another called me 'Lil' Eugene'—they see fit to fill me in on all I've missed. Each has their favorite fable, which they step up and hang like ornaments on my overburdened limbs. There's the one about Father getting kicked by a mule and still finishing his shift. I knew that one, everyone does. Pretended otherwise, of course. Where was he kicked? I'd ask. One man replied, Down in the mine. A little boy pointed at the side of his little head, explaining, 'Wight heow.' A few stories I hadn't heard. Father'd helped to deliver two of the young men I met, from mothers I also met.

Graveside, I'd elected to read from The Village Blacksmith:

His brow is wet with honest sweat,
He earns whate'er he can,
And looks the whole world in the face,

For he owes not any man.
Toiling, --rejoicing, --sorrowing,
Onward through life he goes;
Each morning sees some task begin,
Each evening sees it close;
Something attempted, something done,
Has earned a night's repose.

Walking Mother home, her arm laced in mine, she told
me I'd written the perfect poem to honor Father.
Admitted I hadn't written it, Henry Longfellow had.

I don't believe I've met him, she said. Did he know
your father?

Speaks to her state. She knows Longfellow, or used to.

He did, I decided to say. Mother nodded numbly,
setting my mind to spin off like a top. I started to ask
myself: who knew Odysseus better: Homer or
Telemachus? Was it the bard who, blind, saw
everything? Or the son raised by a myth instead of a
man? Because I know what it is to grow up in a man's
shadow. I am Telemachus. But might I also be Homer?

Anyway. Have also learned something else about
Father: that many a man here who've now paid him
their respects have, meanwhile, not paid him back on a
debt.

Cocksack owes us money, T. muttered to me as one
such debtor was embracing Mother just a single
sidestep away along our short receiving line—well
within earshot, judging by the look that befell the
man's face. Actually, the look on many of these men's

faces was an odd one. One I came to recognize—even flinch at—as when discharging a weapon at a rock: the spite in T. and I's eyes came right back in our faces. Once out of Mother's sight and hearing, these men huddled together in corners and glared at us as if we were the ones who ought be ashamed. At the time, I had no choice but to assume everyone in town knew our family's dirty little secret. I didn't know the dirtiest part yet. (More on that shortly.)

More mourners cycled through, with T. leaning over time and again to whisper some outstanding sum. I put numbers to faces: '300' is a badge-donning officer of the peace. '120' has bright red mustaches & pantaloons to match. Began to wonder what <u>my</u> number is. Anyway, we needn't have so eagerly dug out the hole for Father. He'd already dug one for hisself. The Stewart name and its attendant debt are to be my inheritance.

Weren't the strokes got Father, Tanner said. It's his heart was too fuckin big. Went on to tell me Mother can't hardly afford bacon. Is that not outrageous? Suppose this is how Virginia City really runs: off the books. The bankrupt Bank of Stewart.

What of all these debts, then? I asked.

What of them? Tanner replied, helping himself to more of the whiskey we'd set out for guests.

Well, I said, Mother certainly can't be expected to collect.

T. tapped a finger to his nose, pretending to be

impressed that I'd reached this conclusion all on my own. More mourners approached. Tanner drained his whiskey. We didn't further delve the matter until later. Must pause here.

Okay. Now. After we arrived home from the service, T. and I slipped out to smoke cigars behind the forge. At which time he spit out the plug of a plan he's clearly been gnawing awhile. It is this: the V&T railroad is soon to commence operation. This would be of little consequence, except that it will now carry, among other things, silver from the Comstock down to the new U.S. Mint in Carson City. However, for the time being, the bullion is being transported via stagecoach. Affording anyone so inclined with a precious window in time before such silver becomes a might trickier to intercept.

This is bigger game you're talking about, I said. T. nodded. Still, I wasn't following. As I understood, mother would be square once we'd called in all the debts of the men who'd waltzed through Father's wake. Told T. as much.

Well, he said. That's about half true.

Oh? I said. What half am I not seeing?

T. held his arms wide, like a cigar-smoking Jesus. You're lookin' at him, he said.

The hell are you really after? I said. Say it plain.

Silver.

To what end?

To get square! Tanner said. Goddamn it, Eugene. I'm in over my fucking head. And Mother's suffering for it.

And how's that exactly?

I've been more'n a little unlucky at cards, as of late.

(Must admit, I wasn't shocked.) Tanner, I said.

I ain't after no scolding, Eugene. Ain't proud of what I got us into.

(Us?)

Who is it you owe? I asked.

Oh, there's a fair number...

How much? I said. All together.

Four, he said with a sniff.

Four hundred dollars! I said. Jesus, Tanner.

Thousand, he said.

(My mind still reels at this sum.)

It's come due, Eugene, Tanner said.

And if you don't pay? I asked. If you can't?

T. looked at me, then, and though he has that big black

beard, I can still see fine into the burning holes of his eyes, and at that moment, for the first time I can remember, I peered into them and saw unadulterated terror. Scared me to death.

They're going kill him, Szilard. They've banded together like ranchers whose herds have been attacked by the same lion.

We both had to look away. I couldn't bear another second in his doomed presence. I stormed straight up the road and into the hills, propelled by the steam of spite, muttering like a man fresh from the asylum. Pondering the sheer fucking, skunk-sprayed stupidity of it all, what a man like Tanner's willing to put at stake.

For it goes without saying that these bullion-bearing stages Tanner's after are well-guarded—by men made brave by handsome pay and what self-righteousness seems ever to attend such professions. But also this, per Tanner: the silver is transported inside a fortified safe called The Salamander on account of its green luster, and guaranteed by its manufacturer to withstand a full 48 hours of determined assault. Tanner insists one can counter this particular measure, if adequately (mechanically) inclined.

As I walked, my spite turned to dread. Felt it in the pit of my guts. For I trust in T.'s capabilities as much as I'm beginning to fear my corrupt-abilities. My pace slowed. My mind accelerated. Fact: there is many a man here who owes Father on a debt. Fact: there are many a man here to whom Tanner owes one back. Further—and strange as it may seem—many of these men are one and the same man, though the offsetting debts be of differing magnitude. This town, at its core, is still a small one. Too small. And for too long, its men have benefitted from what appears a heritable speech impediment. That is, a difficulty for Stewart men to pronounce the word 'No' when presented with a hand —be it extended palm up (to Father), or dealt face down (to Tanner). Following? What I mean is, many a man here has come to conclude that he is square with the Stewarts—that, whatever he may have owed The Father was subtracted from what is owed him by The Son. Tanner's been drawing on Father's credit. Drawing cards, specifically.

Now everything's out of whack. To wit: T. coming to me for help. Bastard tricked me once into playing 'particeps criminis'; this time he's all but begging…

Such were my thoughts by the time I'd walked far and high enough to get perspective. I could see myself as others see me, or want to… Father wanted me a literate man. Mother only ever wants that I am happy. Tanner wants an accomplice. Orelia wants me in San Francisco. Hers seems a modest enough desire, except implicit in it there must be some expectation that we live in that fair city decently—not necessarily with the luxury she's grown habituated to, but certainly not roving on a semi-monthly basis amongst the various boardinghouses at which I currently have an outstanding balance. Right? Further, I'd suspect whichever station in life is afforded us—what schooling our child receives, what fruits we eat—shall be the fruits of our own labors, without going hat in hand to her old man, one she loves with all her heart but resents with all her head for his very old man-ness

—his outmoded expectations for young ladies. You know what I'm saying. I'm saying that, without ever saying so, Orelia asks only for what she (or at least our child) deserves, for which I'll need more than two coins to rub together, will I not?

As for myself, I'd ask only to be the author of mine own story.

And it struck me then, as I paused on that hillside, that there might be a way to become all these things to all these people. And I turned heel.

More Longfellow:

Thus at the flaming forge of life
Our fortunes must be wrought;
Thus on its sounding anvil shaped
Each burning deed and thought.

Remember that bizarre tome on whaling Prof. Snyder force fed us? That maniac, Ahab? Well I've glimpsed the fluke of my quarry, and it isn't white, it's green. There's more than silver to be found in the belly of The Salamander, Szilard.

Forgive my family its trespasses, which deliver us into evil.

Eugene

VIRGINIA CITY
OCTOBER 20, 1867

Dear Orelia,

Astonishing: been here two months. Apologies: fully expect to make my return in the coming weeks.

Ours of Oct. 12 passed in the mails. Do you think they shared a roof (or a sack!) at some stage in their opposing journeys? My dusty page tearing at your perfumed envelope, ink smearing, letters crumpling into complementary shapes their authors cannot at present assume… Amusing to imagine, if unlikely. Yet, how likely is anything? Every moment is an egg for which innumerable sperm vie...

Do you tire of my ever-prurient quill, dear? I know it wears me out, being led about by my loins. Try as I might to elevate my discourse, rarely manage to raise it above intercourse. Had our respective sperms found purchase in different eggs in some earlier era—had I been, say, a Roman soldier sent north to war upon the hordes, and you my maiden—the messages I'd've dispatched to you from the front would still have been efforts to make you blush, but in Latin. Although, reckon as a Roman soldier I'd've been illiterate. A fate worse than death!

Found a thin crust of ice in the bucket this morning. The apple tree down the road droops with fruit. Munching one now to break my fast. It's summer that's over, but feels more like the end of winter. Been here waiting out dark days, and now my sap is starting to flow. There are things I will now permit myself to look forward to, chief among these our imminent reunion. I know you still have a mind to come and visit this wild place, but believe me: neither the sights nor smells (nor most assuredly the tastes) would be worth the jostling and discomfort of such a trip. You and your cargo are too precious. Stay put. Soon we'll share a Hangtown Fry and gaze at the glittering bay and I shall regale you. Can already taste your salty, greasy lips. Delicacy. You can count the days on your swollen fingers: I will be there to kiss them before your count's complete!

Only, I must first accompany Tanner on visits to certain parties still in arrears with the Stewarts. Ripe fruit to be gathered, if not exactly low-hanging. But we've a new mouth to feed, you and I! Anyway, it's only men's work, I shan't bore you with the details. But I'm not staying on to rusticate.

Szilard writes that when last he paid you a call you showed off your belly. Told me he could see the slightest protrusion, but not detect any movement within it when you placed his hand there. Hearing this made my blood boil. Szilard can touch you while I can only dream you. A frightening force, jealousy. I see how it could drive a man to murder. Ha ha! I am not plotting to kill my best mate, of course.

The 'inconsequential pains' you mention in your last… poor thing! Just as you know to take all I say and divide by 2, I know to multiply your complaints by 10. When next the doctor comes to call, do please be frank with him about the degree to which you suffer so that

he might provide a proper antidote. I beg you not be so
damn stoic. Don't suffer in silence. Lord knows I don't.

Eugene

VIRGINIA CITY
OCTOBER 25, 1867

Szilard,

The deed I mentioned in my prior letter? Done & done.
I, too, may be. Oh, what terrible things the desperate
do… The story of that day is like a stone in my kidney,
paining me to no end. I must here have a go at passing
it, though it may kill me.

Need first set the stage. Can you hear the orchestra
warming up, Szilard? Impossible to tell by their
inharmonious plucking and tooting if this will be a
comedy or a tragedy. Kill the house lights. A swelling
of kettle drums, the strings intoning en masse. Places,
everyone…

Stage right, a cluster of hardened men, your narrator
among them, huddled yet again alongside the Geiger
Grade. Plumb below the midday spotlight and just a
few switchbacks below the scene of our prior robbery,
this new spot selected for the advantage it affords vis a
vis armored stagecoaches heading <u>downhill</u> to the
Carson mint. Such stages operate only in daylight, you
see, to dissuade all but the most audacious 'actors.'

See us laying in wait behind a stand of juniper above
the road. All of us save Tanner. Who stands stage left,
inside the hairpin. Crouching with me are three men,
all of us within a corral of sorts formed on one side by
the junipers and on the adjoining sides by ropes I
clutch like reins. The ropes are tied to the branches of
the trees so that when I haul back, the branches part
like curtains, granting the men a gap to storm through.

A noise from offstage: coconuts clacking: a horse at full run. Reaching us, the rider brings the exhorted animal to a halt. Takes a canteen from his saddle bag. Savors a long pull. We know this man. Know he's come direct from town. Know he'd loitered in the vicinity of the bank as the stage was being loaded. Know, therefore, that by his taking such a long drink he is not only quenching his thirst but signaling for us that it'd indeed required multiple men to load the Salamander onto the stage's boot.

T. makes a call like a dove, the rider spurs his mount and is gone. We whisper and wink to each other. One amongst us actually rubs his palms together like a greedy Shylock. I've told you how exhilarated my virgin outing as a highwayman made me feel. Well, I might be blamed for overzealousness at my sophomore effort. Call it cocksure. We had ourselves a fine plan, even if it was T's. Watch, then, as I become cock-unsure.

Jitters. Waiting as a single coach passes, going uphill. Waiting as a trio on horseback pass going down. Neither party privy to our presence. Finally, from above, the thrum of heavy hooves. We tug on our masks. I look about. See in each and every eyehole hardened steel. Dust from the speeding stagecoach rising through the trees, the coach itself not yet visible. Its myriad parts can be heard to jangle and creak.

It nears center stage. The switchback is tight. At its apex, a stage driver is compelled to bring the coach nearly to a full stop. On account of the daylight, we wait until the last second. (Violinists saw bows across their thinnest strings...)

Now the coach is directly upon us. And we upon it.

T. rises from behind his boulder and shouts, Halt!,
though he may just as well have cried, Havoc!, for I
haul back against my ropes and loose the dogs of war.
The driver turns. Spotting our onslaught, he rises from
his buckboard, slaps the reins, yells, Yaw! The two
guards stationed atop the coach swivel shotguns,
commence to fire in our general direction.

I let go my ropes. Take up my rifle and rush around the
trees. Am met by one of our number, Rathbone,
staggering, clutching at his face, where a load of heavy
buckshot has taken its effect. His oilcloth mask is
blown away, revealing the tendony inner workings of
his neck, an ivory jawbone. He is screaming, or trying
to. Blood and bubbles issue from a rent in his throat.
Shots are whizzing every which fucking way,
shattering tree bark, sparking against rocks. This must
have been when Tanner shot the lead horse.

Attending to R., I didn't see the beast tumble. (Later
we discovered the bullet hole <u>inside</u> its goddamn ear.)
When next I saw the stagecoach, it looked piled all
upon itself, the horses rearing and lunging, unable to
get past the obstacle created by their fallen leader. With
the coach stuck, the guards leapt off. One rolled
underneath it, the other taking what cover he could
against the horses. The driver let go the reins, threw up
his hands, shouting, Cease fire! Cease fire!

Things quieted. Gunsmoke obscuring everything. A
sulfurous reek in the air. T. advanced upon the stage,
per The Plan. Me, I'd forgotten The Plan the moment
Rathbone became divorced from half his face. He'd by

this point stumbled into some manzanita. Bloody as a butcher. I knew the man a little. We'd worked some shifts together at the mill. Shared a few cigarettes. (During which he'd once confided that he cared for a three-year-old daughter, born of a whore. He didn't know if the girl was his, but there wasn't a doubt in his heart she was his to provide for. Said he'd loved her from the moment she breathed air, a moment he'd been there to witness. Said, That little girl's the only thing I love, 'cept whores. I'd asked, Does the child's mother still... ...Fuck strangers for a livin'? he'd asked. (She does.) Asked him who cared for the child whilst he was at the mill. Oh, he said, they're both of 'em out Kansas City way—least, that's where I keep sendin' half m'earnins!) Do we ever get to decide what we think, Szilard, or when? As I set off down the embankment toward the crippled stage, stuck in my mind's eye was the vision of Rathbone's still-intact face, lit by the cherry of our cigarette, and stuck in my mind's ear was the sound of him saying, 'm'earnins.' Was even muttering it to myself as I descended to my fate, my rifle shouldered. M'earnins, m'earnins...

Was halfway down the embankment when I noticed the guard nearest Tanner make a move. Perhaps this guard had yet to register the driver's order to stand down. Perhaps he disapproved of the order. Perhaps—and this is a question that will haunt me to my grave, and which I have difficulty now even posing—he was raising both his hands (one of which, it must be said, clutched a pistol) in surrender. We'll never know. What we can know is, by the time that pistol of his drew nigh level with my brother, I'd drawn a bead and . . .Oh, Szilard: such indignation I was feeling at that moment. Furious about R. being stuck down so uselessly, so far from his daughter. Furious at T. for being so fucking profligate at poker. My bullet, fired as it was from such moral high ground, passed on a diagonal over the team of horses and found purchase in the guard's buttock.

I submit to judge and jury that this wound was never mortal, though clearly v. painful and certainly debilitating, as evidenced by the screech the man elicited as he fell to the dirt beside the swinger horse. Which animal became quite hysterical. It reared up in its harnesses, sheer terror in its eyes, big dumb teeth bared. Proceeded to stamp its forelegs upon the butt-shot guard. Who endeavored to squirm out from under the horse, but failed. It stomped his chest, his legs. Leaving him groaning and howling most piteously, and me yelling to the driver to get his goddamn horse under control. The timbre of my own voice frightened me. Sounded like Tanner's.

Driver cajoled the horse—Easy, boy, easy!—but to no avail. The animal would not relent. Finally the guard's terrible screaming (and hopefully his suffering) were cut short when the horse stoved in his head. Driver clambered down from his perch, over the backs of several horses, and leapt to the ground. Grabbed the pummeled guard by his feet and dragged the limp body off the road. The horse glaring out the corner of its huge, wicked eye.

One of our number went to see about Rathbone. Tanner ordered the remaining guard to drop his rifle and his gun belt. The guard complied, muttering curses. T. advanced to collect the guns, then went to where the driver crouched over the lifeless guard. The driver made no complaint as T. knelt and yanked the pistol from the guard's belt and plucked his rifle from the dirt.

T. said, Cut that dead fuckin horse out of its goddamn fuckin harness.

Stood frozen in my position, providing cover no longer needed. T. turned to glare out from his mask at me. Now, shithead! he said.

How can one follow an order given so roughly without forfeiting one's dignity? And what in God's name had I done to earn Tanner's ire except to save his wretched life, during a robbery executed to prevent <u>his</u> execution? Suppose I should have calmly replied: Sorry for my hesitation, dear brother—it's just, you've caught me cogitating on the manfuckingslaughter I've just now committed on your behalf, you ungrateful brotherfucking...

Now! T. yelled.

So down the rest of the embankment I scrambled. Sand pouring into my boots. Went to the dead horse. Set about sorting its tangled harnesses, searching for the buckles, whilst T. mounted the stagecoach. He set about liberating a different animal, our intended quarry: The Salamander. T. peered down from his work, saw me struggling with mine.

There ain't time for all that! he shouted. Just cut the damn thing out!

He was leaning all his weight against a long crowbar

he'd brought along to lever the Salamander free of its strap-downs. I, however, had not been prescient enough to know I'd be extricating a dead horse from a tangle of leather and rope. I'd failed to bring a knife to a gunfight.

T. swore to himself, as if I were his fault. Unsheathed the knife he wears on his belt even to church. Tossed it to (at?) me.

I commenced to saw at the bridle. It was soaked in a foamy lather and slippery. Heard the complaint of metal. Looked up in time to watch The Salamander tumble off the stage and into the road with a mighty clang—its contents as heavy as advertised.

T. ordered the remaining guard and the driver to help me in dragging the dead horse off the road. We reluctantly complied. Each of us took a leg, tugged. The corpse canted a paltry few degrees. We have to pull all together! I yelled. I called out, Heave! and we did. Horse budged, bit by bit, its head lolling behind. Blood pouring out its blasted head and puddling in the road. So much blood.

Was about this time we noticed a pair of men sitting their horses at the bend in the road below. Well outside the useful range of a shotgun. Still T. pointed his at them. Warmly suggested they Turn. The. Fuck. Back. They obliged. T. then ordered the driver and guard to remount the coach. Guard hesitated, unwilling to leave his comrade where he lay.

That's my fuckin brother you kilt! the guard said,

looking right at me. Tears streaking down his bronzed and dusty cheeks.

All aboard, T. said, in that tone he takes like everything's funny to him. He calmly raised a pistol at the guard's head. The guard spit at T's feet, then gazed a moment longer down at his brother as if memorizing the sorry sight.

Care to join him? T. asked.

I'll see you pay for this, said the guard, staring at me with hatred in his heart.

He climbed onto the back of the coach.

Off you go, T. said. The driver gave a half-heated yaw and the depleted team was again underway, creaking down the hill. The guard glaring back at us. The coach rounded the bend and was gone. The road quiet as a cemetery.

From up the hill came a flatbed mule wagon hauling lumber and other sundries. The arrival of this wagon—in stark contrast to Rathbone being shot in the face and T. felling a horse and me shooting a guard in the ass and that guard's subsequent trampling to death by a different horse—was perfectly according to The Plan. We were all in a state of shock. Problem was, there was so much still to pull off. We were not out of the woods. Together we all hefted the Salamander onto the wagon bed amongst the other stuff. Draped it with a tarpaulin.

Somehow, Rathbone wasn't dead. An awful stench

about him though. He'd shat himself, and his breath when he drew it was something terrible to hear. We hefted him in alongside the Salamander. The driver shook his head at the folly of it all and with a click of his tongue the mules lurched, and back they went toward Virginia City and on to the mill, blood dripping onto the road through the bed boards.

We returned to town in roundabout ways, T. and I hardly speaking, following a route he knew. We all reconvened at the mill. Rathbone had died in the wagon. R.I.P.

Or, R.W.E.: 'Money often costs too much.' Did Emerson know such mayhem as this, then? How high a cost did he ever pay? Because I'm feeling quite the worthless wordsmith. I can take paper men, cut and fold them into dreadful shapes, tear off their heads if it suits the story. But I am entirely unfit to see real ones, or real horses even, so rendered.

The fire keeps hissing as raindrops sneak down T.'s stovepipe. He left for the mill before dawn. To fondle the money, probably.

Can't hardly stand to be in my own skin today. Have I authored death, Szilard? I shot a man. Did I kill him, though? Or might we blame the scapehorse? Or the ingrate brother? Do tell.

I can't tell.

Curtains.

Eugene

VIRGINIA CITY
OCTOBER 27, 1867

Szilard,

Think it's the 27th, might be the 28th. Am at the
whiskey. Came to a juncture at which I ought probably
<u>absolutely</u> have my wits about me, yet have taken to
drink, and then—surprise!—to ink. Expect my
penmanship and train of thought to come off the rails.
Life has.

Must spill more secrets or run the risk of bursting.
C'est moi. A thing's not a thing until I find vocabulary
for it. Only then can it join The Permanent Record.
Agree? Related query: what do you do with these
letters? Best place for them is probably the fireplace.
Maybe bury them. Or squirrel them away in your
parents' vast attic. I, at least, may one day wish to
peruse them, compelled by the same vulgar instinct
that has me sniffing at my own socks and armpits.
Don't tell me I'm the only one so self-obsessed and foul
beyond redemption?

Where am I? Right. With a balance and a 25-lb
counterweight both certified by some local goddamn
body, we've now determined to've stole 375 lbs in
silver. Were it still 1864 and the Union printing
currency willy-nilly, we'd fetch $3 an ounce instead of
the mere $1 it gets at present. Market Forces! The
Economy! Add these to the list of things I've never
cared to understand. But Lord in heaven, Szilard: it's
still six grand we got! Three zeroes. At such cost, at
such cost.

'Processed' it all in T.'s mill. The manufacturer of The
Salamander may need to walk back its claim to 2-day
impenetrability, or at least admit exceptions for
assaults made by industrial smelters and multi-ton
stamps, which, I can vouch, render the poor thing
defenseless as a sun-warmed watermelon.

Your correspondent must here pause, pour. Pout.

T. made all assets liquid. Poured 'our' share into
containers commensurate with the various debts 'we'
needed settled about town. Plunge with me, if you will
Szilard, into the polluted tub where these monies are
being 're-warshed,' as T. calls it—a clever process, it
must be said: one that delivers to Mother our dirty
money without dirtying her hands. You'd think the
Stewarts were Chinese with all the laundry we do.

This afternoon and into the evening we paid many
visits. Reminded me of Christmases when Mother'd
send me and T. out with ginger cookies wrapped in
cheesecloth to hand out to the other families on our
hillside. In fact, we knocked upon some of the selfsame
doors today. A few of the men we called upon were
loners in sagging cabins, and these visits were short
and sad—like tossing steaks to dogs—but there were
men of A No. 1 standing, too. Men with families. When
darkening the doorways of such households, Tanner
and I would remove our hats. Bid hello to the mother
and children about. Pet the cat. Offer compliments on
the tidy state of the home, the smells on the stove.
Decline coffee and tea, begging instead a brief
audience with the man of the house. Likely as not, said
man had already cut short whatever he was at and
fetched his coat, laced up his boots, and stepped past

us into the cold, bidding us follow, bringing an end to all pleasantries.

T. would at this juncture produce from his sack a small hunk of silver equal to the size of T.'s debt to the man. Believe me when I say that, seeing this, most of the men looked not at Tanner, but at <u>me</u>. Searching my eyes to see whether this wasn't another of T.'s cruel shenanigans. I'd smile, giving each man a glimpse into the gift horse's mouth. Funny: never've felt such a Stewart. Finally on my family's side of a transaction. My bloodshot eyes pleading: Just take it…

Ordinarily when out with Tanner about town, I play The Professor for those we meet. But in T.'s estimation I am always the lowly apprentice, allowed along to be schooled in the way difficult things are truly done. But in these visits to debtors, T. needed to apply a bit of pressure. Whether he calculated my attendance to constitute a full doubling of manpower is another matter. Nonetheless, we were a We, whereas he is merely a He.

Feel I may vomit. Shall here excuse myself to step out & take the air.

All better. So. The deal described to each man was this: the debt we've just now settled needs be paid forward to the grieving Stewart widow, to whom all of Father's debts naturally transferred upon his death. Ain't that right? T. would tell the men.

Let me tell you. There is a particular expression which befalls the face of a man to whom silver has just fallen out of the clear blue sky when that man is then told he must relinquish some or all of that silver—money he's already, in his mind, allocated to a new chimney, or a mule, or likely as not to another silver claim. The look is that of a boy watching Santa Claus reclaim, peel, and eat, wedge by sweet wedge, an orange the boy has just found in his stocking.

S'pose so, the men would mutter, or some such.

Today, T. would say.

In most cases, the man owed Mother less than what T. owed the man. So T. had conveniently provided separate, appropriately sized hunks of silver. That'n there's yours, T. would say. The other'n being Mrs. Stewart's…

Of course, the man would mutter. Or he'd say, Understood. Or, Fine. Or, Fuck you both.

Walking away from one such transaction, the wife and children stopped what they were at in the garden to lean upon their separate implements and gawk at T. & me like they knew exactly what we were, what we were at. Their looks cut through me, Szilard. I killed a man. Or, one's dead now because of me. Whatever crime that's called in the books. It's something. And no amount of whiskey changes it. I'll keep drinking, though, to be sure.

Should I be wracked with guilt or bitter with resentment? Am I allowed to be both? I know something now of what you endured when poor Mrs. O'Rourke's heart gave out under you. Your incessant questioning as to whether your straw broke the camel's back, your struggle to assign blame: was it tough luck or rough fuck? Who can say?

& there he goes…making sport of every damn thing. As if it might get me a victory, or at least a disqualification, but never a loss. But a win and loss together do not make a tie. Still. I'm alive. So, still, is Tanner. Because of me. It's not nothing.

Eugene

P.S. Kept at the bottle after I left off last night. Became so obscure I couldn't get my boots off. And this morning…lord in heaven. Don't recall suffering such morning-after muddyheadedness in our university days.

Anyway, must add by way of postscript that T. and I were passed an alarming bit of gossip this afternoon on our way to the mill. We'd stopped in at a mercantile, found the clerk in conversation with a customer about a certain heist perpetrated on the Wells & Fargo stage two evenings prior.

They're saying it's some brethren who done it, offered the customer. The clerk nodding. They turned to look at us. We pretended their news was non sequitur— nothing to do with us.

Brethren? I inquired innocently. From your congregation, I take it?

Brothers, the customer said, clarifying: <u>Kin</u>.

I think you got that mixed up, Tanner said. Way I

heard it, was brothers <u>guarding</u> the stage, and one of 'em shot in the exchange.

Shot and killt—you heard right, said the clerk. One of Skaggs' sons. But the surviving one says he know'd it was brothers, too, that set upon 'em.

Were the perpetrators not disguised? I butted in, earning a look from T.

Sure they was, the clerk said. But Skaggs says it was the way two of 'em in particular was bickering. Said only brothers talk that way to each other. Suppose it takes one to know one! At this, the customer gave an uncomfortable little chuckle.

Hell, I said. I'm brother to this one here, and damn if I know him from Adam. Man's an enigma!

A 'nigma'? the clerk asked.

Doesn't like oysters on the half shell, I went on. Hard to believe we've got the same blood in our veins.

Can't say I've had the pleasure, said the clerk.

It's a texture thing, T. said, playing along. I looked over at him, half impressed.

Anyways, said the clerk.

I don't like knowing their name, Szilard. His name. Skaggs.

VIRGINIA CITY
OCTOBER 28, 1867

Dear Orelia,

This needs be a brief communiqué, mon amour. Tying off the loose ends of Father's affairs is proving... knotty. Father spread himself far and wide in his largesse. His sons must therefore venture equally far in their quest to settle scores and acc'ts, right wrongs, etc., etc. Been here and there about. Our high purpose: get Mother what she needs—what she's owed. Woman's given too much to this place and its people over the years. Well, bills are come due. One gentleman paid us with a cow and a calf, both of which I had to resell, mother having use for neither.

Yours of Oct. 15 brought me pause. You're too sweet to ever say bitter things outright, but I can read betwixt your lines, dear. Were letters photographs, I'd see your negatives. E.g.: when you say you find yourself daily 'discussing' me and my prospects with your mother, I take that to mean you are actually 'defending' me. Do I misread? Because, in fact, the word you elected to nestle in quotes was 'prospects.' As if they are too fragile to go unguarded amongst the other, bona fide words; or, worse, as if said prospects are themselves prospective, & hypothetical...

Nevermind. I'll leave it. It is not lost on me that my prolonged absence only makes it harder for you to convince your lovely parents of my devotion.

Yesterday on the sidewalk I saw a man I knew as a boy. He was following his flock—homely wife, three kids. A certain gaze of fulfillment upon his face. I've seen the look worn by many a man, but never until that moment had I appreciated it so. It is all I want for Christmas next year, that look upon my own face.

Your letter speaks of Szilard's many kindnesses, the time he carves from his calendar to call upon you and see to your needs. Bordering on Salt Lake City bigamy, this arrangement!, except, the improper ratio: you'll have two husbands if it keeps up!

I jest. God bless Szilard. He's a stand-in for the actor who will soon star in the role of Doting Fiancé. (Yes! There, I've said it. I propose to propose. 'Tis apropos. Prépare-toi!)

Words cannot convey how I ache, at present, to be present for you. And yet you must accept words in my stead. For now.

For now,
Eugene

P.S. Tanner has just informed me we are leaving again this evening for some dusty outpost to the southeast, the name of which already escapes me. Anyway it's not a place, per se. More a cluster of ranches, the citizens mostly beeves. Will be horseback two days getting there, a day or so about, and then straight back. If you do not hear from me in that time, it will not be for lack of love but for a post office. Oh, to be back where a man can buy a stamp and a warm croissant on any corner! I'd kill for less at this point.

VIRGINIA CITY
OCTOBER 28, 1867

Szilard,

Frost whites the rooves and the sage-brushes this
morning. Cannot seem to summon wit, only a falling
feeling in my guts. This feeling is without nuance. It is
fear, plain & simple. Fear founded on fact. Tanner has
slapped me straight. More on that when I have the
time.

Things have taken a turn. An associate of my brother
who keeps books at the deputy's office let slip that the
rumor about fraternal perpetrators has solidified into a
working theory of the case. Frankly, at this point, I'd
welcome them to throw the book at me. Least it's a
weapon I'm familiar with. We're told what evidence
they've got is thin. This may sound like good news. It
is not. Forcing, as it may, the hands of those
demanding justice to take it into their own.
Brotherhood may prove my downfall, Szilard. It is a
crime for which I must plead nolo contendre.

I shall be incommunicado for the foreseeable. Have
written Orelia as much. Disguised the reason of course.
She needn't be troubled by my troubles, not until I've
outrun them, and they become my tales. You, on the
contrary, must suffer the story as it comes, come what
may. You alone can handle it. (I, alone, cannot.) Will
write a longer letter when I can.

Eugene

HELL, NV
OCTOBER 30, 1867

Szilard,

Bet I know better where you're reading this than where
I'm writing it. Let me guess: You're in Jackson Square
or thereabouts, cross-legged in the corner of a café with
a coffee and a cigarette and a newspaper and your
correspondence? Heaven, in other words.

Greetings, then, from Hell. Which, by my calculations,
is two days hard ride south by southwest from Virginia
City. Beyond humanity's fringe. (Hath Hell statehood
yet, or are the Devil & Joseph Smith the last two
holdouts to Uncle Sam?) The desolate aspect of this
place is enough to make you believe a city like San
Francisco is impossible. T. tells me the chalky expanse
I'm squinting at was once a seabed. Seems a rather
important fact, one of many T. knows which I do not.
Perhaps this is why I've entrusted myself so entirely to
him, and his judgment. No longer putting much stock
in my own.

Case in point, the moment he burst in two nights ago and
said we were leaving town right then and there. Didn't
for a second doubt he was right. Of course I still stared at
him, trying to spot some crack in his countenance, some
hint of indecision, which, subjected to my scrutinizing,
might be swayed. Saw nonesuch. I'd been stewing in the
cabin hoping for the best & he'd been out upon the world
preparing for the worst. Even procured us two horses in
fine traveling trim. The pair set him back $200. He started
stuffing saddlebags with hardtack, cornmeal, rolls,
bacon, beans. I asked whether flight might appear an

admission of guilt. He must have considered the question rhetorical. Did not dignify it with a reply.

We could stay put, I offered (as a child offers a stick through the bars of a cage, just to see what the beast inside will do). We could plead innocent, I said.

T. was transferring tobacco from a large tin into a leather sack. I burnished my argument, adding that, flush as we were now, we could afford excellent counsel (and excellent witnesses to boot).

Something in T. snapped. He charged across the cabin, knocking an open can of salt off the table, snatched me up, and pinned me by my collar against the cabin door.

That's enough, Eugene! he said. It's enough!

I gave no fight, merely tried to keep breathing and holding his gaze, which was equally frightful and frightened. His fingers smelled of tobacco. Though he's got an iron shell like Father, my brother's core is brittle. He can, and does, crack.

The hell you think's gonna happen here? he said. You reckon you'll yak your way out of a noose?

I shook my head slowly, no. My heels aloft. Begged T. set me back down. He did not. Kept me in his grasp, stared into my soul. I swear to you brother, he said, you'll never see me hanged.

I nodded acceptance of this. Felt his grip lighten. So we're abandoning all this, I said.

T. glanced about his cramped cabin.

<u>Mother</u>, I clarified. The <u>mill</u>.

We can send word once we're situated, T. said.
Mother's debtors'll make good—we saw to that. She'll
manage, always has.

Financially, I said.

He nodded slowly, a little confused, like financially's
all there is. All I ever brought that woman is worry, he
said. As for you, I'd say she's pretty well habituated to
your absence.

I broke her of that habit these last months, I said.

Yeah. Well. Like I said, we'll send word. You can write
the poor woman pages and pages. Put that <u>gift</u> of
yours to use.

He let me go. We stood with that in the air for a bit. My
'gift' betraying me: couldn't find a retort dastardly
enough to suit. Changed the subject. Asked him where
he saw us headed.

South, he said.

South is not a place, I said.

It's a bearing, he said.

You got a city in mind?

No, he said, just to rile me. But before I could protest, he expounded: I got a <u>vicinity</u>.

Went on to claim various connections & trustworthy 'clients' currently working mines and mills in Inyo county, or thereabouts. Neighborhood of Owens Lake, wherever that is. Good men there, T. assured me. Which I of course took to mean <u>bad</u> ones.

Such was T.'s verdict on the matter. Having pronounced it, he resumed preparations.

Secretly figuring I could still play both cards—flee now, plea later—I pitched in, adding to the packs some paper, a pen. A knife. A pistol. Bullets. Bedrolls. Ralph Waldo. Some walking-around silver. What else does a man truly need? Coffee.

(Tea, for T.)

The salt stayed spillt.

T.'s mount is mottled and cannot be made to walk in the arrears. Mine stands a hand shorter, and yet produces demonstrably more excrement. We ride, therefore, metaphorses. (I dare not share this ridiculous revelation with T., knowing full well it suggests my mind is not where it ought be, that I do not fully appreciate the gravity of our predicament. But you know me. This <u>is</u> fear, for me. Tanner is one to retreat into the hills, while I retract into my head, as a prick does in cold water.)

We lit out in the dark hours. The road quiet save for a solitary Negro dressed like an Injun, donning multiple layers of shirts and coats, even pants, the inner ones spilling from the cuffs of the outers. Yet he was the one asking us questions. Specifically, what had us saddled up at such an hour.

Just getting ahead of the weather, T. said.

There a storm expected? he asked, chewing something.

Of some sort, I muttered from astride my metaphorse (which, yes, I intend to ride into the ground and, when it is dead, to beat).

Stayed off the road after that. Crossed the same dry crick a few times, rode straight up it for a spell. Ascended to a high saddle, dropped over into a drainage. Speaking v. little. No moon. Dark dark dark. Couldn't make out my horse's head. Whilst passing through stands of juniper, had to hold my limbs out in front my face to fend off those of the trees. Stayed a course bisecting the twin twinkles of Fort Churchill and Como.

At long last, a dim blue at the horizon. The terrain opening into a wide basin. Trotted as abreast as T.'s alpha horse and rider will brook. Sunlight bleeding over terra incognita.

I never should've come here, I said.

So go back, T. said.

Home, I mean. I should've stayed in San Francisco.

You did the right thing, coming back for father.

Didn't stay on for him, though.

That was for Mother, T. said.

Funny, I said, it's <u>your</u> debts I find myself paying down.

(No response.)

A man's dead because of me, I continued.

You done the right thing, Eugene.

Doesn't feel right, I said.

You'd have me take Skaggs' place, then? T. asked. You'd see me dead before him?

I didn't say that, I said.

Tanner shook his head. You're saying about as much.

Told him I regretted that it'd happened, is all. That I regretted joining in with him and his brethren, regretted making myself party to the whole doomed affair. All of which, I admitted, were my own damn fault.

I ain't got <u>brethren</u>, T. said. Only got the one.

At this, he drew rein. My horse halted of its own volition. We found ourselves staring across a rift of horseflesh.

Horrible shit can be done for noble reasons, T. said.

Happens every fucking day, Eugene. Then he put his horse ahead. I asked after him what noble purpose was ourn.

You just said it, he said. Our purpose is <u>ourn</u>. We're fending for our family, just like every other asshole walking, Skaggs included. He'd just as soon've killed the both of us protecting that silver. And why? So he'd get paid with some of it. Fendin' for his.

His silver was legally mined, I said. Legally transported.

T. shook his head as if embarrassed. Legal and ethical ain't never been one and the same, Eugene, he said. Silver belongs to the dirt, to God, until some Jew in a three-piece suit in San Francisco says he wants more of it, so some Irish shitheads better go down in the ground and muck it out for him and no matter if some of 'em die doing it.

Informed him my best friend is a Jew.

He sniffed. Sensing I had him on his heels, I added that that life wasn't understood to be fair. That no one was claiming it so.

It <u>is</u> though! T. said. Fair and square! Every cocksucker knows every other'n is looking after his own. That's fair as it gets.

So, there you have it: T. subscribes to Machiavellian self-preservation, or maybe he's only wanting to ease my mind, help justify what I did. Which, sure, I appreciate. It's the least the bastard can do.

Tanner's convinced we're being pursued. Tonight at dusk as we were crossing a valley he told me that sometime forenoon he'd glanced back at a gap in the mountain we'd just surmounted and seen a group, horseback, outlined against the sky. I asked how come he hadn't felt the need to share this information with me at the time and he said because he wasn't sure it meant anything, that it could have been just some men. When I asked why he'd now decided to alert me, he pointed back at a similar but different gap in a similar but different mountain, and I followed his finger to where I myself saw some minuscule men on minuscule horses, picking their way down a massive slope.

How many you see? T. asked.

Three, I said, squinting. No, four. How many you see?

More'n two, he said—meaning, more than us.

The terrain we were at the time traversing was tricky, carved out here and there and everywhere by steep canyons. We'd crossed many a plateau only to find it dead-ended in a cliff. I asked T. how far back he reckoned the men were.

Half a day, he said. Or half an hour. Seeing as we ain't capable of holding a bearing in this damn maze and maybe they got it solved.

Think Skaggs is among them? I asked.

T. shrugged. All I think is, if it was you been killt, it'd be me chasin' the Skaggses.

He spurred his weary horse on, and I mine. It grew
dark. We've not glimpsed that party or any other since.
Saw only a boy with a dog and a flock of sheep on a
distant hillside.

OCTOBER 31

Third day out. Still in Hell. Am told it's 'Nevada Day.'

This afternoon stood my stirrups to stare out across the
hardpan. Felt I was looking at the edge of the earth. Yet
can see no further into our future than my horse's next
step. We keep looking over our shoulders. The
horizons of Hell take on many shapes, but none have
yet materialized into men.

We've covered a fair piece of ground. It covers us back.
It's a crust baked into the creases of our skin. There's
dust in our eyelashes, in our assholes. I long for the
baths on Washington Street.

You know I crave company. I'm my Mother's son.
Drawn to cities, conversations. But for perhaps the first
time in my life, the only man I wish to see is my
brother. And the only place I can escape is these pages.

Thinking constantly of Orelia. Wonder whether she
carries a son or a daughter, and when/if I'll get to see
her/it again/ever.

There are few roads here. What roads there are we
avoid. Today at noon we came to a riverbank and
rested in a stand of cottonwood. Lovely, really. We sat
in shade, listening to the river on the rocks, the horses
chomping tall grass. Felt like a Sunday afternoon from

our youth when Mother'd set us loose after church &
chores and T. and I would disappear into the hills and
I'd be forced to play cowboys and injuns, fingers for
pistols. What bloodthirsty games boys cotton to.
Shouldn't all that hiding and seeking have prepared
me for this, then? All those hours spent holding
deathly still, peeking out from some bush to spot my
brother's approach, scared shitless he'd flanked me
and would at any second pounce. That awful feeling
when you're trying to be quiet but your heart is
pounding so hard you're sure it's betraying your
position... it wears on boys and men, both, I can say.
Wears 'em to the bone. Anyway, I drifted off under
those cottonwoods. Dead to the world. T. shook me
awake some time later. Felt like a minute, though by
the change in the sun it had been much longer. Don't
think T. slept a wink.

NOVEMBER 1

Spooked a party of antelope this morning. They raced
away across a plain into a spume of dust. This route
would be a death march in August, and may prove to
be still.

Am growing my whiskers to mask my appearance.
Still no sign of our pursuers, if pursuers they be. It's
only the sun itself that seems intent on killing us. Am
left to conclude that it hates us, personally. Rode with
it at our back all morning. That means we're moving
away from it if I'm not mistaken. Tell me then: why is
it getting warmer? Glad for my Panama hat.

Tonight T. snuck into an outpost barn and stole a few
buckets of barley. We were standing in the moonlight,

my brother and I, our mounts butting their velvet
muzzles against our palms, chomping away, when T.
told me I ought be aware that certain of the bricks at
the base of Father's forge were not in fact brick, but
silver from the Salamander, disguised in soot and dirt.
That, should circumstances dictate, I should avail
myself of what bricks I might need.

We ought make Mother aware of that, I said.

Oh, T. said. She's aware.

(Of course. As, of course, you are now aware, my
friend—shows how much I trust you...or, how little I
know you to want for silver.)

Metaphorses munched away, oblivious to the concerns
of men.

The evening wind is whipping through, drying our
day's sweat on our skin. The sun here rules the roost. I
squint and steam against it all day, but the moment it
slips away I start to miss it, and to shiver. The wind
never abates, just switches from hot to not.

Cue coyotes. (I do not joke, they're howling now, out
taking their pasear in the tall moonlight. Where they
live, what they eat, I couldn't guess. Probably they live
as Tanner and I do these last days: in a path, not a
place.) Hobbling the horses tonight, I explained to
them it wasn't to limit their wandering so much as to
prevent them stealing our pistols and shooting
themselves.

We're holed up in a three-sided windbreak formed by

rocks that look to have plummeted to earth solely for this purpose. And yet! Of course! Wind this evening out of the single cardinal direction left unprotected. Were we to have a campfire, we would smoke ourselves out. Not that T. allows the luxury of fire.

Asked him if we are outlaws now. He argued he's been one for years. I said I'd only ever been an outcast. Regretted this admonition the moment it left my lips. He stroked an invisible violin, told me to get some shuteye. That's what he tells me whenever we stop. He intends that we move on before first light. I said, Supposing I stay behind.

He looked at me askew, said, You fixing to just sit in here, then, jotting letters?

(Yes, I thought. Maybe.) As if anyone other'n you cares what's in that head of yours! he said. Well, stay here and it's liable to get blowed off. Then everyone'll know what's in there. He laughed.

Blown, I said.

T. shook his head, said I'd correct the grammar of St. Peter hisself, that I'd get myself blacklisted from Heaven just to prove I was cleverer than everybody in there.

I believe I'm going to Hell, I said.

T. tipped his hat, said, Meet you there, mon frere.

And with that he leaned back against his saddlebag, causing the silver inside to settle and clink. He shut his eyes, his face fell slack, and he was soon snoring. How can a man brimming with such fury and spite achieve serenity at the drop of a hat? Probably he's accepted we're doomed, and so no longer frets over it. (By the way: French? Fucker has some. Picked up from a prostitute, je suppose, amongst other, itchier infections.)

NOVEMBER 2

Up a tree. Have been for some time—half a day, half a lifetime. Szilard, how have I come to this? Astride a limb, boots dangling nigh forty feet off solid ground. Pants and shirt caked in sap. Treetop sways in the wind as if to chuck me out, its ancient conscience probably sensing the treacherous creature in its clutches. It <u>has</u> graciously provided shade—a gift I shall never again take for granted.

Can only sit and stew. Nothing to occupy my nervous mind except furtherance of this letter. Have been here long enough to see the sky go from clear blue to blood red. Feel honor bound to stick it out here until it goes black.

It was near noon when T. noticed the men again. Same we'd seen previous, pursuers now to be certain. Appeared they'd upped their pace, having gained the very rim upon which T. and I had taken our breakfast. As such, we spied them from across the canyon we'd spent the morning descending and ascending, our path a 'U.' Had they been a murder of crows and not of men, the distance to catch us up would have been halved. A rifle shot separated us. We could make out their various hats. One yellow, two brown, one black.

When the breeze was right, we heard their voices, the huffing of their horses. They did not hesitate at their rim but started right into the steep switchbacks. So we set out from ourn, across a plain toward some foothills.

Tanner addressed me without looking over. Brother, he said, I'm going to tell you something. Told me he'd been cogitating on a matter of importance for two days, and that if I saw fit to give a word edgewise, I had to first think on it for as long as he had. Only then, if I still saw fit to argue, well, we'd Cross That Bridge When We Came To It. Then he ordered me to unfasten my saddlebag.

I argued.

Goddamn it, Eugene! he said. He reached back even as we rode and grabbed at the straps. I slapped his hand like a prude whose undergarments he'd sought to unclasp. Finished the task myself. Took the bag into my lap. My horse, puzzled by the shifting load, slowed. Well? I said.

T. said, Them who's tracking us ain't going to lose our trail, not in this soft soil. They're following two horses. So be it.

He directed my attention to a massive pine on the far side of a clearing. A specimen of the species, taller and fuller than its brethren, perhaps on account of the extra sunlight it was afforded near the periphery of the forest.

See it? he asked.

Tanner, I said.

We're gonna stay the course, he said. Right under that there tree. And you're going to reach up and nab one of them low branches and yank your carcass up off your mount.

And then?

Climb, he said. I'll ride on with your horse alongside.

Where to?

Just up the trail a spell.

I huffed. Drew breath enough to air numerous grievances. T. silenced me with a look. Not of impatience. The opposite.

He said, Don't fret, Eugene. We'll reunite very soon.

Where? I asked. On the fucking bridge we get to cross when we come to it?

I said, You aim to start a gunfight.

If they want one, he said.

Suppose they only want to capture us, I said.

They do, T. allowed. So's they can hang us at the nearest elevation convenient. Like that Frog they dangled in front of half the goddamn county. I told you, Eugene, I shan't be made a spectacle.

I looked ahead. We'd come almost to the tree. T. reached over and stole the reins from my hand. Ordered me to stand in my stirrups. I obeyed just in time for the low limb to catch me across the chest and knock the wind from me. Next thing I know my boots are kicking air and I'm watching my brother plod away. The image is burned into my eyes: three horses' asses.

Thank you, Brother, Tanner called back matter-of-factly, without turning to look at me.

Goddamn it to hell, I growled through my teeth, struggling to get a leg up.

Are these the last words my brother and I shall say to each other? Because putting them now to paper, I see we somehow got our lines swapped. T.'s the one who ought be cursing the world, I ought be grateful.

Dutifully ascended, branch by branch, until I reached my present rung. I sit facing north, one eye watching the east for the party come to do us harm, the other looking west toward my brother, wherever in hell he's gotten to. I move little more than my pen. Listen as hard as I ever have. My backside has lost all sensation.

Will these pages ever reach San Francisco? Will I?

West is gone purple. Know not if Tanner is alive or captured, only that those two are for him mutually exclusive. Dear God, Szilard. They—the men—came & went. Was sitting here as I described. Heard a man's voice on the wind, the clop of shod hooves over rocky ground. Could swear I smelled tobacco smoke, so

sharp have my senses become in these days on the
lamb, these hours on the limb. Knew the men were
drawing nigh, but dared not shift upon my branch so
as to gain a better look.

Soon enough, there they were, dead below me. Could
have pissed on their hats. And probably I did piddle a
bit. Four men, six horses. Hot on our trail. Armed to
the teeth. Their pace neither hasty nor leisurely.
Inexorable, I'd call it. Felt the cold undercurrent of
death coursing below, that chilly layer you feel with
your feet when floating out in the bay. The men were
no longer distant and two-dimensional, they were
right down there in their dirty shirts. I could hear the
swishing of their horses' tails. Couldn't see faces,
which were hidden below brims, but the one in the
black hat was Skaggs, I'd swear to it. The way he sat
his horse, all high & mighty. Knew at any moment he
was going to turn in his saddle, push back his black hat
and point his big pistol up at me. But no. Though I
quivered in my nest and surely reeked of fear, I went
undetected. Maybe if they'd brought dogs…

No sooner had they appeared below than they were
out from under the tree and away, penetrating into the
shade of the forest, dead reckoned on the route T. had
taken.

Excruciating, the minutes that ensued. Stayed put,
feeling yellow. Hiding up in the air while Tanner was
down there somewhere, boots on the ground, heels
dug in, I had no doubt. Wanted to call out to him, give
him some warning. But was he even within earshot?

He'd waited until the curtain rose to hand me a copy of

the script. I seem to play only a bit part anyway, shuffled offstage early and forced to listen from the wings as T. delivers his soliloquy. (I imagine that, were Tanner to hear Hamlet start in on his legendary & longwinded question, my brother would cut the Danish prince off after a couple couplets. As soon as it was suggested to take arms against a sea of troubles, Tanner'd say, Yes. That.) To kill or be killt. That is my brother's only question. It has always been, I think.

Gunshots. Couldn't say the distance. Two, close together, followed by a smattering. Differing calibers. Another volley. Coming in staccato, ones and twos. Then a silence, pregnant as Orelia. More shots. A terrible minute, during which could be heard hollering. Another three shots, close together: crack(echo)! crack(echo)! crack(echo)! Finally, a fourth, separated from all prior. It echoed and re-echoed in the chambers of my ears and heart throughout the stillness that ensued. It echoes still. I am beside myself.

Tanner would have returned this way by now, had such been his intention. Or the posse would have, had it been theirs. There are simply too many possibilities. Surely Tanner got the jump on them. So has he killed some of their number? All? None? Who fired that fourth shot? What is to become of all of this? Will I ever see Orelia again? Will I ever meet my own child? Am I any better off now, alone and afoot, not knowing where in Hell I am? Once you're in Hell, does it even matter which direction you go?

It is gone too dark to see my own scrawling. Shall now allow myself to climb down from this tree like the apes from which we are said to have evolved. In search of knowledge. It being the antidote to fear, or so says RWE. But riddle me this, Ralph: what if it's knowledge itself that I fear?

NOVEMBER 3

God save us all, Szilard: Eugene Stewart is in a church, praying for his soul. Didn't take long for this ape to find religion.

Amber light is pouring in through stained glass. This is a humble house of God, and a drafty one. Slept what little I could last night in a pew. A knave in a nave. Communion cushion for a pillow. Asked too much of it: nothing could support a head so heavy as mine.

After leaving the tree, followed the path my brother and our pursuers took into the forest. Even in the dark, could see marks made by the horses through the pine needles. Came to the spot where Something happened. The tracks chaotic. Deep gashes in the dirt. Brass shell casings scattered about. Stood in that moon-dappled glen, everything the color of gunmetal, and looked about, holding my breath. Sensed I was being watched, that at any moment the night would be split by gunshots and I would be riddled with lead, hot and vindictive. Heard only an owl.

Picked a track and followed it. Found it circled back. Followed another. It veered through some aspen toward a boulder I'd seen on my approach but which upon closer inspection was not a boulder but a downed horse stiff with rigor mortis, its lips peeled back in some final agony. It wasn't figurative, this horse. Wasn't one of ours. Was dead though. Gutshot.

Plus an extra, gruesome eye socket, dead centered on its long face—a bullet hole. Mercy shot. Had <u>this</u> been the haunting fourth report?

The glen looked no different than the forest around it. Leaving me to wonder how it came to be the site of Tanner's stand. Soon I glimpsed my answer: a granite outcrop situated on a rise a little off the beaten path. Had to will my feet to carry me there. Approached slowly, curving around behind it, wondering whether I was tracing my brother's final footsteps. He wasn't there. Still, think I saw what he'd seen: a clear line of sight afforded through the rocks.

I breathed in my brother, stood yet again in his boots, squinted down the sight of his gun. Drew my bead upon the men who'd come for us. Was able—and grateful—to occupy my brother's space, if not his time. But timing is everything, is it not? My gun was imaginary, the men I targeted only ghosts. Had the steel in my grip been cold and the blood in the men warm, <u>I</u> would have hesitated. This is how I know Tanner fired and fired and fired. I know his courage well because I know my cowardice. I fell there and then to my knees and wept and did not rise again for a time.

Further along, found the tracks converged and carried on, more southerly than before. Thought I saw blood on some pine needles, but stooping to inspect could not well discern the color in the thin light. Pocketed the needles. Have them here now. The stain is such a dark crimson as to be nearly black. Is it my brother's blood? Did it drip from a captive or a corpse? I am at a loss.

Followed the tracks for miles through the woods. They
led here. Some sleepy hamlet at the base of the Sierra.
The homes all quiet and dark. A cur trotted out of a
livery stable to bark at my passing. I spied a church.
Felt drawn to it. The door was unlocked. Lay my
weary body down. Curled up, cried some more.

I risk my biscuit here. Tanner would be furious at me. I
care not. Cannot go on not knowing what's become
of him.

Helped myself to the body of Christ from a breadbox.
Stale. Considered washing it down with some of His
blood. Abstained. Stood before the altar, chewing,
contemplating, wanting for butter, wanting for my
brother. The morning light upon Jesus' wooden
countenance makes him look to be winking at me.
Filled my canteen from the font, lifted it in toast. Doubt
v. much I'm in God's grace.

What icon would we hang upon altars had the Romans
preferred the noose to the cross? What if they'd had
pistols? I've heard crucifixion actually kills by
suffocation—it's your exhausted shoulders collapsing
into your lungs that finishes you off. Has Tanner died
for my sins, or his?

There's a painting on the wall here of a silhouetted
foursome—Joseph, Mary, baby Jesus, a jackass. They
trudge single file past pyramids. Placard reads, 'Holy
Family.' I think we know for certain now who's the
savior in mine and who's the jackass.

The priest is arrived. Bearing the most terrible possible
news. It's exactly what I'd feared, and what Tanner

foresaw and made manifest. Gunned down in a glen. Goddamn it all to fucking hell, Szilard. My brother is gone to join my Father.

Dead.

Forever.

All the night I clung to some obtuse hope I'd awake from this dream and find myself seated across from Tanner at a restaurant, a cigar protruding from his beard, a twinkle in his eye. A ticket in his hand. He hands it over. A train departing presently for San Francisco. This has all been just a nightmare. Life as I know it is not over. Mother will not die of grief, nor I of guilt.

The priest tells me Tanner was buried. His grave surely shallow, unmarked. I probably passed it—him—in the night.

Utterly beside myself. Care not a lick what becomes of me at this point. The priest says the posse rode yesterday evening into town and boarded at various of the local dwellings. They intend to ride back north today. The priest came to the church this morning before dawn. Heard me snoring. Has already ratted me out. Father Judas.

Unfair of me. He seems a gentle and reasonable man, a man of the world, perhaps the only in this town who can read the bibles in these pews. He read me, didn't he, even as I slept? Went so far as to nab my pistol and hand it over to the posse.

I'm told Tanner in his ambush took the life of one man and wounded another in the leg. This brings precious little comfort. So much spilled blood has made a terrible mess. I try to believe all of us anteed up for the hand we're being dealt, that we knew well the stakes. But what pot was there to win? This is not justice. Not that of men. Maybe it's the justice of nature. Maybe that's the only kind there ever was, or will be. Forever and ever. Fucking hell. Amen.

Is it impossible, this feeling I get, of <u>pride</u>? That the priest recognized me as the shoe to match the one already dropped? He does not seem to fear me, this priest, any more than I him. There is pity in his eyes when he gazes on me. The strange paper of these latter pages is his. He procures it from a newspaper office up the road, tears it himself into letter-sized pages, hence the irregular edge. Apparently I've made it back to California. This town is 'Coleville.' Not big enough for a post office or a schoolhouse, just a church.

Seems the priest holds some sway in this town. Says I'm welcome in his church for so long as I seek the salvation it offers and not just the shelter it also does. The Lord absolves, He does not aid nor abet. Apparently the posse, knowing they were hunting two men, were afraid for their lives as they made their way here in the dark—assuming another ambush, some retaliation. They, of course, took me for a murdering son of a bitch—thought they were dealing with a second lion, not a common pussy.

They've gathered this morning across the road from the church. With me now accounted for and disarmed, they've taken to drink. Their leader having agreed to respect the sanctity of this church for so long as his men are readying to roll out—a process that, by the sound of it, entails shouting the Lord's name in vain and taking target practice at what bottles they drain. (Topping off their bladders for a proper dowsing of my grave?) They've begun roasting some animal on a spit —a goat? A dog?

The priest, bless him, bargained with these pagans on my behalf, brokering my surrender while I was gorging on his God. I am to be taken alive. For how long I am to be kept in such condition is, per the priest, not something the posse cares to discuss.

They aim to do me as they did my brother, I told the priest. He did not argue.

I almost envy my brother. He was taken truly alive, guns ablaze. Skipped out on such a shit end as I will surely get. A neat dodge, that.

Dogs know when their day is come. They slink off to some corner to see through the most private of acts alone. With a dog's dignity. Whereas I will likely have for my final view an array of top-heavy assholes, all of whom hate my guts, standing about spitting and cracking wise. While I strangle to death or bleed out the hole in my back, they'll assess the angle of the sun and figure in their heads how much ground toward home they'll be able to cover today.

Priest tried to loan me a bible. Informed him I am otherwise affiliated. Held up my copy of RWE. Priest's not heard of him. I gifted him mine.

He's agreed to mail this letter, which has swelled considerably since it was began in Virginia City. Scanning it, I'm made nostalgic. It recalls for me a time when Tanner was still with me, our fate still up in the air. An uncertain time, certainly, but certainty is overrated.

I miss my brother something terrible. Miss not knowing where we're going. When next I see him I will astonish him with the warmth of my greeting. Which may fall short of the heat of our new environs.

The priest has a sad smile. Something doomed about it. I gave him all my silver. Thanked him for his kindness. He lifted his palms. I'm lucky he's a man of the cloth, for he has been merciful to a sinner, giving me cover enough to scratch out this confession, such as it is. He says it is not faith alone compels him. He, too, has a brother. Says he understands the particulars of that bond. 'Commiserates,' was the word he used, actually.

I had two brothers, in point of fact. One by blood, one by ink. Have. (The tenses of my verbs seem in flux.) For I still have you, & Orelia, & Mother, & my child. For so long as I can keep pen to paper...

I might be forgiven a disorientation in time. Feeling rather divorced from the sequence of my own story. There is The Present, sure. As I write, it's loitering outside the door with guns loaded. Can hear its impatient mutterings, its peels of laughter. Sometimes it knocks and the priest meets it at the door, holds it at bay. It sounds a righteous mob out there, and rightly so. But I am channeling Tanner. Perhaps in his passing he bequeathed me some of his prescience. Because it is from some higher vantage I can see clearly where I am. The End. Just as Tanner foresaw. Which is to say, all now is past, and tense. Am writing furiously. Later—as later as possible—I shall open that door and stride out into the clutches of my captors with arms akimbo, feeling the sunlight upon my face as never before.

Am beyond redemption. The only thing in this church that'll get saved today is a stack of paper & ink. The priest has promised to post these last letters for me, God bless him.

Promise me you'll not give up on the magazine? Swallow your pride, talk to your father. Let me be the lesson on what comes to those who tarry.

Will write Orelia now. Convince her to marry another.

I am a squid who squirts ink to distract, to escape!, but it will not save me, not this time. Swim along without me, brother. The leviathan rises, mouth agape. I am not long for this earth.

Eugene

P.S. Whilst writing to Mother, was startled to see the priest crossing the altar, waving toward the back of the church and shouting: No! Please! Knew by his frightened tone—knew even before I'd turned—that it'd be Skaggs.

You are not welcome in the Lord's house, the priest said. We have an arrangement!

Skaggs removed his black hat and held it in his hands. His thin hair plastered against his head.

I aim to honor our arrangement, Father, Skaggs said, calm as can be. You needn't shout.

Skaggs took a few steps toward me, his spurs jangling in the cavernous space. Pistols dangling off his hips.

Just getting a look at him, Skaggs said, as if I weren't sitting there.

Well? the priest said. Are you now satisfied?

I am, Father, Skaggs said. I am, and I ain't.

Please go, said the priest. We'll be out in due time.

Skaggs stared at me then. The church brimmed with silence, but through the walls we could hear the crowd. Men and women peering in the windows. Children being held up to see.

Them out there's celebratin', Skaggs said. I just wanted you to see: I ain't. Don't expect I ever will. This ain't nothing to celebrate. Nothin' good about it. It's just something needs be done.

I'm sorry, I said. My brother and I—we never meant...

Tell it to him, Skaggs said—nodding either at the priest or Jesus. I ain't got no ear for it.

I said nothing.

You got one hour, he said.

I felt the urge to thank him, but he'd already turned his back. He shouted into the back of the church: You're lucky I'm a Christian, Stewart! Or you'd already be lyin' in the dirt, the way you left my brother.

And you mine, I said, Skaggs.

Amen, he said, and he was gone, back outside, the noise of the crowd swelling as he rejoined it. I turned to the priest. His head was bowed as he mouthed some prayer. He crossed himself.

COLEVILLE, CA
NOVEMBER 2, 1867

My Dearest Orelia,

I am so v. sorry. Yours truly has not been true, or, at
least not entirely forthcoming.

Fear not: it's nothing to do with adultery or the like.
Only flesh I've put hands to is horseflesh. And not in
the act of congress, I'll add. (Lord in heaven! Did not
intend to make light. But can't restart this letter.) What
flippancy I'm feeling must owe to a hope I harbor that
this letter will, in fact, be <u>mine</u> to receive. That you'll
never see it. So why not amuse <u>myself</u>? See, if I can
find a way to untangle myself from this mess I'm in—
slip the noose, as it were, and <u>is</u>—I will race without
rest or so much as a sip of water straight to San
Francisco. Beat this letter over the pass and intercept it
at your door. Such that you will take receipt of this
dirty correspondent instead of his dirty
correspondence.

However. Should I fail in this effort, then my second
highest hope—oh! this kills me—is that you press on,
sans moi. I think I am overcome, my love.

I miss you to the point my whole body aches, my
stomach churns. My head has overflowed for days
with visions of you, every time I curl into a ball
beneath my blanket in a howling wind… yet never
before this moment—right now, this one—have I wept
over us. I <u>knew</u> my love would be requited. Knew I'd
see you again. I was never in doubt. Pull you to my

chest, make us whole. To see now that's most surely not to be… my heart breaks, sinks to the depths…

Alas. Here it is. The Truth. I have played the highwayman and robbed a stage. Twice.

Why? Well. Because my brother asked it of me, on behalf of our family, the finances of which are much dwindled. Said dwindling partly my doing, partly Father's, and mostly Tanner's. It's no part Mother's. This family that no longer exists. The Stewarts are halved. Father dead as you know, but Tanner now too.

The men who hunted him down have tracked me to a little town a thousand miles from anywhere. From you. Szilard can more thoroughly, if roughly, detail for you how so much calamity came to pass. His account may add color, but it will never justify my leaving you (and our child) behind. I don't expect that can ever square.

You once described for me the death of the young editor of the Evening Bulletin, shot outside his office by the editor of a rival rag. How the city mourned him. You were trying to cheer me, convince me that writers could be loved, that I oughtn't quit the craft. You said all the stores closed, all the bells tolled, crape and mourning was hung all about, flags lowered to half staff… Well. I will not receive such a send-off. Other than you, Szilard, and Mother, no one will miss me. I know not where my body may come to rest.

Our child will never know me. I will be an absence, an abstract. An ache, not a pang. I will write The Peanut a letter and ask that you pass it along when you feel the time right.

When a Digger Injun man dies, the widow smears her head with pitch and wears that sticky helmet for months. I prefer it be memories that stick inside your pretty head. (Remember the evening we were so late to Szilard's concert that we skipped it, went window shopping and 'window bought' him such fine gifts in apology!) As with pitch, the stickiness and fresh scent of me will wash away in time. Perhaps all I can ask is that you take comfort knowing that I died doing what I enjoy—what I seem to have been born for: making light of sexual congress with livestock.

If I die, Lord, let it be with my tongue in my cheek, luscious thoughts of Orelia in my head, a smirk on my lips...

RWE tells us 'a man is to carry himself in the presence of all opposition as if every thing were titular and ephemeral but he.' Reckon this is why I write. Or, how. That is, I've always assumed the words might be worth holding onto, by someone. You. The world has been a parade, and seems all I've managed to do is lampoon it from the stands. What giggles I've mined from you over the years are my Comstock lode.

I wish you all the luck life can bring. If this letter reaches you in my stead, as I hope against hope it won't, marry another. I am sorry beyond words. I love you beyond them, too, though they are all I have left to give. These 'window gifts' and I will forever be

Yours,
Eugene

COLEVILLE, CA
NOVEMBER 2, 1867

Dear Mother,

Last I wrote to you was from San Francisco, to say all
was well. You wrote back posthaste to say all was <u>not</u>
well, that Father was poorly, and I ought come home.
That was the last letter I wrote to you. This is The Last
Letter I will write to you.

To say it short, as I am forced to: I am as sorry as a son
can be. What I have to reveal to you is terrible for its
import, but more so because I must reveal it at all—
you should have known some of these things sooner.

First & worst. Tanner is dead. Killed in a gunfight.
He'd holed up to ambush a group of men who'd been
tracking us for days. It will come as no surprise to you
that your youngest son, my 'little' brother, died
fighting. He managed to take out one of their number
and badly wound another. His grave is somewhere
shallow and unmarked in the forests northeast of the
city from which I now address you. By all
appearances, these foul men are v. soon to do me the
same.

The issue they took with us is not without a certain
validity. T. and I did indeed rob a Wells & Fargo stage
about a week ago, during which robbery I came to
shoot one of the guards, a man by the name of Skaggs,
who I believed was fixing to shoot Tanner. You may
have heard this about town. It's true that Skaggs was
sadly and subsequently stamped to death by a horse.
There were two Skaggs brothers guarding that coach

on that fateful day. The one still alive wishes me no longer so.

I pray you survive such a tidal wave of bad tidings as this. (A flock of magpies is called a 'tiding,' were you aware? A 'tiding of magpies.' Oh, Mother, I already miss our chats, the love we share of such bookish morsels…) Your grief for Father was only just beginning to ebb, though it will be a lifelong sorrow, I know.

I wonder if life is just too sad to survive. Your life, especially. But survive is what you must do, Mother. You must! For amongst all this ruination and darkness, there is a glimmer of purest light. You are to be a grandmother.

I'd been waiting to tell you at a more decorous moment, but there it is. Orelia is with our child— which shares your blood, and Father's, and Tanner's, and mine. To be born this summer. May God grant it to suckle at the breast of California, far from all this incivility.

I would say to you: Go. Leave all this horror behind and head straightaway to San Francisco. Look up Orelia, who as you know lives with her fine parents on Pacific Avenue, and my dear friend Mendel Szilard on Sansome Street. They will see you properly situated.

Before Tanner and I 'vamosed,' we paid visits to a fair number of men. We left each to understand that they pay you back on whatever debt they'd each, respectively, been harboring from Father for 'services' he'd rendered them. (Services I understand you were not altogether ignorant of, at least not to the extent I was.) Still, it is likely that even the most honorable of these men will take the Stewart Sons' deaths as reason not to make good on their debts to their mother. To Hell with them. You live in Virginia City. There are resources in abundance for those savvy enough to know where to look. <u>Forge</u> ahead, Mother. Gather up the bricks life has lobbed at our family and rebuild, best you can, on a fairer shore.

Your loving and remaining son,
Eugene

COLEVILLE, CA
NOVEMBER 2, 1867

Dear Peanut,

You are still months from arriving at this soiree, but
I'm afraid I am shortly to leave it. This letter, then,
must serve by way of introduction. I see no other way,
not from where I sit. At university your father was
quite the procrastinator. A paper would come due and
he would stay up all the night huddled at the lamp,
scanning pages, furiously scribbling. This has a similar
feel. Writing under deadline. My whole life I've been
killing time, waiting for a body of work to accumulate,
garner accolades. Who was I trying to impress? Well,
my Father…& your Mother…& mine…&, I see
now, You.

Through the window I see men who wish me gone.
The cold turns their laughter vaporous and it
comingles with their tobacco smoke and rises into the
morning air to dissipate. Soon they'll lead me out of
town and give me what I suppose I have coming. Their
horses are tied up in a row to a fence. At the end of the
row is a mule with a potato sack saddle. My mount, I
expect. Life's a joke, why not death?

Gallows humor. Am beyond tired. Need a nap. Shall
not succumb to sleep though, or I'd waste what
remains of my life.

You'll notice I'm inclined to be frank here with you. By
the time you read this, it will be clear your old man did
not 'pan out.' The road he's been traveling was a cul-
de-sac. Here's a lesson he was too late in learning:

what days we get aboveground are, each & every singular one, a gift.

None promised.

I keep going down dark tunnels. Death's at the fore of my mind. I was not done. Am not. Haven't met <u>you</u>.

You deserve to know from whence you come. Here is what I can tell you: I was born January 5, 1843 in Cork, Ireland, to Harold and Imogen Stewart. On December 28 of that same year my brother Tanner was born—of the selfsame Imogen, though such may seem to fly in the face of biology. 'Irish twins.' My parents— suddenly having twice as many mouths to feed on an island that would soon yield less than half its usual potatoes—eventually boarded one of the crowded sail ships bound for America. I was 4, Tanner 3. I remember next to nothing of the journey.

Mother had family who'd fled before us and gained purchase in Missouri. So it was there we headed first, sharing a wagon with two other families. Father worked as a journeyman blacksmith. Mother grew a garden and marveled at its bounty. Tanner and I did what young brothers do. We argued over the rules and score of whatever we were playing. We competed at games, chores, critters, girls. We competed at falling asleep, waking up. We fought constantly. How could we not? We were inseparable.

A few years later, gold was discovered in abundance in California and thereabouts. My father heard tell of blacksmithing jobs in the mines paying double what he was drawing in St. Joseph. Back into the wagon we went. I remember <u>that</u> journey. I was 7, had read about the Comanche, and so kept my eyes trained at the horizon for a party of be-feathered savages come to slay us. I spent so much of my boyhood and manhood afraid.

Don't do that.

We resettled in Virginia Town, an ink stain on an otherwise blank map of unincorporated and lawless Territory. The Town became a City, the Territory a State; however, my present predicament would suggest that the law in these parts remains largely in the hands of large men.

The Stewarts made a decent stand. Father and Mother grew to be pillars of the community, such as it was. Tanner, too. As for me, I came to detest the place and avoided the sight of it by keeping my nose forever lodged in a book. At 18 I was sent to Santa Clara to attend the college there. I studied literature. You would think my father would have disowned me for being so soft. Quite the contrary. He encouraged the softness, demanded it even. As if it raised his station to afford a son who spent his days and nights doing nothing but making up stories.

My father, your grandfather, was a man of enviable horse sense and good humor. On 4th of July he'd sandwich black powder betwixt his anvils. When lit, the report could be heard—we were later told—clear to Carson City. The only part of me he insisted <u>not</u> go soft was my upper lip. His own was kept hidden behind mustaches which resembled the business end of a push broom. He told my brother and I to 'do battle with the world for so long as the world would show fight.' My brother, your Uncle Tanner, heeded that advice to his dying breath.

My Mother and I exchanged long letters whilst I was at college. Through me, she lived out the intellectual life she'd abandoned. Of your grandmother, suffice it for you to know that she sings while she tends her garden or her stove. Irish ballads have but two registers: suicidal and silly. Her pitch is perfect in both.

Tanner & I never sent each other letters, yet it is he I've always known best, whose views and news have always been plainest to me, even at great remove. For I could trust that whatever I got up to in San Francisco, he was up to the opposite in Virginia City. I stayed out until sunup arguing minutia; he awoke at dawn and reaffixed his nose to a grindstone. My brother was no saint, but he was an honest sinner. The competition for me became: Be the most different. I was proud of myself for what I became. Right up to the day I came home.

Let me offer some advice, my dear child. Consider making of yourself something <u>useful</u>. Something that gives you leverage on the physical world, not merely a vantage from which to stand back and laugh at it. Still, seek the latter, too, on occasion.

I do not regret that I saw a world my family never got to. Frankly, I hope it's the world you live in. I learned its streets, its secrets, its sundry citizens. Was riveted. Drew inspiration. Wrote stories. A few of which garnered attention. Mostly, though, I made mischief. In which earnest pursuit I came to gain a true friend:

Mendel Szilard. May you, too, be blessed to know a spirit so kindred. Szilard and I are made of the same stuff, only he's a polished silver spoon and I a dirty nugget.

I met maidens. Fell head over heels for one. Orelia. Your mother. Fairest of them all. Love of my life. I've now disappointed her, to say the least. I pray she knows I did not mean to leave her alone these last months, nor in the years to come. This does not excuse me.

I pray you two enjoy a bond. That you take utmost care of one another. I pray—though it pains me deeply —that your mother finds for you a father and for herself a husband, and that they are one and the same man, and that he's not a turd, like me. I am a bastard for making you one.

I have so little time left. What else to tell you? For some reason I keep returning to a night in St. Joseph. Father'd been much displeased with me. Over what I cannot now recall. He used the lash on us no more often than other fathers, though I'm convinced he used his better. To be lashed by a man whose arms are the strongest in town, whose stock in trade is the concise application of force, who believes things and boys take shape only through cycles of heating and beating...it is a pain in one's young ass. Alas, I stayed up until I heard Mother and Father snoring. Slipped out of the bed I shared with Tanner. Grabbed a satchel I'd prepared, containing books, light, a knife—all a boy needs to start fresh. Climbed out the open window into a hot and muggy night.

Off I went through Mother's garden, the corn high, the tomato plants fragrant. Across fields, drawn to the great river, the Missouri. It was a fair piece to cover. I was barefoot and anxious, as I went in those days. The fields and the woods teemed with malicious, nocturnal creatures. I could hear their pulse and call, their skittering in the branches. Whispered to myself, urging courage: You can do this, Eugene. By yourself.

But no. Couldn't leave Tanner to fend off the lash alone. Or, really, I missed having him along. On our adventures he was always scouting ahead like a dog, while I stuck to the trail, my head in the clouds.

I retraced my steps to the sleepy house. Clambered back in the window, woke him. He rubbed his eyes. I held a finger to my lips, pointed with my eyes out the window. He didn't for one second hesitate. I have never forgotten that.

Once away from the house, he asked first where we were going, then why. The order of those questions… that is Tanner. The river, I told him. We're running away.

His third question was, again, Why? Father, I said. He did not ask a fourth question. He'd heard my lashing that evening just like everyone else within a mile of the forge.

We got to a stand of cottonwoods we knew from our daytime raids. Here we settled our little boy backs against a big trunk. My hindquarters smarting. I lit a candle and read Tanner a story. He found the knife in my bag and sat idly whittling a stick into a spear. And

there we stayed, joined at the hip, listening to the
water moving out there in the gap made of darkness
that separated us from the other shore, and it was there
we were found in the morning by a friend of our
father's, one of a number who'd joined in a search
party.

Wish I could give you the gift of a brother or a sister.
Someone with the same blood, their back to the same
tree. Someone with whom to gaze out at the black &
mysterious & ever-moving river.

If and when you read this, I will likely be gone. God
knows where you'll find me. Elsewhere.

But look here. In these words. In the period at the end
of this sentence.

Seeing these pages stack up. Haven't time to write a
short and smart letter, only a thick and rambling one.
Will keep writing until…well…

My own father never much cottoned to writing, but the
man comprehended craft. How things can be honed
almost to holiness by repetition and pride in one's
product. As a lesson in how to be a better anything,
one needed merely sit and watch your grandfather in
his forge. I hope you find something like that,
something you can turn to when all else turns to shit.

This letter is probably the very last thing I will do. I'd
expected to one day pen my masterpiece. But it seems
I've already done it. <u>You</u> are my masterpiece, though I
can claim only co-authorship (and hardly that). Still, I
shall.

I take solace simply knowing <u>of</u> you. Bless you and keep you. Long lost though I am to you, I will always be

Your loving father,
Eugene Stewart

Harold E. Szilard, Ph.D.
William Nixon Professor of Geophysics, Emeritus
Dept. of Earth and Planetary Sciences
University of California
Mail Stop 103
Berkeley, CA 94720

Janet Curtis
Director, Special Collections
University Libraries
Mail Stop 217
University of Nevada
Reno, NV 89557

15 October, 1951

Dear Ms. Curtis:

I write to inquire whether the enclosed letters might be
of interest to you. I meant to bring them to your
attention years ago. I am prone to procrastination.

Please allow me to explain. I used to consider myself
very busy. Time in those days yawned before me. For
decades I lived and breathed geophysics. My lab was
forever coated in pulverized dust. This ruined both of
my lungs (pulmonary fibrosis) and, it has been argued,
both of my marriages. Rocks can be blamed for
warping my sense of time, too. The doctors tell me I
have six to nine months. To a geophysicist, this is as
precise an estimate of time as can be made. The author
of the enclosed letters—my biological father, Eugene
Stewart—likely knew the time of his demise with even
better precision. In the pre-dawn hours of November 3,
1867, he was cornered inside a church in Coleville,

California by a 'vigilance committee' and later that day gave himself over to its custody, having spent the intervening hours writing what were his final letters. How very like him.

So I assume. I never knew the man. He was last seen astride a mule, being led out of Coleville by his captors, his hands bound. His body was never found. Nor were the members of the 'committee' ever officially identified, let alone prosecuted.

My attorney assures me that what criminal revelations these letters contain are no longer of concern to the courts. That they may be of interest to posterity is a matter I leave to your professional opinion. It would seem a shame for them to end up in the dust bin.

Reading my father, one may come to conclude he was a silly man. Yes. But I don't think he was a shallow one. Certainly not as he stared down his doom. Nor do I think he was a singular one. To me he seems a man like any other, unique and universal. A man of his time. Perhaps a victim of it. But not a sucker. He died before his time, that much is certain. He lived high on hope, debilitated by doubt. He was the child of immigrants, granted no easy quarter. His story ends tragically. I only wonder if it might have some broader purpose. This is of course my reason for contacting you.

At the time of my father's disappearance I was not yet born. My mother, Orelia Szilard, was then living in San Francisco. She and Eugene had yet to marry. Soon thereafter, in a gesture of propriety, my biological father's best friend, Mendel Szilard, asked my

pregnant mother's hand in marriage. This spared my
mother's reputation, and mine.

A section of my family tree may be helpful here:

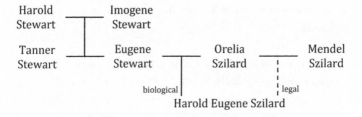

It's possible you know my mother by her pen name,
Owen Forthright, whose feminist writings brought
much-needed notoriety to what was then a fledgling
'Left Bank' magazine. Her husband, Mendel, was the
magazine's founder. This is why, for much of my life, I
mistakenly believed it was from Mendel (not my
mother, or Eugene) that I inherited a certain
appreciation for words.

Growing up, no one knew me for what I was, and am:
the bastard child of a thief and killer. I didn't know
that's what I was, either. I'd only heard of Eugene as
my father's best friend—practically a brother, I was
told. Uncle Eugene, my parents called him (with a
wink I never noticed).

I am an only child. My mother died in 1931, within a
year of Mendel. Near her end, as she was drifting in
and out and I sat vigil beside her in a UCSF hospital,
she told me to go immediately to her house (which had
survived the great fire of 1906) and fetch from her attic
a small box. I found it to contain letters my father

wrote separately to each of my parents during what
was to be an ill-fated stint in Virginia City, Nevada.
He'd gone home to attend to his father's dying, and
stayed on afterward for a time to help with family
business. I learned from these letters that I did, in fact,
have an uncle. Uncle Tanner. My real father's real
brother.

I learned also that the old woman in the photograph
that hung in our hallway all my life, with me as a very
young child propped on her knee, was not, as I had
once been told, a great-aunt, but was in fact my own
grandmother, Imogene Stewart, who'd moved to San
Francisco soon after Eugene's disappearance. Though I
was too young to remember her, she lived with us for
nearly two years before her death, and bequeathed to
me a sizable inheritance. I later put this money toward
a lengthy and self-indulgent education, and as down
payment on a small house in the Oakland hills. I had,
then, no idea of the true source of my providence. I
have, now, some confidence that both my grandmother
and my father would say the money was put to
good use.

I will never forget the evening I spent in the quiet of
my mother's kitchen reading the enclosed letters. They
were the most profound moments of my life. Initially, I
was furious with my mother for not sharing the truth
with me earlier, and I would have said as much to her
the next morning when I returned to the hospital, but
she was in no state for it. I only asked her if what the
letters said was true, that Eugene was my father, and
she looked at me as if for the first time in her whole life
—as if, perhaps, I was Eugene himself—and she
nodded, and gave a smile, and tapped my wrist. I have

long since forgiven her profound procrastination. It runs in our blood. Whereas, from my father, I fear I inherited a tendency for the dramatic. My ex-wives would attest.

Please do not get me wrong, Ms. Curtis. I was raised with love. I am grateful for the upbringing I was afforded. Still, it seems within one's rights to lament never meeting one's father. I am so much older now than he ever was. I have this strange vision where I'm reading to him—Ralph Waldo Emerson—and his eyes are closed while he mouths the words. There is, at least, some consolation in the intimate sense of my father that can be gleaned from his letters. I've all but memorized them.

And I know him even better now, in writing this letter to you. For I, too, write knowing I am dying. I suppose we all know this, with every letter we write. Or, we should.

I do not have children of my own. There's no one to pass this brittle stack of paper to. I'd be honored to see it somehow preserved. Perhaps it even merits publication in some modest form. My father would be tickled pink were such the case.

I eagerly await your assessment and reply. I'd only beg that you not procrastinate so awfully as I have. I wish to see my father put properly to rest, as he did his, before I too am called home.

Sincerely,
Harold Eugene Szilard

NOTE TO THE READER

Dear Reader,

Thanks for reading my first collection of short stories! I hope you enjoyed it – that it entertained, informed, or inspired you in a meaningful way.

When I put a piece of writing into the world, I'm dying to know how it lands, whether it resonates, how it makes others' think and feel. I write to form connections – connections between ideas, experiences, and most of all, between people.

As such, please consider reviewing *The Mayfly* on Amazon or Goodreads. Reviews close the loop of the connection for me, and are the lifeblood of an independent author. I read every one and they help to make my writing better.

More about my work can be found at readrogers.com.

Thank you!

-Ben

ALSO BY BEN ROGERS

Silicon Valley Tech meets The Cocaine Trade.

Can you program yourself into a winner?

In the San Francisco Bay Area, tech innovation is King, and money is God.

Vik Singh watched his immigrant parents work their fingers to the bone chasing the American Dream. But standing at his father's funeral, he realizes one thing - hustling will get you nowhere. All you need to get rich is one big idea.

And when he meets Los, a small-time drug lord with visions of grandeur, Vik makes a plan worthy of Jobs and Zuckerberg:

Design a drug sale app.

After all, market disruption is everything.

From his comfortable cottage in Lake Tahoe, Vik writes the code that builds a cocaine empire. When his app attracts an infamous drug cartel leader, it seems like a natural expansion move. And for a while, life is Swiss bank accounts, luxe coke parties, and falling in love with Remi, a beautiful and ballsy woman with secrets of her own.

Then he discovers he is being watched.

The DEA is closing in, the cartel is getting suspicious, and he can trust no one. As things heat up, Vik discovers the real price of easy money.

And that price could be his life.

If you're a fan of Breaking Bad, Mr. Robot, and Dark Mirror, this is the book for you.

PRAISE FOR *THE HEAVY SIDE*

"Vik Singh, who believes above all in elegant code compressed by 'pressure and hard thought,' tumbles into the drug world after leading a blameless life. Rogers' precise language makes the twists of Vik's code as involving as the particulars of his getaway plan in this astute thriller."

— **JENNY SHANK**, AUTHOR OF *THE RINGER*

"The Heavy Side will be one of the smartest and best literary works you will read this decade. Rogers updates traditional literary themes...through the languages of literature and of programming code. In doing so he blends an authentic love story and an intense thriller into a unique, gripping human story."

— **CALEB S. CAGE**, AUTHOR OF *DESERT MEMENTOS: STORIES OF IRAQ AND NEVADA*

"A vivid thriller made all the more engrossing by its narrator... Lyrical... Haunting. Very highly recommended."

— **MIDWEST BOOK REVIEW**

"The Heavy Side *is a devilish joyride of a novel, a literary thriller that's as original as it is mesmerizing. From Tahoe to Mexico, a star-crossed couple can't escape their coiled fates, even when--especially when--they most need to. Ben Rogers writes like a maestro--readers won't be able to put down this book.*"

— **MATT GALLAGHER,** AUTHOR OF *EMPIRE CITY*

"*A caper that starts with a clever protagonist--the likes of whom we don't see often enough... This is carefully crafted fiction that springs from the well-organized mind of an engineer with the soul of a storyteller. Rogers has created a 'killer-app' of engaging prose.*"

— **MARK MAYNARD,** AUTHOR OF *GRIND*

"*Filled with tremendous writing about the meaning of Code, and what coding a masterpiece might be like, as well as a primer on the economics of the illegal drug markets with deep insight into how drug cartels operate... It fills a spot on the book shelf next to the mesmerizing works of James Ellroy.*"

— **JOSEPH G. PETERSON,** AUTHOR OF *THE RUMPHULUS*

I wanted to shake the globe.

I wanted to hide in the corner.

I wanted to get it over with, everything over with. Remember what they named that pent-up barrel of uranium, the one they dropped on Hiroshima?

Little Boy.

All boys play with fire.

Oby is a closet pyromaniac. His backyard shed is a secret lab where explosive recipes are tested. His house burns down twice under suspicious circumstances. Parents, teachers, mountain men, and arson inspectors are all concerned. But Oby just can't help himself. His genius lies in napalm.

Oby's biggest question is: Will he land the Nobel Prize? Or is he stuck in the fattest part of the bell curve?

PRAISE FOR *THE FLAMER*

"A story of love, told like an explosion—a novel not only about a boy's romance with fire, but also with language, people, and the whole wide world. Rogers has crafted one of the wisest, funniest, strangest novels I've ever read, narrated by one of the most unique characters I've had the pleasure of meeting in American fiction. I treasure this book."

— **CHRISTOPHER COAKE**, AUTHOR OF *WE'RE IN TROUBLE*

Named one of Five Overlooked Books It's Impossible Not to Love.

— **BARNES & NOBLE**

"A highly original and delightful debut."

— HIGH COUNTRY NEWS

"Like Harper Lee and Mark Twain, Ben Rogers has tapped into regional America to scribe a coming-of-age story that is universal in its truths."

— H. LEE BARNES, MEMBER OF NEVADA WRITERS
HALL OF FAME

"A witty, Nevada-based coming-of-age story."

— LAS VEGAS REVIEW JOURNAL

"Rogers gives us a precocious young man with fiery tastes and curious charm."

— DON WATERS, AUTHOR OF *THESE BOYS AND THEIR
FATHERS*

"Rogers gets the coming-of-age novel right."

— THE NEVADA REVIEW

*"*The Flamer *is a diabolically funny, explosively tender portrait of youth, a mad scientist's coming-of-age story. Brainy and splendidly profane, Ben Rogers's writing is incendiary and hypnotic. We watch with an arsonist's glee as his boy genius lights the fuse of his own volatile adolescence. A sizzling debut."*

— CLAIRE VAYE WATKINS, AUTHOR OF *BATTLEBORN*

ACKNOWLEDGMENTS

Many of these stories appeared first in literary magazines. Thank you to the people who work at those fragile and crucial institutions, and thank you to certain among these people for plucking my little stories off the river bottom and giving them wings. Special thanks to Roxane Gay, co-founder of Pank Magazine and extraordinary author, who boosted my spirits immeasurably with her assessment of my story, and to Christopher Morgan at Arroyo Literary Review for nominating my story for a Pushcart Prize.

Thank you to the early readers, and immeasurable improvers, of these stories, including Claire Vaye Watkins, Adam Dedmon, Mena Dedmon, Gabriel Urza, and Kenny Ching.

I owe Donnie Curtis in Special Collections at the University of Nevada Libraries a high five (whoo-pshh!) for guiding me to the treasure trove of Alfred Doten's diaries (https://clark.dotendiaries.org), and Walter Van Tilburg Clark for that weighty contribution to Western American History.

Thank you to those who help me 'broadcast' CQ Books,

including Lindsey Nicole, Katarina Zivkovic, Shaun Loftus, Ilsa Brink, and Xavier Comas.

Thank you to those who've championed and/or coached my writing over the years, including Michael Sion, Caleb Cage, Christine Kelly, Danilo John Thomas, Brian Egan, Marian Young, Christopher Coake, Curtis Vickers, and Mignon Fogarty.

Thank you to those friends not already mentioned, including Joe Goodnight, Matt Herz, Kam Leang, Ben Clyne, and David Torch.

Thank you to Tyler and Julia, Judd and Lindsay, Reid and Logan, Pam and Steve, and all of my family.

Thank you to my parents, Jim and Sandy, who give and give, and cheer and cheer.

Thank you to my accomplished and humble and beloved girls, Quinn & Sydney.

Thank you last to my first, best reader, always: Jill.

ABOUT THE AUTHOR

 Ben Rogers' work has been published in The Rumpus, PANK, McSweeney's Internet Tendency, The Portland Review, Arroyo Literary Review, Wag's Revue, and elsewhere, and has earned the Nevada Arts Council Fellowship. He is also the lead author of *Nanotechnology: Understanding Small Systems*, the first-ever comprehensive textbook on nanotechnology, and *Nanotechnology: The Whole Story*, both of which earned the CHOICE Outstanding Academic Title Award from the American Library Association. He studied engineering and journalism in college and has worked as a business analyst, a reporter, a teacher, and a scientist at various labs, including Oak Ridge National Laboratory and NASA's Jet Propulsion Laboratory. He is currently the Director of Engineering at NevadaNano and lives in Reno with his family.

www.readrogers.com

Made in the USA
Las Vegas, NV
02 December 2021

35814770R00156